ABIGAIL AND ALEXA
SAVE THE WEDDING

Also by Lian Dolan

The Marriage Sabbatical

Lost and Found in Paris

The Sweeney Sisters

ABIGAIL AND ALEXA
SAVE
THE WEDDING

A Novel

LIAN DOLAN

WM

WILLIAM MORROW

An Imprint of HarperCollins*Publishers*

ABIGAIL AND ALEXA SAVE THE WEDDING. Copyright © 2025 by Lian Dolan. All rights reserved. Printed in the United States of America. No part of this book may be used or reproduced in any manner whatsoever without written permission except in the case of brief quotations embodied in critical articles and reviews. For information, address HarperCollins Publishers, 195 Broadway, New York, NY 10007.

HarperCollins books may be purchased for educational, business, or sales promotional use. For information, please email the Special Markets Department at SPsales@harpercollins.com.

FIRST EDITION

Designed by Michele Cameron

Library of Congress Cataloging-in-Publication Data

Names: Dolan, Lian, author.
Title: Abigail and Alexa save the wedding : a novel / Lian Dolan.
Description: First edition. | New York, NY : William Morrow, 2025. |
Identifiers: LCCN 2024041515 (print) | LCCN 2024041516 (ebook) | ISBN 9780063270657 (hardcover) | ISBN 9780063270671 (ebook)
Subjects: LCGFT: Novels.
Classification: LCC PS3604.O427 A64 2025 (print) | LCC PS3604.O427 (ebook) | DDC 813/.6—dc23/eng/20241001
LC record available at https://lccn.loc.gov/2024041515
LC ebook record available at https://lccn.loc.gov/2024041516

ISBN 978-0-06-327065-7

25 26 27 28 29 LBC 5 4 3 2 1

For JCC

Who always had a cocktail napkin for every glass

ABIGAIL AND ALEXA
SAVE THE WEDDING

Part One

From the Website of Dearly Beloveds and Betrotheds

Dear B & Bs . . .

As wedding season approaches and families are aflutter, it's time for my annual column directed at Mothers of the Bride (MOBs) and Mothers of the Groom (MOGs). Think of this as the ultimate public service performed by your Aunt B. You're so welcome. My goal is to make every wedding a joyous and heartfelt celebration, filled with goodwill toward all. Add in a few lovely touches, some good behavior, and plenty of cake and you have the makings of a memorable day. If you can just keep your mouth zipped about every little thing. In other words, pull it together for one single day, MOBs and MOGs, and everyone at the wedding will benefit. How hard could that be? As you know, my motto in all things is "Propriety first."

I think of these nuggets of wisdom not as rules, but as wishes. My wishes for you, Mothers and Others who care, so you can be your best self throughout the process. But a gentle reminder that while my position has evolved over the past thirty years of writing about all aspects of matrimony, much as weddings themselves have evolved from a spectacle with well-known standards and traditions to a free-for-all of personal expression, one idea remains steadfast: Dear MOBs and MOGs, this is not your wedding.

Big Kiss & Wedding Bliss,
Your Aunt B

Chapter 1

THE CALL

The Mother of the Bride

"Mom! It's me. It's us. Sorry to call so early there. I have some news."

News! Despite the early hour in Montecito, California, Alexa Diamandis was all ears. *Could Penny be pregnant? Please, let it be that.* "Give me two minutes. I need my coffee," she said to her only daughter while positioning the tablet on a stand in the kitchen, as she did every morning to take video calls from all over the world. Her family lived in Greece. Her friends lived in England. And her business was travel. She was used to early-morning conversations in her small but airy California kitchen. It was why she rose at five most mornings and put on her face first thing, at least a modified version of her face. Moisturizer, a light coat of foundation, a swipe of mascara and lip gloss. She even had a rotating collection of velour tracksuits that worked well on camera, like the soft pink one she was wearing now. But first, coffee.

Alexa worked the magic of the espresso maker, grinding, pounding, pulling, and steaming until the dark elixir dripped into her tiny cup. Her morning routine started with a quick shot, followed by a more leisurely cappuccino. She loved this gleaming machine as much as she'd ever loved any object and most people. Except Penny, her daughter, the light of her life despite being her complete opposite in personality and preferences. A grandchild would be a tiebreaker of sorts, Alexa thought. "Hold on, I'm almost done."

Alexa's back was turned to the camera, but she heard her daughter laugh and then explain. "She's a fiend about the coffee. She's Greek; she doesn't function without it. Give her a minute." A man's voice answered back, something about how they should have waited to call.

Alexa didn't turn, but she knew it must be the boyfriend. Chris? Chess? Ah, Chase! Yes, he was a charming guy, the type you do bring home to Mother. She scrolled through her mental files to conjure up an impression of him. She'd only met him once, on layover in New York City, and Penny had brought him to dinner unannounced, disrupting Alexa's plans for a serious mother-daughter talk about Penny leaving her corporate public relations job and coming back to work for the family business. Instead, it was an evening of first impressions and impressing, everyone at the table aware of the stakes. From the moment she met him, Alexa knew he was a serious contender for Penny's heart.

Chase looked to be every bit a Chase, Alexa supposed. Dark hair, normal build, good suit. In politics. As she recalled, he grew up outside the city in suburban Connecticut and now worked for the Mayor of the City of New York, as he said multiple times. He talked about the city like it was a small town and, of course, he worked for the mayor because who else would he work for? Alexa liked him, liked his confidence, liked the way he held the door for her daughter but also let her tell a story without interrupting. This new generation of men had qualities that Alexa admired. They could share the spotlight in a way the men of her generation disdained. Still, did Penny really need him to live a satisfying life?

Funny, when she and Penny talked most afternoons on Penny's walk home from work, Chase was rarely a topic of conversation. The

Diamandis women talked about work, friends and family, the latest celebrities whom Alexa had seen at Bettina, the star-studded pizza place of choice in Montecito, but almost never about men.

But that was fitting, because men had never been a part of their daily life as mother and daughter. One thing she knew for sure: Chase and Penny would make handsome babies. She swallowed down the single shot of espresso and went to work on the cappuccino.

"Steaming milk now," Alexa called over her shoulder to the couple in her pan-Euro accent, an asset in a town like Montecito, a Pacific Coast gem with European aspirations. The Positano of California. Over her decades as a resident of the hamlet, she'd used her background as part of her brand, working with clients to plan their dream vacations in the Greek isles or the Amalfi Coast. Her gentle Mediterranean lilt informed by a British university education had served her well in this sophisticated beach town. So had her hustle. It's why she needed her coffee. Steam, press, pour, foam, layer. Perfect.

Turning with cup in hand, Alexa positioned herself at the marble-topped island, a spot she knew had great morning lighting that blew out her wrinkles on camera. "Now I'm human. Tell me your news!"

Penny, lovely Penny, who with her olive skin and green eyes didn't need good lighting to look stunning. She'd been blessed with favorable genetics and a strong sense of self that shaped her style. Even on a Sunday morning, she looked pulled together, polished, in a white linen shirt, small gold earrings and necklace, and her hair swept up in a messy bun. A swipe of color popped her smile. No filter needed. The couple appeared to be huddled together on Penny's couch in her Upper East Side apartment. Alexa recognized the art on the wall, the work of a painter on Patmos, her own birthplace and the island where Penny spent most of her summers. The slashes of blue and pink in the painting brought a little bit of the Dodecanese to Manhattan. It soothed Alexa.

"Are you sitting down?" Penny asked dramatically as she held up her left hand. "We're engaged! Isn't it gorgeous?" She thrust her ring into the camera. It was a stunning light-blue square-cut gem surrounded by baguettes of a light-pink stone. Sparkly and special, like her daughter. Like the painting. But Alexa refused to get weepy. Or swept away. She stayed as pragmatic as ever. "Is that an aquamarine?"

"Yes, three carats with tourmaline baguettes. No blood diamonds for us," Chase said, looking satisfied and proud of both the rock and his newly acquired vocabulary. "The mayor knows a guy."

"Chase picked it out all by himself!" Penny said, as if this act alone made him marriage worthy. But did it? He had failed, Alexa noted to herself, to inform her of the proposal. It wasn't as if she expected him to ask for Penny's hand in marriage like it was the Middle Ages. And she didn't want to react like her own Greek father might have at the slight, with a torrent of patriarchal language and a curse on Chase's family. But some sort of advance notice would have been appreciated. She would cope with that slight later.

Penny continued because that was the purpose of the call: to tell the story. "He got down on one knee at the top of the Empire State Building. The lights of the city were amazing. Nobody else was there. It was so romantic, Mom."

Alexa knew she needed to react in exactly the right way, or her daughter would never let her forget it. She had one chance to get this right. That was the tricky part about being an only parent: Her reaction was the only reaction. There was no backup, nobody to smooth out the rough spots, to fill in when she failed. She willed herself to smile and raised her voice half an octave. "How thrilling. Wonderful for you both. Do we need to talk about your plans now?"

She hoped not.

This was so unexpected, and she had so much on her schedule for the rest of the year. A long engagement would be ideal, twelve or maybe even eighteen months. And maybe Penny would want to get married on Patmos at her family's hotel. It would be practically free. And then the happy couple could have a long honeymoon somewhere she could use her connections to get them a good deal, like Croatia, even though the service was terrible there. "Do you have a date yet? Or a place?"

"We can follow up on that next week, Mom," Penny answered like a pro. Alexa knew her daughter worked the calendar months in advance, planning five steps out while everybody else was still on square one. It was what made them both so good at their jobs, and, Alexa thought, at their lives. "We want to enjoy the engagement for a bit."

"A lot of it will depend on our work schedules," Chase added, to Alexa's satisfaction.

"Whatever you two decide will be the right thing, I'm sure," Alexa said, a line she had heard one of her friends use with her adult children. She didn't believe it, but she was committed to selling the sentiment. She lifted her coffee mug in a toast. "Welcome to our family, Chase." She even choked up a bit as she said that last part.

Of course she did. Because what Alexa Diamandis was really thinking was, why on earth would anyone ever get married at all?

Chapter 2

THE CALL

The Mother of the Groom

"Mom. Mom? Are you there?"

"Hello? Hello? Chase, is that you? Wait, what button did I hit? Did you call me? Or did I call you?" Abigail Blakeman asked, then pulled her phone away from her ear to stare at it. It was new. Not the latest version, of course, because those were expensive and complicated and really more computer than phone. She bought the reasonably priced older version, which would soon be obsolete. It seemed smaller than her last phone. Or her eyes were rapidly deteriorating. Or her joints were swelling. Either way, she was constantly dialing people she didn't want to speak to and hanging up on people she did want to talk to. She missed landlines.

"I called you, Mom."

"Well, that's nice." And surprising on a Sunday morning. Her eldest child, Chase checked in every few weeks, usually when he was in the back of a car stuck in Manhattan traffic en route to a meeting. The tactic ensured that the call was no more than seven minutes, half of which was Chase giving instructions to the driver. The other half was Chase apologizing for being so busy that he hadn't had time to call.

Chase was the chief of staff for the Mayor of the City of New York, Timothy "Timmo" Lynch. It was an impressive title and an impressive accomplishment for a B student who'd just turned thirty. Abigail couldn't stand the mayor even though he was a well-respected Independent who was fiscally conservative and socially progressive. An Irish immigrant, the son of a construction worker and a schoolteacher, young Mayor Lynch had used his University of Galway education, street smarts, and charm to make his way to Harvard for an MBA, then to New York City to build a financial empire. When Timmo decided to trade in his career in finance for a career in politics, the voters fell for this naturalized US citizen with his Irish accent and Gabriel Byrne looks.

Abigail thought the mayor was smug, too charismatic for his own good. And Chase had picked up the same skills, the easy conversation with everyone from world leaders to old ladies, the ability to break down complex ideas into simple, digestible chunks of information. Her son had even started dressing like his boss, in handmade suits when Brooks Brothers' ready-made suits were perfectly fine. She loved Chase, but she wished he'd find another line of work, maybe even one where no one knew his name. Politics could be so tawdry. You could get dragged through the mud through no fault of your own. Or just a tiny little fault of your own. Why couldn't he have a high-powered career and make gobs of money, but in something not so objectionable? Like law.

"Are you and Dad around today?"

"I am. Puttering in the garden," Abigail lied. In truth, she was drinking coffee and staring out the window at the sailboats bobbing on their moorings, using the first weekend of the summer season as an excuse to skip church. It was a blue-sky Connecticut day in Fair Harbor. She might rally and do a little weeding later, but for now, she was content to do nothing. "Your father's golfing."

"Penny and I thought we might come out for the afternoon. To stop by. There's something I want to tell you."

Immediately, Abigail had two thoughts. The first: *I wish I had spent the money on that gazpacho at Nutmeg, the specialty market.* The second: *He's finally getting out of politics and going to law school.* "We'd love to see you. For lunch?" she asked cautiously.

"No, we'll arrive around two. Penny and I will take the train out and then walk to the house."

Abigail was relieved about the lunch. She really didn't keep company food in the house anymore. "Wonderful. Your father should be home from the club around then and do his usual, fall asleep on the couch while watching more golf. Sarah might even be home. She's teaching some sort of clinic or something this morning." That was it, the totality of the Blakeman family: Abigail Ellsworth Blakeman, sixty-five, mother of two, former private school development person, now working the front desk for minimum wage at the senior center; George Blakeman, late sixties, former stockbroker forced out under suspicious circumstances and for overall underperformance, now a competitive bridge player; and Sarah Ellsworth Blakeman, twenty-seven, living at home, the health teacher and head coach of the junior varsity field hockey team at Fair Harbor High School, unattached and uninterested in men or women. All co-residing in the circa-1834 center-hall Colonial on the water in a small, picturesque village on the Gold Coast. Travel sites called it the Nantucket of Connecticut.

Only Chase had escaped to Manhattan, forty miles down I-95 and a world away. "We'll see you then, Mom. Thanks."

"Love you." She did.

"You too, Mama," Chase said in return, like he always did.

***

FOUR HOURS LATER, after Abigail had done a quick cleanup, made fresh iced tea, and defrosted some brownies from the Mother's Day gift basket her son had sent after missing brunch, changed into a linen shift dress, applied sunscreen, and arranged some of the early blooms of her showstopping blue hydrangeas in a pewter pitcher, Chase burst through the back door with Penny in tow. He added energy everywhere he went, and this bolt lit up Chez Blakeman. "Hey, we're here."

"Wake up," Abigail hissed at George as she made her way through the house from the patio. He was sound asleep and still in his golf clothes.

"I'm awake," he insisted, as if a second ago he hadn't been snoring.

Abigail shook her head and made her way to the kitchen—the new kitchen, is how she thought of it, even though the remodel had been during the first term of the second Bush administration. "You came in through the back door!"

"Since when are we allowed to come in through the front door?"

"Guests are allowed in through the front door," Abigail said, nodding at Penny, who was even more striking than she remembered with her dark hair, olive complexion, and bright eyes. Abigail expected all California girls to be blond and bikini'd. But Penny was wrapped in layers of sophistication, with her floral maxi dress, espadrilles with ankle ties, and the silk scarf in her hair. She didn't look like the preppy girls from Fair Harbor whom Chase had dated in high school. Nothing like them at all, which Abigail took personally.

"Good to see you again, Penny," Abigail said, extending a hand. She'd only met the girl a few times; it didn't seem like a hug-and-kiss situation.

Penny swapped a bag of bagels into her other hand to shake properly. "Thank you for having us."

Thank you for having us? This is Chase's house. He's not the guest, you are, Abigail thought. "You brought my favorite bagels. I look forward to breakfast tomorrow. Though I limit myself to only half a bagel at a time."

Chase came in for a proper hug and said to his mother, "One day you should really go for it, Mom. Cut loose and have a whole bagel."

"Your mother looks amazing, Chase. She should keep doing what she's doing. No carb shaming! Right, Mrs. Blakeman?" You can take the girl out of California, but you can't take the California out of the girl.

"Thank you," Abigail said, thinking about whether now was a good time to invite Penny to call her by her first name and then deciding against it. She wanted to remain Mrs. Blakeman until she knew exactly where this relationship was going. "Why don't we go out on the porch? There are drinks and brownies out there."

"We just finished lunch," Chase said. "We grabbed some food at Nutmeg's and then ate it at the park. I don't think we're hungry, are we?"

"We can take a brownie for the train ride back," Penny suggested.

Abigail tried hard not show her disappointment. They ate in the public park instead of accepting her lunch invitation, albeit a tepid one? And now they were going to take her Mother's Day brownies to eat on Metro North? Who ate on Metro North? Again, Abigail dug deep. "Wonderful plan."

***

THE PATIO OFF the back of the house, overlooking the harbor, was a point of pride for Abigail. The blue-gray slate. The white vintage Brown Jordan furniture that she maintained herself because the professional refinishers were a fortune. The multitude of Gertrude Jekyll pink rosebushes surrounding the enclosure. And the view! The view led the eye down the rocky slope to the water and out across the harbor to the vibrant marsh on the other side. When visitors exclaimed that it was "a million-dollar view," George always responded, "Let's hope it's a three-million-dollar view." And there was knowing laughter all around.

Not only did Abigail hope, but she also prayed it was a three-million-dollar view. Every night.

"Do you want something stronger than iced tea?" George asked, alert and awake now, even though he was still in his pink golf shirt and lime-green shorts.

"Not right now," Chase said, giving his sister, Sarah, a hug. She had arrived on the scene, fresh from the field hockey pitch. It didn't matter what time of year it was; for Sarah, it was always field hockey season. "You reek," Chase teased.

She put up her hands in an inviting gesture. "You want to see if you can do more burpees than me? Let's go. In the grass. I am the champion of my league team, which is coed." Nothing got Sarah more fired up than a squat thrust competition. Abigail hoped that someday, somewhere, someone would appreciate those thigh muscles.

"Sit, sit!" George instructed, and the entire group did as they were told. It was a lovely view. "What brings you out on a Sunday afternoon?"

"We have something to tell you," Chase announced, then reached for Penny's hand. "Last night I asked Penny to marry me and she said yes." Chase could not have looked more pleased and Penny could not have looked more radiant. The announcement was more of a proclamation than an announcement. The mutual adoration seeped out of their pores. If love was a scent, these two would reek.

"Congratulations!" Sarah shouted, jumping up and moving to embrace the happy couple. "I'll finally have a sister!"

George followed suit with some generic words of encouragement and went off to get a bottle of champagne.

Chase and Penny turned to look at Abigail at the same time, all anticipation. She knew that this response would set the tone for the rest of her relationship with her future daughter-in-law. And still, she couldn't help herself. "So, you're not going to law school?"

***

TWO HOURS LATER, all the champagne was gone and the happy couple had recounted for the second time that day what would become the mythology of *them*: the Buying the Aquamarine not Diamond Ring Story (the mayor knew a guy in the jewelry business); the Proposal Story (the mayor knew a guy who could keep the Empire State Building open late for the occasion); and the Cozy Late Night Supper Afterward at Bemelmans Bar Story. (Again, the mayor and a guy he knew meant no waiting in line.) Finally, the story of the After-Party, which Chase had arranged with their friends at Dorian's Red Hand. It had all been perfect.

Then, there was the discussion of everything they didn't want to discuss yet, like the date, the location, and, as Sarah put it, "the hideous bridesmaids' dresses." Penny declared that no decisions about any of that had been made in the nineteen hours they'd been engaged. And Chase added that they wanted a breath to enjoy their new, affianced status before choosing napkin colors or cutting the number of guests in half. Abigail pretended to buy all the denials, but one look at Penelope Diamandis told you that she locked things down as soon as she could.

After the nonstop talking and the laughter that Chase always brought into the house, the couple seemed spent, so Abigail went into the kitchen to pack up the brownies to go before the five sixteen train back to Grand Central. Chase followed her in.

"What was that about law school?" Chase asked, grabbing a seltzer out of the fridge.

Apparently, he wasn't going to forget her faux pas. "I'm sorry. I don't know where that came from. I mean, I do. You said it once and you know I hate all the politics of . . . politics. Law would be a nice quiet career for you, that's all." *And lucrative*, thought Abigail, but she would never say that out loud to her son. Most nights, she lay awake worried that there wouldn't be much left to leave her children if she and George lived as long as their relatives had, well into their eighties. There would be no house on the Connecticut shoreline to split; they'd get a condo in Hilton Head if they were lucky. A law career with a steady, solid income would be Chase's hedge against a diminished inheritance. And Sarah? She would have to marry well.

"I think I said I wanted to go to law school once when I was sixteen. Mom, I love my job. I work for the mayor of the greatest city in the world. And now I have a gorgeous, smart fiancée who is accomplished on every level. Please let her know that you think she's great, too."

"I do!" Abigail said defensively while adding some cheese and crackers to the to-go bag, along with hand-sanitizing wipes and napkins. She hoped to God they snacked at the station and not on the train itself. "It seems so sudden, that's all."

"We've been dating since last September. Weren't you and Dad engaged in less than a year?"

Busted. "Yes, but we were a little older and had been in the same circle. Penny is someone out of the blue."

Chase cocked his head. "What does that mean?"

Abigail wasn't going to back down or be ashamed. She wanted to stand up for her people. "There are so many nice girls here in Fair Harbor. I assumed you'd settle down with someone we knew. Get married at the club."

"Mom, I haven't dated someone you knew since sophomore year in high school when you forced me to take Molly Yang to Cotillion."

"She's a lovely girl. She's a nurse at my dermatologist office. Gorgeous complexion," Abigail added in case there was a slight chance Chase would change his mind in exchange for free skin care products. "Penny is lovely. I just worry, you know."

"About what?"

Abigail dropped her voice to a stage whisper. "About the no-father thing."

Chase barked a laugh. "First of all, you know that's medically impossible, right? And second, she doesn't worry about it. Her mother is very proud of the fact that she is a single mother by choice. So is Penny. I wouldn't mention it when you meet her mom in a few weeks. We're going to arrange a dinner in the city. Try not to be a snob. It's that DAR thing with you, isn't it?"

"I'm very proud to be a Daughter of the American Revolution. As proud as Penny's mom is of her status." Indeed, Abigail Ellsworth Blakeman was prouder, there could be no doubt. She had a direct relative on her father's side, Oliver Ellsworth, a founding father of Connecticut and a signer of the Constitution. She had the family Bible and reams of verified genealogy to prove it. On her mother's side, she was related to an eighteenth-century Hartford seamstress and a shop owner, a couple she wished had had the good sense to acquire real estate or master the printing press when they'd had the chance so there would be some serious generational wealth, instead of only the appearance of generational wealth.

The point was that her lifelong membership in DAR came with deep roots and satisfaction. Some women could play tennis. Other women had great fashion sense. For Abigail, she had her connection to the Revolutionary War and that was enough. "I worry that you don't know what you're getting into genetically, that's all."

"Like the Alzheimer's and baldness on your side of the family? And the heart disease and high blood pressure on Dad's? I'm not sure I feel better knowing what lies ahead."

"Don't be fresh." She loved her son's quick wit but not when it was aimed at her.

"Penny has all the father figures she needs. She spent every summer in Greece with her uncles. Her grandfather on Patmos is still alive."

Her grandfather on Patmos? Sudden realization dawned on Abigail. What if the wedding was on some Greek island in the middle of nowhere? It would be bad enough to have to go to California. The inconvenience of it all. The expense! But Greece? Nothing was worse than a destination wedding on an island. Nothing. Before she got carried away with the misery of travel by ferry, she refocused on her son.

"And she has a godfather who is like a father to her. She is very close to him. Fittingly, he's a member of the House of Lords. Is that good enough for you?"

Abigail was laser focused. "He's a British lord? How is that possible?"

"Remember at Christmas when Penny mentioned that her mother went to college in London? Simon Fox is her college mate, as they say. That's Lord Simon Fox to you and me. His title is something like Baron Plumley. Or Plumfield. Penny sees him all the time. He comes to New York for work, and she's spent holidays at his estate in the country. Somewhere with lots of apples because he makes hard cider when he's not in Parliament. I'm sure he'll walk her down the aisle."

Abigail's brain started to explode. Her disappointment at Sarah not being the first to get married at St. Mark's down the street with a tented reception in the backyard and the remote possibility of an announcement in some decent publication was being replaced by a rush of exhilaration. A British baron! Walking Penny down the aisle! Along with her family's own founding father credentials and Chase's ties to the mayor, the event was a shoo-in for a prime wedding announcement placement. And Penny being half Greek must count as diversity, Abigail thought. This whole event could be NYT "Vows"-worthy and who knew where that could lead?

Abigail made a mental note to get in touch with her prep school roommate Bernadette Caruso, formerly of the *New York Times* but now known as wedding etiquette doyenne Aunt B. Bernadette might even be open to covering the wedding herself for her matrimonial digital empire, Dearly Beloveds and Betrotheds. Maybe this unknown girl from California would be an asset.

If only they could have the wedding here, in this historic house in this historic village, maybe, just maybe, Abigail could work this wedding to their family advantage. It would be untraditional to have it in the groom's backyard and not the bride's, but it would be so lovely. She'd have to talk with Bernadette, who would give her the straight scoop on whether a historic house in Connecticut or a godforsaken island in the Aegean was a more desirable location in terms of attention. Her media-savvy son would thank her, no doubt. And wouldn't a gorgeous wedding photo spread on a well-respected site increase the real estate value of the house? George would have thoughts on that.

In the meantime, she tried to smooth things over with Chase. "I guess a little diversity in the gene pool is a good thing."

"I know it's good for politics."

"What does that mean?"

"Penny's background and her ties to California will play well with national voters and donors."

Now it was Abigail's turn to cock her head. Whose voters? The mayor was foreign-born and terming out; he couldn't run for president. And he said that being mayor was the only political job he wanted. What was Chase talking about? She handed him the snack pack. "What voters?"

"Mine. But we've gotta get going if we're going to make the train. I'll explain next time," he said as he gave her a one-armed hug. "Please tell Penny something nice before we leave. Like, welcome to the family."

***

THE BLAKEMANS WALKED the beautiful couple to the door en masse. Abigail realized it was now or never for her gesture, so she pulled Penny into a genuine hug and announced, "We're delighted about your news." She released her hostage and added, "Please, call us Abigail and George. You're family now." That was a phrase that Abigail had never uttered, nor a sentiment she'd ever felt about anyone but her actual family, and it sounded like a line from a cheesy TV movie. But she supposed that was what people said in situations like this.

"Thank you, Abigail. And you too, George, for the champagne," her son's fiancée said. "I can't wait to be family. Or as we say in Greek, oikogéneia."

"And a beautiful okeefenokie you'll be," George joked, causing the rest of the occupants in the front hall to cringe. Sincerity was really his strong suit, not humor, Abigail thought.

Almost as an afterthought, Sarah asked if she could get a picture for her socials. Abigail echoed the sentiment. Finally, she would have something to post besides pictures of hydrangeas and sunrises and banana bread, her specialty. She could imagine the caption, like she'd seen all her mom friends post: "She said YES!" Of course Penny had said yes to her son, and Abigail wanted the world to know.

"Let's go out on the front lawn. The dappled light is beautiful there," Penny directed, as if she had scouted the location on her way in. "Oh, and please don't post anything until we get our photos back from the Empire State Building later this week. Chase thought of everything, even a photographer. Remember, when it comes to weddings, the bride posts first!" Penny cooed, though it came out as a warning.

"I think the bride goes first from now on in everything," George said, trying to recover from his previous comment, but only generating more cringe. Abigail thought he looked like he needed another nap.

Penny nodded. "That's sweet, George. So sweet . . . and true."

Sarah and Abigail snapped their shots and there wasn't an un-flattering one in the bunch. After Penny and Chase approved the photos, the three remaining Blakemans stood on the front porch, waving as Chase and his future bride, hand in hand, hurried to catch the train back to the city to start their new, fully upgraded lives together.

Bride first, bride first, Abigail repeated in her head. As the mother of the groom, she would have to remember those words.

From the Desktop of Dearly Beloveds and Betrotheds

Dear B & Bs . . .

As promised, my short and not-too-sweet list of wishes **for the Mothers of the Bride:**

Be supportive, but not overbearing.

Offer opinions only when asked. Never offer criticism.

Just because you've written the check doesn't mean you get to write the guest list. Be grateful for one table.

Channel your need for attention into something productive like learning calligraphy to address the envelopes.

Be the mother you wanted at your wedding.

Stay hydrated, but not with vodka martinis.

Enjoy the accomplishment that is your adult daughter.

You won't regret looking your best on the big day. But your daughter will be the most beautiful one at the wedding.

Never, ever wear white.

Repeat as needed: **not my wedding, not my wedding**.

Big Kiss & Wedding Bliss,
Your Aunt B

Chapter 3

THE REVEAL

The Mother of the Bride

Alexa Diamandis pondered who to tell and when as she pounded out her daily walk on Butterfly Beach, a stretch of sand walkable from her house that took her back to her Patmos beginnings. Ever since she was a little girl, she worked out the sticky details of her life with a brisk morning walk on the beach, followed by a swim in the sea when the weather allowed. And there was no more beautiful spot in the world to help her make sense of her reluctance about announcing Penny's engagement than the slice of Montecito that was Butterfly Beach. The wild Pacific Ocean, the white sand sliver, the glamorous view of houses that ringed the cove, the impressive mountains that surrounded this bubble of luxury. She loved this special spot and had chosen to bring up her daughter here.

And now that daughter was choosing a man in Manhattan over this paradise.

She wished she was the type of mother who could scream for joy, make sure the moment was captured for posterity, and post to social media with descriptions like "My baby girl has found her true love." The mothers of Penny's Southern Methodist University sorority sisters seemed to own that corner of the internet, with heartfelt messages and a professional photographer on hand to capture the "surprise" proposal. As the SMU Kappas dropped one by one, engagement after engagement, Alexa marveled at their Insta-gorgeous announcements.

But Alexa wasn't that type and she never would be. A lifetime of taking care of herself, both financially and emotionally, had rendered her too pragmatic to wax poetic on social media about Penny. Or anything, really. Of course she was happy for Penny and Chase. She also hoped they would elope and get on with their lives. Maybe take a fantastic trip rather than spend time and energy doing the seating chart or ordering party favors. She'd rather contribute to a house down payment than a one-off wedding, an eminently practical idea no one ever mentioned in those glowing "She said YES!" posts.

Normalize "She said ESCROW!" Alexa thought.

If she were completely honest, there was also the fact that a tiny piece of her would never understand giving yourself over to another human being.

Alexa was a tender but tough twenty-four-year-old when she landed in Los Angeles in the eighties. She had spent her childhood in Greece, first on Patmos, an idyllic island near the coast of Turkey known for being the birthplace of the mystic Saint John, author of the Book of Revelation. Alexa's mother, Leni, was American-born, the child of immigrants who had left Greece for the icy winds of Chicago. Leni, however, was sent back to the family homeland in Greece in disgrace to ride out an unwanted pregnancy when she was eighteen. After giving birth to a son, she fell in love with an island innkeeper, Yiorgos Diamandis, and married him. Or maybe she just fell into a pleasantly useful relationship that meant she wouldn't have to move back to Chicago and her cruel family. It was all the same in those days. Arrangements were made for her to stay in Greece.

Leni and Yiorgos owned and managed a growing number of

inns and restaurants on the island serving the summer and religious tourist trade. In addition to raising Nikos as their own biological son, the couple added three more children, two noisy boys and their darling Alexa. It was a sweet life of hard work, sunshine, blue water, and unconditional love until Leni was hit by a drunk German tourist on a moped when Alexa was a teenager. The loss was shocking; the loneliness overwhelming. Her mother was dead, and Alexa learned to rely on herself.

Deciding that life on a small island in the company of four men wasn't the ideal situation for a smart and heartbroken girl, Yiorgos sent Alexa to an international boarding school in Athens in the care of her posh uncles, successful hoteliers with multiple properties in cities all over Greece. Alexa had spent time in the capital city over the years with her cousins and felt drawn to the culture and vibrancy of Athens life. But her first year without her mother was like going through a meat grinder and coming out the other end a pulverized version of her former, carefree self. She hid her insecurity behind dark sunglasses, black clothing, clove cigarettes, feigned ennui, and the Cure. Throwing herself into school meant not having to think about loss, and her good grades gave her a chance to move to London and enroll in King's College.

In London, Alexa spent many hours smoking in cafés and drinking in clubs while perfecting her English and a slightly cynical worldview. Every summer she returned home to Patmos, passing along her observations about the Brits to her uncles and father to incorporate into their hotels. Electric teapots in every room. Fresh flowers in the lobby. Books on the shelves. When she returned to school every fall, she went through a period of mourning, grieving the loss of her mother, the sun, and her tan in that order.

After finishing her degree, her plan was to get a job with an international hotel company based in London, but a busted love affair and the endless rain broke her spirit. When a British pal suggested a summer in Los Angeles, surfing in Malibu and working an hourly job, Alexa jumped at the chance. Because of her mother's American heritage, she was a dual citizen. A breezy summer in California seemed like her birthright.

But a random conversation in the baggage claim area during a very long wait for luggage led to a surprise job offer. The professional-looking couple, who claimed to be in the movie business, had two young sons who needed a nanny. Would she be interested in a summer on the beach taking care of the boys while they worked on their next film?

Yes, she would.

Little did she know that the beach was in Montecito, ninety miles north of LA, an idyllic town with a large contingent of Hollywood's brightest, which included her new employers. The wife was the writer and director and the husband was the producer. Together they were power players. The gig would last a decade. But within weeks of arriving at the modern house that was both the couple's home and their office, Alexa was making her impact felt. She was savvy, smart, and knew her way around technology. Plus, she was a whiz with numbers and had strong organizational skills after a lifetime of working for her parents' business. Once the kids were in school, Alexa would assume a senior role at the film company in operations, which meant more travel, accounting, and hiring and firing. She was well suited for the round-the-clock schedule of the film business, and the film business loved her European upbringing and British-tinged accent. For a while, it was a love match.

But the real draw for Alexa was Montecito. She felt at home in the seaside town the minute she arrived with her backpack and her Walkman. It reminded her of any Mediterranean island, with stunning houses built up the hillside, rocky sandy beaches, sunny days and cool nights, spectacular sunsets, and so many beautiful people. But Montecito had a touch of magic, an earthiness overlaid with sophistication. It was the perfect blend of beach and brains, taste and twist. It was star-kissed well before the biggest stars even moved into the neighborhood. And being in California meant that she could reinvent herself as needed, to hide the scars of her loss. She became a better, more confident version of herself, fueled by California's sunshine and optimism. Alexa was smitten and she never wanted to leave.

So she didn't. When the couple asked Alexa, then in her thirties, to move to LA proper and run their film company, she declined. She was ready to put down real roots, to stop living on movie sets and airplanes and maybe have a baby. She bid farewell to the biz and marched into a local travel agency she'd had her eye on. The older gentleman who owned the business, Addison Kent, knew everything about travel but was struggling to transition to a digital world. Alexa promised him that she would double his profits in less than a year if he gave her the opportunity to update his systems, streamline his process, and bring the company into the computer age. Plus, she wanted to add luxury tours of Greece to his offerings, executed with her insider knowledge of the country. For all that, she wanted a percentage of the company. She had grown up as a nonconsensual participant in the world of hospitality, thanks to her family's businesses. Now she wanted back in.

Addison, on the edge of sixty and exhausted by his demanding clients, took her up on her offer. The good people of Montecito would come to trust Alexa with their travel as they trusted Addison. They were used to someone else doing most tedious tasks for them. Booking travel was no exception, even when booking travel switched to this new online nonsense. They wanted to have a few conversations in a proper office with a real person where they could toss out phrases like "cruise through the Mediterranean" or "cooking school in Provence" or "family Christmas in London," and someone with a certain taste level, insider knowledge, and computer skills could simply make that happen. This clientele wanted full service and no surprises. And Alexa Diamandis knew how to provide both.

Eventually, she would buy out her friend and mentor and Kent

Travel would become Odyssey Vacations with Alexa as sole propri-
etor. The offices were redecorated in the blues of Greece. A con-
cierge position was added to provide beverages and quarters for the
parking meters during client meetings. And well-designed itinerary
folders became standard issue for every trip. Her people were paper
people.

On the personal side, she added a lovely historic 1920s condo at
the end of a cul-de-sac in what locals called the Lower Village to her
portfolio, a real estate decision she never regretted. She was settled,
successful, and she was ready for that baby.

And now that baby was getting married to a New Yorker! Someone who might take her precious Penny away forever. While it was
grand to be a citizen of the world and hold those two passports—
Greek and American—she couldn't quite grasp that Penny had
chosen New York over California. She'd worked so hard to create a
perfect childhood in a perfect town for Penny. Maybe, just maybe,
she'd have to succumb to plan and pay for the perfect Montecito
wedding. Then her Penny would see the light and return to California.

As Alexa walked through the door of Lucky's Steakhouse, she
spotted the crew who could make her plan a reality: the Merry Widows. And they were already through their first round of vodka sodas.

***

WHEN CAROL "TOOTS" Bixby had asked Alexa to plan a ladies-only
spa vacation a dozen years ago after the death of her husband, Bix
Bixby, neither understood it would be the start of a beautiful circle
of friendship. Toots was grieving, but not devastated, at least not
yet. The overwhelming grief would come once she recovered from
the exhaustion of his illness and funeral. Bix was twenty years her
senior and, as his second wife, Toots had put in some hard time on
the caregiving front as her husband's physical and mental health

diminished. Even his grown children agreed that she had earned her prenup payout and then some, a fact they acknowledged by not making a peep when the Montecito house went to Toots outright. They owned the oil company after all. What was a single piece of residential real estate compared to natural gas fields?

Toots, at the time an energetic former interior designer in her mid-sixties, cornered Alexa after Feldenkrais and begged, "I need two weeks away somewhere with lots of body treatments, a few fun coconspirators, and a discreet staff. If you know what I mean. And I don't want to see any of my neighbors, so not Rancho La Puerta or Miraval. Also, I want to make no decisions more complex than lemon or lime in my drink, so you must come, too."

Alexa nodded, understanding the assignment. "There's a place in Antigua." She recruited a handful of other Montecito women, all second and third wives, now widows, in the same circumstance: Mitsy, Roxanne, Ming, and Frannie. Thus the Merry Widows were born, and remained a vibrant force collectively, traveling, socializing, and playing mahjong together while talking, laughing, and empathizing nonstop.

At first, Alexa was on the outside, the hired hand paid to put their yearly trips together. But over the years and the global destinations, she was swept into their circle. She was not a widow, but she shared their desire for independence in her later years.

Tonight was their monthly dinner and the timing couldn't be more perfect. Penny had texted her that afternoon and given her the go-ahead to announce the engagement. The official photos would be up on Penny's Instagram any minute. Alexa guessed that once Penny checked the engagement photos off her list, the wedding planning would begin in earnest. She could sense that Penny had plans in the works but wanted to save the details for some reason.

"I have exciting news," Alexa declared as soon as Bernard, their usual waiter, placed her sauvignon blanc in front of her.

"You're retiring!" guessed Ming, a former financial planner who had worked her golf handicap down to a respectable plus ten in retirement.

"You're finally going to introduce us to your mystery man," said Mitsy, who'd held the title of widow the longest and with the most pride. Though she was not interested in marrying again—too much paperwork—she suspected Alexa of having a secret lover or else why would she smell so delicious all the time?

"I hope you're not sick," declared Roxanne, who believed that work killed and sunshine cured. She was convinced her late husband, a CFO, suffered his heart attack because of too many meetings and not enough vitamin D. She worried about Alexa.

"You finally agreed that we should all go to Antarctica on our next trip," shouted Frannie, who was slightly hard of hearing but up for the adventure travel that the rest of the Merry Widows avoided.

Alexa laughed and waved off all the speculation. "No, no. It's more . . ." She struggled for the correct word in the situation. What word could convince her that she was happy about all this? "More personal than all your speculations. Penny, my Penny, is getting married. To a lovely young man from New York. He works for the mayor!"

The Merry Widows oohed and ahhed and peppered her with questions about the ring, about popping the question, and, of course, about Chase. Penny had worked many of the Merry Widow trips over the years, either manning the phone at Odyssey Vacations or as Alexa's right hand on site in Provence and Porto and Sardinia. They had a genuine fondness for her daughter and Alexa soaked that in. Maybe this would be more fun than she thought.

"What's the scoop with Mummy and Daddy Blakeman?" Toots asked.

Alexa repeated the debrief she'd gotten from her daughter. "Real Connecticut Yankees, according to Penny. That's the correct term for the type with the old house and the old Labrador?" The Merry Widows nodded, always willing to fill in Alexa's cultural gaps. "The mother worked at a private school in development for many years, and the father was a stockbroker. Now they are retired and play golf and bridge. One sister. Penny says she's not sure how much money they have. The house is a bit shabby, but that's the way those people like it, right? Well-worn, like their Volvos."

The group shook their heads, as if allowing an upholstered armchair to show some age was a personal failing. Redecorating was a legitimate hobby in Montecito. Didn't they owe the universe well-appointed living rooms? "I'm meeting them in two weeks in New York. Penny and Chase have arranged a dinner in the city on Friday and then the parents are holding an engagement party at their house on Sunday. Is that normal?"

Mitsy Fairchild, a Pasadena native who migrated north to Montecito, self-identified as the group's Emily Post and jumped in. "Yes. Very traditional to do it quickly after the engagement, that way you can keep it simple. It's a drink, some nibbles. An informal acknowledgment that gives friends and neighbors a chance to meet the bride. Or the groom, depending upon who hosts the party. It's very flexible these days. And those New Englanders will be checking you out. So wear one of those gorgeous silk dresses you picked up in Athens. You'll wow them."

Toots added, "Penny may collect a few small gifts, like monogrammed coasters. But you will be able to gather a lot of intelligence for the wedding planning. About the MOG."

"The MOG?"

"Mother of the Groom. MOG. And you're the MOB. Mother of the Bride. You have a lot to learn about American weddings. According to tradition, the MOG is supposed to . . ." And at that point, the Widows chimed in like a Greek chorus: "Wear beige, stand back, and shut up." Laughter erupted.

"And what am I supposed to do as the MOB?" Alexa asked.

"Call San Ysidro Ranch to book the date and write a blank check," Ming answered, referring to the local luxury resort. "But as a financial advisor, albeit not yours, please don't get in over your head."

San Ysidro Ranch was where Jack and Jackie had honeymooned and where the lucky few held their weddings. Alexa had never been invited to a ceremony there, but she could imagine the classic nineteenth-century California ranch nestled up against the mountains and perfumed in lavender and roses and twinkling in white lights and fairy dust as the ultimate wedding venue. She couldn't imagine the costs. Truly. Was a wedding there one hundred thousand dollars? Two hundred? A million? Whatever it was, it was out of her league. Alexa sensed Ming was an ally. "Well, I'm hoping I can convince Penny to have the wedding here next summer. Something lovely, personal. Something that I can afford. But still special."

The more she talked about it, the more Alexa got on board with her own idea. Of course Penny would have the modest wedding of her dreams. Beautiful young people from both coasts would attend. A small cadre of family would come from Greece to represent their heritage. Her dear friend Simon Fox would be her escort for the weekend. A small, select group of her local friends, like the Merry Widows, would add to the party. It would be a joyous, charming, sunny California celebration, admired by guests for its authenticity and good vibes. And with the naivete of a woman who had never fantasized about such an event, never mind planned one, she believed she could produce a simple, personal, affordable wedding in Montecito.

There was a collective squeal of enthusiasm from the Merry Widows. Much to their credit, her friends didn't want to burst her bubble quite yet with the cost of a venue or the logistics of the tent or the impossibility of booking a caterer in the summer. Ming bit her tongue before divulging stories about clients, the half-million-dollar weddings, and the divorces two years later. There was no reason to spoil the fun tonight. Let the hard truths be saved for tomorrow.

"The minute you have the date, call San Ysidro Ranch and book the honeymoon suite. That will be my gift to the bride and groom!" Toots and Penny had a special relationship, forged in the early days of Toots's widowhood when Penny spent a whole summer in one of her guest rooms working as Toots's personal assistant. Truthfully, she got the job because Toots was lonely and sad in her grand house, but neither one would ever admit it. That was years ago but they still adored each other. Toots waved her hand and her wrist full of gold bangles in the general direction of their waiter. "Bernard, we need Veuve! We have a wedding to plan!"

From the Desktop of Dearly Beloveds and Betrotheds

Dear B & Bs . . .

My list of wishes for the Mothers of the Groom:

Beige looks terrible on almost everyone, so skip the first part of the adage, "Wear beige, stand back, and shut up." But the last two bits are good advice.

Act as if it's lovely to be included in any part of the wedding planning, even if you disagree with every decision.

Offer no opinions, only validation to the Bride and her mother.

Just because you've written a check doesn't mean you get to write the guest list. Not even one table. Maybe not even one name.

It's all out of your control—the venue, the meal, the flowers, the guest list. Try to enjoy the freedom of not being in charge.

Channel your need for attention into one nifty cha-cha for the mother-son dance.

Be the mother-in-law you wish you had at your wedding.

You won't regret looking your best on the big day. But your daughter-in-law will be the most beautiful one at the wedding.

Never, ever wear white.

Repeat as needed: **not my wedding, not my wedding**.

As always, I look forward to answering your questions in future columns, even the tedious ones about forcing your poor bridesmaids to plan a bachelorette party in a foreign country and to pick up the tab for you. (No. Hard no.) Or the ones where you question the need to feed the guests that take a day, drive for hours, and graciously attend your ceremony. (Yes. Hard yes.) And, of course, the classic dilemma about your estranged cousin who put their Venmo QR code right on the Evite to streamline gift giving. (I have no words. No. Words.) See, all tedious. But send the questions anyway and I will plow through them with diligence . . . and love.

Bonus! Here's a secret I can share! For my very first **Your Aunt B Goes to the Wedding** profile of this season, I'll be attending the nuptials of Ashlee and Damien in Charleston. I've been promised Spanish Moss Meets Modern Nautical. We shall see, won't we?

Big Kiss & Wedding Bliss,
Your Aunt B

Chapter 4

THE REVEAL

The Mother of the Groom

Abigail Blakeman carefully lifted the lemon bars on the silver tray out of the back of her Mercedes sedan. She'd made her signature baked good to accompany her announcement of the engagement to the team at the Black Rock Senior Center. She'd gotten clearance from the bride to "post on her socials," which made Abigail laugh. As if she had the technical skills and energy to manage a multitude of platforms! She still wrote notes on Crane stationery. The truth was, she wasn't waiting for Penny's permission anyway. She had her whole story ready for the crew at Potluck Tuesday. Plus, while these were her coworkers, they weren't really her people. Who would they tell?

The first time Abigail ventured into the BRSC, as she would come to know it, she was a recently "retired" private school development person who was seeking discretion and conversational Italian lessons. She'd lived less than ten miles from the facility for decades and never considered it a viable option for leisure-time activities even when she crossed the threshold into senior citizen status. Why would she? Abigail and George Blakeman were club people—golf, tennis, and yachting—the last being in name only as they rarely sailed anywhere and the time they spent "at sea" was to join friends on their sailboats moored in the harbor for cocktails. But the roast beef sandwiches and holiday parties at the Fair Harbor Yacht Club were top-notch and seemed worth the dues when they had money. But the last ten years had seen their clubbiness seep away, at first monetarily, and eventually emotionally.

George Blakeman had spent the bulk of his career achieving modest to no success as a stockbroker, a true beneficiary of the old boy network. He ultimately gave up the pretense of managing anyone's money, especially theirs, when he was forced out of the firm—by his Pomfret roommate, no less—after a few questionable trades. (At least questionable to his clients, who didn't know they were happening at all.) He turned his sights and their fortune to professional bridge, a game for which he had a knack and now endless hours of time. But the drip, drip, dripping away of their wealth started long before George left finance because of his terrible investments, and it accelerated with his gold watch and sad send-off party.

The prospect of them living on Abigail's salary was laughable. She'd spent twenty years as the warm, cheery, and underpaid director of development at the Silliman School, an expensive private high school known for its low expectations and pottery program housed on the former estate of the heiress Cecelia Silliman. The main building was an English Tudor gem with, sadly, no water view. The school was a way station for C students, weirdos, and second sons and daughters who'd been booted from legit prep schools. The parents loved Abigail and gave generously because she took the time to get to know their offspring and could say to them at school events, "Benton is so gifted in ceramics," or "Layla makes everyone smile all the time." True statements that reassured his parents that Benton, who had very few friends and smelled like cheese, was good at something. Or that Layla, who'd been goth since the second grade, was totally likable despite the tongue stud. That's all parents wanted, a sense that their Bentons and Laylas would one day be fine. They wrote checks to Abigail because she filled them with reassurance.

But when Silliman's beloved headmaster retired and the board, headed by a tedious tech zillionaire, went all in on academics and hired a STEM-focused head of school, Abigail found herself in over her head. They wanted her to run capital campaigns, network with the high-net-worths, and even apply for grants. It was all too much. She returned to her beautiful office filled with antiques and hand-woven rugs after the Christmas holidays prepared to give notice for her departure at the end of the school year. She'd give the parent community enough time to organize a gracious retirement event and maybe a scholarship in her name. But by noon on the first day back, she was informed that her services were no longer needed and by that Friday, she was gone from Silliman. Barely even an acknowl-edgment for twenty years of service, except the flower arrangement sent by the Wiggins family, whose four Silliman graduates had a long history of poor test scores, underbites, and plenty of import-export money.

It was then that Abigail, who'd always managed the house-hold finances, started the cost-cutting measures and the excuses in earnest. One by one, she shed the pieces of her identity visible to the outside world that were sucking up cash. She dropped the membership at the yacht club and switched to a golf-only plan at the country club. (She never really liked tennis anyway, except the outfits. She would miss the cute skirts.) She jettisoned her charity commitments, like the hospital auxiliary and the home for women in recovery, which always seemed to come with a rather hefty sug-gested donation in addition to hours of volunteer time. She wrote the membership chairs lovely notes, explaining that now that she and George were retired, they wanted to do as much traveling as possible, which of course was a lie.

They stopped attending fundraising dinners, luncheons, and any event with a silent auction. Truth was, Abigail didn't really miss most of the social activities. She was over small talk and feigning interest in other people's children. Her go-to excuse for not attending became something vague about using all her free time to finally organize the house and do a little downsizing. She felt like she sold it to her fellow Fair Harbor mothers and wives, who nodded in agreement, as if Saturday night were the natural time to run old stuffed animals to the Goodwill.

But it was with the heaviest heart that she withdrew from the Coventry Garden Club, an organization devoted to beautification and that had once favored hands-on gardening over galas. Recently, the focus had changed to luxury group trips to events like the Chelsea Flower Show or private tours of the Alhambra in Granada, none of which she could afford, even in the good old days. Her resignation from this group felt like cutting the last tie to her privileged life as she knew it, but she told herself that nobody noticed that Abigail Blakeman was fading away. She was simply reorganizing.

She thanked her stars that she had the sense to secure her lifetime membership in the Daughters of the American Revolution with a hefty donation in the early aughts. She'd never give up her heritage.

Beyond the social connections, there were no opera tickets or Broadway matinees or dinners out at eateries that were not at the golf club, where they had to use that monthly minimum. The Mercedes was old, but not quite vintage, so she kept it as clean as she could to fool people. Thank goodness both she and George favored simple tailored clothes that never went out of style, at least in her opinion. She felt like they were at least keeping up appearances. Weren't they?

Abigail felt a visceral relief when her daughter, Sarah, chose to play field hockey at the University of Connecticut, a state school, rather than at Connecticut College, an expensive private school. Sarah assumed her mother's tears were sentimental, that she was reflecting on her daughter's years of hard work, morning lifting, and unrelenting focus on her sport, but really, Abigail wept because she knew they could hold it together financially for a few more years, until they could finally sell the house.

The damn house was both the golden goose and the clapboard noose. When George's aunt Eleanor had left them 4701 Water Street, it seemed like a dream come true, a genteel address that ensured a lovely life. When the couple first met in New York City, they used Aunt Eleanor's coastal home as a getaway from the city. Over the weekends, Abigail and Eleanor grew close, bonded by a love of hydrangeas and gin and tonics. And George was like the son Eleanor never had. When she died, a proper Yankee death with little fuss, no one was surprised the house went to her nephew and his wife.

New parents at the time, Abigail and George eagerly left New York City to start their suburban dream. Abigail would give up her job at Merrill Lynch in the marketing department to stay home and care for Chase, meet other mommies, and get a Volvo wagon and a Labrador. George would commute in and out of the city on the train and have two separate lives: a Manhattan Expense Account life during the week and a Connecticut Golf Dad life on the weekends. It felt like they'd earned this lifestyle.

The only catch was the caveat in Aunt Eleanor's will that they hold on to the house for thirty-two years, a specific number that neither attorney nor family could explain. But Aunt Eleanor wanted George and Abigail to stay put—no sales, no sublets, no substantial remodels that changed the profile of the house. (As if the zoning commission would allow such a thing in a registered historic home.) To ensure that George and Abigail didn't become house poor, the practical Eleanor had even created a monetary trust for home maintenance. Abigail had complained to her friends that the Ghost of Aunt Eleanor controlled their every financial move. But over time, she came to see the aunt's will as a document that protected George from himself. Who knew how many times he might have mortgaged the property to finance a bad investment?

Even with the provisions in place, George had managed to burn through the trust by their tenth wedding anniversary with home improvement projects executed by the most expensive contractors in town. "This roof was worth every dime. It will last fifty years," George had promised at the time, not anticipating Hurricane Sandy and other extreme weather events. Still, 4701 Water Street increased in value, as the whole town benefited from the explosion of wealth in the area in recent decades. The truth was that the house was their financial salvation—but they couldn't list it for two more years.

Abigail prayed every night they could make it through the next twenty-four months, sell for over the asking price, and move to a resort community near Savannah. Or Hilton Head. Or anywhere with low taxes and an even lower cost of living. Abigail and George could leave the Nutmeg State with their heads held high, as if this were their plan all along.

This engagement had given her renewed hope that could happen. Maybe if she could convince Chase and Penny to have the wedding in Fair Harbor, there would be press and photos and the house would sell itself at top dollar. It looked gorgeous in the summer with the garden in full bloom and the view. No one would even notice the fading paint job. Until then, she would pinch her pennies, keep making excuses, and stash away those paychecks from the BRSC in what she thought of as her slush fund bank account.

She applied for the job as a front desk clerk as a combination whim and act of desperation. She needed a break from life at home with George and she couldn't afford to go anywhere or do anything. The initial Conversational Italian class beget Zumba beget Morning Joe and Mojo, or Mojo Mojo, as the regulars called it, a class where they drank coffee, walked on the treadmill, and talked.

The more time she spent at the senior center, the more at home she felt. Her fellow seniors had so much to share, from unusual recipes to off-the-wall medical advice to stories about their personal lives that bore no resemblance to her own life whatsoever. These

people had messy, complicated, loud lives, so different from the va-
nilla existence of her neighbors in Fair Harbor. And she loved being
around them.

When Cecily, the sharp young director of the center, interviewed
her for the front desk position, it was a match made in heaven. Cecily had confidence and credentials, and Abigail wanted to be in
her orbit. Even if it was at fifteen dollars an hour for fifteen hours
a week. In return, Cecily praised Abigail as a "steady, mature presence." Exactly the role she wanted to fill.

Now she happily set off to her job two days a week and spent
another two mornings a week at the center working out and socializing. She'd never really bothered to explain to George that it
was a paying job that got her out the door. He'd assumed she was
volunteering, giving away her time and talents for free like she had
done for so many other organizations. It was what capable, educated
women did in Fair Harbor: take their advanced degrees and experience and give back to the community with endless hours of volunteer work. It never would have occurred to George that it was a real
job and it never would have occurred to Abigail to tell him. Money
was their second-least discussed topic; sex was the first.

Even her friends, the few she stayed in contact with after the
great purge, assumed she was volunteering her time. "You've become
so devoted to the senior center. It's so admirable, helping those poor
old people," Arletta Draper declared after a catch-up chat in the
produce section of the Stop & Shop. Arletta was at least seventy-five
herself but saw nothing in common with the retired social workers,
teachers, plumbers, and bank tellers whom Abigail served.

Abigail had been that way once, too. But if the last few years
had taught her anything, it was that there was no cultural divide a
baked good couldn't bridge. And while her lemons bars were sweet-
and-sour citrus perfection, they weren't any better than Phillipa's
wedding cookies or Ronetta's sweet potato pie. She couldn't wait
to tell the team about her handsome, talented son, his sophisti-

cated fiancée, and the sparkling but frugal drinks-only engagement party she was hosting "for the neighbors," even though the guest list included several Silliman board members, her Mommy and Me group from 1998, the DAR stalwarts, and the few former clients of George's who'd managed to make money. (She certainly didn't want the BRSCers to feel left out, but she wasn't ready to share her three-million-dollar view with them yet.)

Abigail pushed open the doors, silver tray balanced in one hand, and felt great about her life for the first time in years.

Chapter 5

THE MEDIA PLAY

The Mother of the Groom

"Hi, dear."

"Hi, Mom," Chase said, for once at a normal volume, not in a hushed tone that suggested he was in a car heading somewhere downtown with his boss. "Do you have a sec?"

"Yes," said Abigail. "I'm glad you called; I have very exciting news about the engagement party. But you go first."

"I wanted to let you know that Penny's mom's old friend Simon Fox will be joining us for the party. You know, the British guy I told you about? He's in New York for business, so I hope you don't mind if Penny invites him."

Mind? My goodness, she was thrilled. A real-life British lord at her drinks party. He would understand the concept of drinks and mixed nuts only. She had wanted to keep it tight—time-wise and money-wise. Plus, she could show him which properties in the neighborhood the British had burned to the ground during the Revolution. How exciting! "Of course not. We're delighted to have Penny's *godfather*," she said with a wink. Could he be Penny's real father?

"Mom, please, please, don't make a big deal of this."

"Of course not. It's our secret. But I am looking forward to meeting Lord Simon Fox. Do you know who else will want to meet him? My special guest, Bernadette Caruso. She was my roommate at Ethel Walker. Then I went to Bryn Mawr and she went on to Barnard and Columbia J school and then the *Times*, of course. Now she's *the* Aunt B, the wedding guru. Her coverage of society weddings is sublime. She's old school when it comes to weddings, but new school when it comes to media. Aunt B is going to be at the party. Do you know who she is?"

"Yes, Mom. You've mentioned her a million times. And every woman I know has quoted Aunt B about something since we started telling our friends we're engaged. It's like they memorize her columns," Chase said with a mix of admiration and bemusement. "Will she be there in a professional capacity? Is she covering the engagement party?"

"I don't know exactly. I think she's thinking about covering the wedding, so she's surveilling the party to make sure it's up to her standards. At least she still has standards, not like the *New York Times*, which doesn't even print the names of the parents and grandparents in the 'Vows' section anymore. Who are these people getting married in a barn? We don't know."

"Mom, please don't say stuff like that out loud this weekend." Chase laughed.

"You know I won't. I just miss the old days when lineage mattered. But Bernadette does live right up the coast in Niantic. A Fair Harbor wedding would be an easy trip for her."

There was a substantial pause on the other end of the phone. Chase was making calculations, which was literally his job. Every day, he maneuvered the mayor of New York to this meeting or that meeting. One interview over another. To lunch with this donor instead of coffee with that advocacy group. Every minute was a considered choice, and now his mother was offering up an unexpected option of her own: coverage. He decided to tread carefully. No reason to put his foot down just yet. "Remember, Mom, this is Penny's wedding. And she wants to make it significant for her and her mom, so that may mean California."

"It's your wedding, too. And Connecticut is significant to you and to me. Plus, wouldn't an article about your tasteful wedding benefit your career?" Abigail wasn't naive about her son's ambitions. His comment about running for office had been top of mind over the last two weeks. Well, not quite top of mind. Roping in Bernadette and scouring the RealReal for designer mother of the groom dresses at a bargain were number one and number two. And ordering the monogrammed cocktail napkins and securing a decent bartender for the party were numbers three and four. But supporting her son's future, even if it did include working for a loudmouth like Timmo Lynch, was in the top five of her concerns. "And don't pretend you don't know that. Penny's in public relations, so she gets it, too. Tell her Aunt B will be there and I'm sure she'll be thrilled."

Another pause. "You didn't pitch Aunt B on the British lord connection, did you?"

"Of course I didn't," she snapped. Of course she had. Vaguely. In her note to Bernie, she referred to Lord Fox as a beloved godfather and dear family friend, possibly more. "The point is that Bernie's coming as are many other lovely and socially prominent people who want to meet Penny and wish you both the best. Think of the party that way and you'll both enjoy it."

Chase was silent for a beat. "Sounds good, Mom. Penny and I appreciate your effort." Now he was back in chief of staff mode.

"We're looking forward to dinner Friday night with Penny's mother. And what time should Sarah pick you up at the train station on Sunday? Have you made your plans?" She tried to keep her voice light and breezy but she'd be furious if they hadn't thought through the train schedule. The party was an efficient ninety minutes. Being late wasn't an option. They had to be there before guests arrived and stay until they all left.

"Penny booked a car. We're leaving the city to be there in plenty of time. She said her mother really doesn't do public transportation."

A car! For the whole evening! The expense seemed outrageous. She could have ordered the beef tenderloin platter or the mini crab cakes, maybe both, with the cost of the car service from the city. The waste. When the quiet car on the train seemed fine. Still, Abigail managed to zip it. "How lovely. It's drinks and nuts at the party. But I've some sandwiches and salad for all of us after the guests leave."

"Oh, that's okay. We're headed back into the city for a late dinner with Simon. Penny's people eat late, especially in the summer. She always says there's on time and Greek time. I'm learning."

Abigail tried not to sound deflated, outdone by European sensibilities. Did she still have time to cancel the order for the Caesar salad with grilled shrimp from Nutmeg? She hoped so. "We have so much to learn about Penny's family, don't we?"

"I gotta go." Chase's standard sign-off.

"Bye. See you—" The phone call ended. "Friday."

Chapter 6

THE DINNER

The Mother of the Groom

Abigail thought she had prepared herself for Alexa Diamandis. For the last two weeks, ever since the engagement, she'd been scouring the internet searching for photos and articles and mentions of Penny's mother. And there was a treasure trove of information on her future in-law. Alexa was a business owner, after all, and an active citizen of Montecito, land of a thousand charity events. Plus, her job was to take people on vacation, so she ended up tagged in scores of photos of tanned, happy people beachside in Mykonos or at historical sites in Sicily. Abigail knew that she was striking but not beautiful, tall-ish, and had one go-to smile for every picture captured of her. She had practically memorized Alexa's bio on the Odyssey Vacations site, so she knew, too, all about her idyllic childhood on Patmos, her uni days in London, her Hollywood decade, and her glamorous career in luxury travel.

Alexa was one of those women who had aged in place, meaning that Abigail could still see the eighties undergrad and the focused career gal and the bold single mom in her sixty-something face. Some people disappeared into their later years' appearance, no trace of their young days left, thanks to injectables and surgery. But not Alexa. She was all she had been.

Abigail was ready to be warm, curious, and generous with her new relative, treating her like you might a visiting minor royalty who didn't quite understand the language. Abigail, after all, was well educated in all things, but especially tact. Despite her world travels, Alexa was the guest and might feel out of sorts here on the Upper East Side in the small private dining room of the charming neighborhood Italian place. Abigail, on the other hand, felt right at home, even though she hadn't lived in this zip code since the nineties. It was Chase's home now. Still, she'd go out of her way to make the mother of the bride feel comfortable.

Just then the curtain blew open and in stepped Alexa Diamandis.

Abigail was not prepared to be so intimidated. Alexa did, in fact, carry herself like royalty. She was statuesque, not slender, but her height allowed her to carry the extra weight. Her long black hair, swept up in an elegant bun, was gently streaked with silver and set off her gray eyes. She was a well-preserved sixtyish woman whose skin looked like it had been dipped in olive oil and then polished to a sheen. And she was wearing a long, flowing white silk dress splashed with a bright blue abstract print and shaped by a gold belt. She looked like she was going to a much better event after dinner and it was probably on a yacht.

And the fact that she arrived alone made her entrance more legendary.

After she greeted Penny and Chase and then George, she made her way around the table to Abigail, freshly bobbed and highlighted in her tailored navy-blue Tahari dress that she'd picked up at a very good resale shop in Darien. Alexa did the double kiss, which Abigail was sure was meant to throw her off, and whispered in her ear, "We are family now."

She smelled like lemons and sunshine and Abigail knew in that moment that everything she had fantasized about the wedding would never come to pass. It would not be at her house in Connecticut with an all-white tablescape featuring hydrangea and rose centerpieces. It would not feature fun New England–y fare like clam chowder bowls and a rowboat full of local beer. She would not be the second-most-striking woman at the wedding, next to Penny, of course. And there would not be a stunning feature of the classic Connecticut event in Aunt B's column. With one double kiss of Alexa's lips, Abigail knew that she would do exactly what everyone at the senior center advised her to do as the mother of the groom: wear beige and shut up. "Yes, we are family."

***

A CACOPHONY OF small talk, laughter, toasts, and dinner orders followed the initial greetings. Questions were asked with inconsequential answers, like how was your flight and how often do you get to New York City. Abigail was having a hard time finding her voice, but George was skilled at these sorts of interactions. There was a reason that he'd kept his job for years, despite the underwhelming results for his clients: his broad but shallow knowledge of all sorts of topics and his erudite cultural references. It was clear that both sides of the table had done their homework. Alexa asked about Sarah and retirement and bridge. But all the chitchat was a warm-up before the main event. Chase had promised that the wedding plan would be revealed at the dinner.

In the gap between the first course and the three pastas that Chase had ordered for all of them to share, Abigail gave her son a look that she hoped registered as "It's time." He took the hint and his fiancée's hand. Abigail had to concede that Penny looked lovely in the creamy white dress she'd chosen, as the new rule seemed to be that brides wear white to any wedding-adjacent festivities. She didn't need the resort-wear flash her mother brought to the party to draw attention to herself, Abigail thought.

"We wanted to fill you all in on a few decisions that we've made with regards to our future," Chase announced. He looked so handsome, Abigail thought, filled with pride in her part of his good looks. *He certainly got the best parts of George and me*, she thought. Not like poor Sarah, who seemed to have received most of the worst. Like her father's cankles.

Penny jumped in right where Chase left off, akin to a scripted presentation or a sign of their single-mindedness. "First, let us say that it's truly special to have you all here at our favorite restaurant and we're looking forward to the engagement party. Thank you for hosting on Sunday, Abigail and George." The use of their first names was jarring to Abigail, but she smiled to cover the wincing. "We know this is the first of many blended-family events. It's really something to see our parents in the same room. It feels real now!" Penny had been the president of her sorority at SMU and she still carried that smooth, singsong delivery of a young woman in charge. The two of them were quite a pair.

The plates of carbonara, cacio e pepe, and arrabbiata arrived and, without losing a beat, Chase served the five of them a sampling of each while speaking. It was like he'd been interning with a big Italian family on the weekends. "We have a few announcements here, so if you can hold your questions until the end, as we say in the press room, that would be appreciated. First, our plan is to be married rather quickly and here's why. And no, you don't need a shotgun, Alexa." There was genuine laughter from George, and fake laughter from the MOG and the MOB. "As you know, my current job ends later this year as Mayor Lynch terms out. And at his encouragement, and the encouragement of others, I've been asked to consider running for Congress. There's a district in Queens—Astoria—where an incumbent will be retiring at the end of his term in eighteen months, and the mayor thinks I'm a great fit. Yes, Queens. Big Greek population. I'll be running as an Independent, like the mayor. I'll have the full backing of Mayor Lynch and continue to work for him in some capacity even after he leaves office, so I can pay the bills and do my due diligence at the same time. And yes, I will be moving there to establish residency and get to know the place—and Penny will join me in Queens as soon as we're married. Now, Penny, I think this is your department."

Penny turned to Alexa. "Mom, we'd like to be married in Montecito around New Year's Eve. We know getting married on New Year's Eve would be too expensive, so the Friday night before is the date we'd like. Not a huge wedding, but a special wedding. I can't wait to plan it with you. I know you don't do client trips over the holidays anymore, so I thought it would be good, timing-wise. And I get that the family might not be able to come from Athens and Patmos, so we'll spend our honeymoon in Greece next summer and celebrate with them then. I can show Chase my other home."

Abigail's head started to swim. Did Penny just say she was not planning on inviting the Diamandis family to the wedding? Would her family be cut out, too, because Connecticut was too far away from California? As she was considering how she would tell her one remaining aunt and her three cousins that they wouldn't be invited to a wedding that was sure to get press coverage, the announcement continued.

The words of the happy couple started to come out at a rapid pace and made less and less sense to her. Squeeze in the wedding before the campaign starts in earnest. Only have one bridesmaid, which will be impossible because she has already been in seven weddings and feelings would be hurt. Rent a house in Astoria that could also be the campaign headquarters. Rent an estate in Montecito for the family and the reception. Mediterranean mezzes and lemon cake. Leaning toward a beach picnic for the rehearsal dinner. Maybe the mayor can marry us. Certainly, the mayor will endorse him. All the guests in shades of blue. The mothers need to coordinate dresses. Their friend Ree, the graphic artist, is going to design the campaign logo and the wedding logo. *Wait, weddings have logos?*

For the couple who two weeks ago claimed they hadn't made any plans, they certainly seemed to have made all the plans now. Abigail guessed they were hiding something.

Penny looked pleased as punch. "We appreciate your support so much. On such a quick timeline, we're going to need all your help."

"What do you think?" Chase asked with excitement in his voice.

Abigail was stunned. She looked at her counterpart and, much to her surprise, the mother of the bride also seemed shell-shocked. This pleased her. Abigail could only squeak out one question: "Queens?"

Chapter 7

THE DINNER

The Mother of the Bride

"Queens?" Alexa gasped at the same time as Abigail. The whole thing was so unexpected. Her Penny had gone and planned her whole life without consulting her. How could that have happened? In the past, they had talked about everything. Even in the last two weeks, they'd talked every day, mainly about Penny's crushing work schedule, thanks to a demanding client and a new project. But Alexa had believed her when she said that they hadn't started the wedding planning. Now, boom. This. A lifetime of decisions laid bare between the pasta course and the main. And she was hearing them all for the first time, like she was an outsider. *Like she was an in-law!*

Sure, she was invited in now to help with the tedious decisions, like reception venue, but the big decisions, like spouse and house, were already made. She couldn't wrap her head around the idea that Penny would be living in New York, never mind Queens near the airport. The airport! From the California Riviera to the shadow of LaGuardia. And if Chase won his election, he could be in Congress for decades. They might move to DC, the dowdiest city in the country, awash in women in navy-blue suits with below-the-knee skirts.

She'd never come back to California. To Montecito. What had Alexa done wrong?

As Chase was explaining that there were some cool parts of Astoria and it was closer to Midtown than people thought, Alexa searched her Penny's face for some sign that this was all conjecture and that when the two of them, mother and daughter, got a moment alone, they would make the real plans together like they always had. But Penny gazed at Chase as if he were going to save the world, but first, he was going to save her.

This was all Alexa's fault.

She never should have let Penny wear all that pink and be a cheerleader in high school instead of on the debate team. When she picked college in Dallas instead of Berkeley, Alexa kept her mouth shut. She joined that sorority and Alexa played along, flying in for endless events that made no sense to Alexa, mother-daughter this and mother-daughter that. Alexa, motherless since fifteen and not used to American-style education, was shocked at the outlay of money and effort that went into activities unrelated to academics. Penny, on the other hand, seemed to genuinely embrace the Kappa lifestyle.

Then there was the move to New York after graduation. Alexa could see now that was a mistake. Too much freedom and independent choice. She should have made Alexa intern at Odyssey for at least two years before agreeing to supplement her rent on the Upper East Side. She never thought Penny would love New York. Or meet a man up to her standards. And she never thought she'd move to Queens.

Every Greek immigrant in America knew Astoria, Queens, of course. It was the first stop in the country for thousands of immigrants from her homeland and many put down new roots there and never left. Alexa had made a conscious decision not to move to Astoria, a place where the old-school values still ran deep. She had wanted a fresh start in California. Now it felt like her daughter was rejecting her unconventional upbringing. She was moving to Queens but not inviting her Greek family to the wedding? That would go over well with the Diamandis clan in Athens!

Penny interrupted her thoughts. "Mom, we'll have all day tomorrow to go over everything. I know we'll need to talk budget. I understand," she said, as if her mother were a small child instead of the woman who had raised her all on her own and paid her college tuition in cash because that's how much she loved her.

Alexa was trying hard to keep a smile on her face when George piped up. "Count the Blakemans in for the rehearsal dinner. And, if you need a tent for the big day, we'll cover that. Won't we, Abby girl?"

Alexa caught the sudden flash of rage on Abigail Blakeman's soft, lined face. Her simple ash-blond bob was still in place. Her soft pink lipstick had been reapplied somewhere between the artichoke carpaccio and two bites of the cacio e pepe she allowed herself. But her décolletage was streaked an angry red, visible thanks to the split neckline of her sheath dress, a tasteful, if uninspired, choice that Alexa had seen on dozens of women at home. Alexa didn't know exactly what Chase's mother was angry about, but she knew repressed fury when she saw it. Alexa was holding her tongue out of pride and good manners. Abigail was stuffing her feelings out of habit. That was something to remember, Alexa thought.

There was a slight nod from Abigail. "Of course we will. Our pleasure."

Just then the servers swept in and cleared the table. The head server, using quite possibly a fake Italian accent, announced, "It's now time for your entrées. And then, we celebrate the beautiful couple with cake. Enjoy."

Alexa didn't know how she was going to make it through two more courses.

***

THEY PARTED ON the sidewalk outside the restaurant on Seventy-Eighth Street and Second Avenue. The Blakemans hustled into a cab and headed to Grand Central to catch the ten forty train home. Alexa wanted to walk a bit but didn't want the young couple to feel beholden to walk her back the ten or so blocks to the Lowell Hotel, where she was staying thanks to a professional courtesy rate. She pretended to order a rideshare and assured them that she would wait near the valet for safety. "You're tired. No need to wait with me."

As soon as they were out of sight on the way back to Penny's place nearby, she'd make her way back to the hotel on her own. She needed to walk off her emotions.

But Penny had more surprises. "So, now that Abigail is gone, I wanted to tell you that Kalliope Moon is in town doing a trunk show in SoHo. As soon as I saw it posted, I called Sofia at the boutique in Athens. You know, the saleswoman who helped us last when we did that trip with Westmont alumnae. Those women bought the boutique out. She told me there will be four wedding dresses at the trunk show. She wouldn't send me photos because she said I had to see them in person. They agreed to hold them for me in exchange for some social media posts on my personal accounts. But only until noon. It could be chaos at the sale. I thought we could start the day at your hotel for coffee and be at the shop by eleven. Can you imagine, a Kalliope Moon wedding dress? I didn't think I'd even have the option on such a short timeline. It would be my dream."

"Just you and me?"

"Yes. That's why I waited until Abigail left," Penny whispered, as if someone nearby were wearing a wire and might inform her future mother-in-law of the slight. Not that it was officially a slight in terms of proper wedding etiquette, but so many of her friends had included the mother of the groom in the dress-shopping experience that she felt a bit selfish for wanting it to be special for the two of them, mother and bride. She hid behind her groom, who knew nothing about dress shopping. "I feel kind of bad not including her, but Chase said she wouldn't mind. Right, Chase?"

He nodded, oblivious to any devastation his permission would cause.

So was Alexa. She was happy to be included, but it wasn't anything she expected. Alexa had watched the dress-buying shows on TV when she was at the hair salon and couldn't believe the nonsense she witnessed as groups of friends and relatives, in sashes and drinking champagne, challenged the bride on her choices. Nobody needed ten people in a dressing room badgering the bride about her weight or her taste. At least Penny had retained enough judgment to know that.

As for Abigail, she rationalized to herself, but not out loud: *Chase's mother has Sarah. That's her chance to go wedding dress shopping.* "A Kalliope Moon dress would be a dream." An expensive dream.

It was already starting, the expense creep. As soon as the words "wedding" and "dream" were said in the same sentence, the budget blew up another 25 percent. A budget they hadn't even established yet. "I think you'll look stunning in anything. But I love that you want a Greek designer. Classic but modern. And, of course, our heritage."

"Thanks, Mom. I'll see you in the lobby around nine. Is that too early?"

Penny understood the first morning on East Coast time could be tough for Californians. "Let's say nine fifteen. I won't be late." She smiled at her daughter and then turned to her future son-in-law. "Thank you for dinner. It was delicious and eventful. Sleep well." She glanced at her phone screen to sell the lie. "Four more minutes. Off you go. I'll be fine."

Chapter 8

THE CAB RIDE

The Mother of the Groom

"What were you thinking?" Abigail snapped as soon as they settled in the cab headed south on Park to Grand Central.

"I didn't encourage him to run for Congress!" George countered.

"Oh, I can't even speak about that now. I'm going to need some time to process, as young people say. I thought I knew what might be coming, but it was so much worse. Why on earth would anyone want to be a congressman? I don't understand his need for attention."

"I think our son actually wants to do good in the world," George responded with a bit of awe in his voice, because doing good beyond tossing a few bucks to a charity had never really occurred to him.

"Again, we're not talking about that situation right now. I'm talking about your offer to pay for the rehearsal dinner and the tent! The accepted wedding rules say the dinner the night before is on us. But why did you throw in the tent! Do you have any idea what tents cost?"

"Honey, please," George said, nodding toward the cabdriver, who was both speeding and playing with his phone.

"He has those ear birds in. Or earbuds. Whatever they're called.

George, we can barely afford to go to a wedding in Montecito, never mind host a wedding in Montecito!"

"I made a small gesture. Dinner and a tent, that's it," said the king of small gestures.

"You pay no attention to our finances, but somehow you feel you've earned the right to be extravagant," Abigail hissed. She had held her tongue for most of the last five years, quietly mopping up the messes George made, overly enthusiastic when his bridge-playing pivot earned dividends. She really didn't want to be a shrew about money. She didn't deserve to be forced into that role, she thought. "We haven't been to a fundraiser in three years, but yes, let's lavish a wedding tent on a family we barely know."

"Here we go again," George mocked, as if every day they had conversations about weddings. "You're the one hosting an engagement party. Can we afford that?"

"Not really. That's why it's ninety minutes long, with limited drink options and roasted nuts. No beef tenderloin, no French cheeses. Roasted nuts, George! That I bought in bulk at Costco and will heat up before serving so they seem special. Just nuts!"

"Just relax."

There would be no relaxing for Abigail Blakeman. The entire plan laid out tonight was counter to everything she believed in: politics, California, ethnic food at a wedding. She was in a full-blown panic. How had her dull, predictable, easy life spun so out of control? "George, take a guess at the cost of that tent at the Silliman School fundraiser years ago. The beautiful white one with the lights, the dance floor, the sides in case of rain or cold?"

"Five grand. Tops."

"Sure, for the scaffolding to hold the tent up. Try twenty-five grand with labor, lighting, the sides, the heaters, the dance floor. And that wasn't even the best tent they offered. One with the florals and the twinkle light entrance. Slap the modifier 'wedding' in front of anything and the cost goes up another ten percent."

"We won't need to pay for the dance floor," George scoffed as if he'd suddenly become an expert in special event etiquette. Then he considered the fact that Alexa was a single mother and maybe it would be the polite thing to do, throw in a dance floor. The last wedding he'd attended was a country club affair a decade ago in Ridgewood, New Jersey, for the daughter of a client. He had a vague memory of jumping up and down on the dance floor to "Born to Run." Honestly, he really had no idea how weddings worked anymore. He hated when Abigail was right. "Let's hope they have an indoor wedding and there won't be any tent. Besides, it's always warm in California, right?"

"I think they have some sort of winter in Montecito. Our friends, if we're allowed to invite any, won't travel to Southern California over the holidays. They go skiing in Vermont. Congratulations, a small gesture for a bunch of strangers. We won't have access to that kind of cash until we sell the house. You better start winning some of these bridge tournaments so we can pay for your small gesture." She hated speaking like this, hated being this person. But, honestly, what life did he think they were living? Not the one she had married into, that's for sure.

George was silent as they pulled up to Grand Central. Abigail turned to him as she slid out. "Don't forget to give the cabbie a huge tip, Diamond George! Or should I say Diamandis George?"

Now the cabbie was fully focused on his passenger. George handed him a twenty and said, "Keep the change."

From the Desktop of Dearly Beloveds and Betrotheds

Dear B & Bs . . .

Of all the questions that pour into Aunt B's mailbox, the two areas that modern brides find most vexing are The Dress and The Guest List. Today, we tackle The Dress. My advice below is based on years of tears, tantrums, and taste. The tears and the tantrums from others; the taste is mine.

Let's get the most common question out of the way up front. Do I need more than one dress for my wedding? No.

Thanks to social media, many brides believe they need A Ceremony Dress, A Reception Dress, A First Dance Dress, and An After-Party Dress. (My goodness, will these brides and grooms NEVER leave their own weddings? Don't they have something better to do? I hope so or the marriage itself will be a long row to hoe.) If you have enough money for four dresses and want to spend the better part of your wedding in a cramped anteroom with your stylist and her team rather than with your new spouse, your family, and your friends, then there's nothing I can write here to sway you. But a gentle reminder that you have the rest of your life to wear special-occasion dresses, even white ones, which is really all Dresses Two through Four are.

If, as part of your heritage, you wear multiple dresses to your multiday celebration, that is wonderful. Ask your own aunties for advice. I'm sure they have it.

If you are getting enormous pressure to wear your mother's 1986 Priscilla of Boston dress complete with capelet, or your grandmother's yellowed lace and satin number from the bottom of the dress-up closet, or your future mother-in-law's puffed-shouldered relic with the hideous fringed headpiece, hear me now: You do not have to wear someone else's dress unless you truly want to wear it. If you need to show someone in your life this paragraph, please do. You're a grown woman and you can choose your own dress. You're welcome.

But if you, like me, believe in one and only one wedding dress, then this advice is for you.

Choose a dress in your budget. There are lovely, beautiful, elegant, perfect dresses at every price point. Don't get talked into something you can't afford.

Choose a dress you love, not one that your entourage loves. Long, short, mermaid, ball gown, sweetheart neckline. Bohemian, Grace Kelly, princess, minimalist, renaissance faire. Lace, satin, velvet, beaded, sequins, feathers. Make sure that when you look in the mirror, you love your dress.

Choose a dress that suits your body the way it is, not the body you wish you had. Buying a dress three sizes too small and putting all the pressure on yourself to drop the weight before the wedding will result in a miserable Bride-to-Be. Look your best, of course. But not at the expense of every joyful aspect of getting married. Counter with good fit. Good fit makes simple design spectacular. Good fit and good sense make for a beautiful Bride.

Choose a dress you can wear for ten hours. If you don't regularly wear structured couture gowns, then don't wear one on your wedding day. You will be miserable in the corseted bodice and the fitted mermaid bottom.

Choose a dress that leaves something to the imagination. Sexy dresses make guests uncomfortable, like your Aunt B. Save the skin for your wedding night. (If you ever leave the after-party.)

Choose a dress that is timeless. You'll thank me on your twenty-fifth wedding anniversary when you look at your wedding photos and think "Beautiful." Instead of "Was I under the influence of an influencer?"

Big Kiss & Wedding Bliss,
Your Aunt B

Next Week: Should I force my bridesmaids to learn complicated choreography to a nineties hip-hop anthem in hopes that it will go viral?

Chapter 9

THE DRESS

The Mother of the Bride

Of all the traits passed from mother to daughter, the one that Alexa was most proud of was her daughter Penny's ability to make things happen, quietly and gracefully. Alexa had watched her own mother, Leni, welcome tourists from all over the world, those seeking meals after closing time or a room for two that they could share with five people, and her mother had accommodated these strangers as if they were family. Leni would commandeer sightseeing guides or boat tours on the spur of the moment for their hotel guests. She almost never said no and almost always succeeded in making the visitors' trip memorable. She had a network of others in the trade, from bartenders to cabbies on Patmos to innkeepers on other islands, in Athens and the Peloponnese, not an easy task in the days before the internet. They worked together to keep the tourists satisfied and the economy humming. The guests appreciated the effort so much that they sent their friends and relatives from Germany or England or Australia or Canada to their small island for vacation instead of the splashier Greek islands like Santorini or Mykonos. It was playing the long game in what travel experts would call word-of-mouth marketing now. The currency of human connection.

Alexa herself absorbed the lessons of hospitality and used them to her advantage in her Hollywood career, saying yes to any request and then figuring out how to make it happen afterward. When she started Odyssey, she learned that high-income clients had high expectations, like special shopping hours at boutiques, meals created just for them by the chef, a tour of the vineyard that went into the cellars normally closed to the public. She had to make those experiences happen in new cities all over the world. She learned to work from the ground up. Her signature move? Picking up the phone and speaking to the shopgirl or the restaurant manager as if that person were the CEO of the company. Her tone said, "I respect you and we're all in this together to make something special happen." She knew that her daughter had watched her and learned to speak to every individual with the same attitude to create opportunities where everyone could benefit even if it required extra effort.

When Alexa and Penny approached the Kalliope Moon trunk show, the line stretched down Spring Street and around the corner. Eager shoppers stood holding their iced coffees and their cell phones, waiting for their turn to view the merchandise inside, clothing and housewares that would look at home in the Hamptons or Ibiza or Capri. Or Montecito. Two women in navy blue monitored the line, allowing a select few in at a time. Alexa watched as Penny approached them with a broad smile and open arms. She could hear a few words of greeting in Greek, reestablishing the connection that they had made years ago in Athens when Penny was still leading tours and would bring her clients into the boutique after hours for what could only be described as a cocktail-fueled shopping frenzy.

Her Odyssey patrons snapped up caftans and palazzo pants and dresses of all shapes and sizes in Mediterranean-inspired colors and patterns. Some shipped entire sets of dishes or sheets and towels back to their homes in Dallas or Palm Beach or Dana Point. The shop owed Penny and Penny owed the shop. The circle of commerce closed.

And now, all of that back-channel planning, scheduling, and communication was paying off. Today, Penny was the client and she was going home with an exclusive Kalliope Moon wedding dress.

She turned to her mother, her proud mother, and said, "They've been waiting for us."

Sofia, who'd managed the shop in Athens for over a decade, nodded with recognition at Alexa. But today, instead of speaking with the familiarity of one working woman to another, she treated Alexa as her honored guest. It reminded Alexa so much of her own mother, who would have treated a stranger in her modest hotel on Patmos with the same care. Sofia cleared a path and ushered the mother and daughter past the gaggle of New Yorkers waiting their turn. "Madam Diamandis, Mademoiselle Diamandis, welcome to Kalliope Moon SoHo. Please follow me. May I get you a coffee? Cava?"

***

"Oh, Penny . . ."

This was the moment that Alexa hadn't known she was waiting for. The moment her daughter, the heart of her being, stepped out from behind the curtain in the small showroom that had been reserved for them, in the dress that would become her wedding dress.

Kalliope herself was there to assist them, and there was no doubt about which of the dresses would become Penny's. After hugs, kisses, and small talk about mutual friends in Athens, the designer listened to Penny describe her dream dress. And then she disregarded the bride's wishes for simple and sophisticated. Instead, she brought out a stunner from the back room. It was a silk and lace confection with a skirt of many layers of flowy fabric, gentle pleats, flutter sleeves, and a deep V neckline. The color appeared to be cream at first glance, but as Penny moved around the room, layers of various shades of blue, seafoam white, and blush peeked through, giving the skirt the effect of rolling waves. Hints of lace highlighted the bodice, including the deeper V back of the dress. Scattered around the bottom of the dress were handsewn crystals in rose, blue, and silver. It was a completely unexpected choice by Penny, who favored tailored clothes and neutral colors. It was a romantic but modern mix with nods to both her Greek heritage and her beachy California upbringing. It looked like it was made for her, save for a few alterations.

"You'll never guess what it's called," Penny said, stepping up on the riser after allowing Kalliope to add a pearl and silver accent belt at the waist and then a similar headband with a veil that put Alexa over the top emotionally.

"Penny's dress?" Alexa guessed through tears.

"Practically. It's called the Penelope! Can you believe it?"

Alexa could. In Greek mythology, Penelope was the loyal and clever wife of Odysseus, the Greek hero who took his sweet time coming home from the Trojan War. During the decade of her husband's wandering and philandering, Penelope held down the home front, staying loyal to her husband while fending off young suitors with a clever trick. She vowed to marry again when she had finished weaving the funeral garment for her late father-in-law. She wove by day and unraveled her work by night, thus delaying another marriage indefinitely. Eventually, her scheme was revealed by one of the servants.

While Penelope was often written off by readers and scholars as too loyal and faithful of a wife, Alexa admired her steadfastness not to marry again and her clever way of staying single. Creative, gentle but firm in her resolve. That's how Alexa thought of her daughter, who had made her way in the world through her gentle manner, her creative brain, and her firm resolve to get exactly what she wanted out of life.

As Alexa stared at her daughter in her creamy sparkling ocean dress, she knew that she must want every bit of the life she had described last night—as Chase's wife, his political partner, a Queens dweller, and a weaver of dreams. There would be no talking her out of that, she knew now. Loyal, faithful, clever, creative Penelope. Her Penny.

"What do you think, madam?"

Penny looked at her with the same expression she used to get her first car. "Mom?"

She nodded at her daughter. "It's perfect. I love it. We'll take it. Yes?"

"Yes."

Neither one of them had asked the price.

"Now, madam, shall we move on to our mother-of-the-bride dress?" Kalliope asked, filling Alexa's glass with more bubbly.

"Absolutely. Apolýtos," Alexa agreed, swept up in the romance of it all.

From the Desktop of Dearly Beloveds and Betrotheds

Dear B & Bs . . .

Some weeks, my mailbox resembles group therapy more than wedding etiquette. When that happens, I scuttle my regularly scheduled content for a Very Special Episode of Your Aunt B.

This week's Group Therapy Topic: Difficult Brides. (No, I won't call them by the other name, a derivative of that of a very angry prehistoric reptilian monster, because I think that slur is all kinds of misogynistic. And probably other awful things as well.) If you are a Bride-to-Be or identify as the Bride in your coupling, this short list is for you. Please understand, I know that weddings can be stressful. It's a new life experience that involves a host of skills from budgeting to diplomacy to menu planning to very strong opinions on typography that you might not have previously developed. I am on your side, Brides, giving you a wide berth as you make your way through this virgin territory. (Wink, wink.) I encourage others to do the same, allowing grace for the crazy that may come before that dear sister/friend/cousin walks down the aisle.

That said, you must do your part, Ms. Bride, to minimize the friction and maximize the love. A few rules to bear in mind:

You're not the first person to be married, and you won't be the last. Sorry, dear one. You are part of a long tradition that stretches back thousands of years. A wedding is two people committing to each other until death do them part surrounded by the family and friends who will support them on this journey. It's not really **your** day. It's simply **a** day. If you understand your place in this continuum, you will find the perspective you need to proceed with civility. Honor tradition humbly.

The people you include in your wedding, like your bridesmaids, should hold a special spot in your heart. Respect them and their boundaries. Remember, their primary purpose is to bear witness to your relationship with your future spouse. They don't work for you. They shouldn't go broke being your friend. And they are real people with feelings who can only forgive so much. Be kind.

Details fade, but the vibe doesn't. Modern brides face a cavalcade of choices from the ridiculous (position of the hand-lettered signs indicating the porta potties) to the sublime. (To wear a wedding veil or not? Yes, wear a veil because it's your one chance and veils are magical.) Resist the temptation to get so lost in the particulars that you forget the purpose of the day.

As the years go by, the lasting memory won't be about the appetizer choice, but the overall feeling of the wedding. Was there unity? Was there joy? Was there love? Those are the most important details.

Big Kiss & Wedding Bliss,
Your Aunt B

Chapter 10

THE BEGINNINGS OF THE MIDDLE

The Mother of the Bride

Beware the emergence of Bridezilla, the Merry Widows had warned Alexa. It all starts out with hearts and roses and ends with tears and threats, they had said that night at dinner a few weeks ago. Even the best-behaved brides will have moments, they assured her. It comes with the territory. The only way MOBs can survive is to rely on good friends for strength and assume that one day, after the wedding, they'll get their girl back.

But Alexa couldn't believe that Penny would turn on her the way Ming's daughter, Tessie, had, by issuing an order via a strongly worded text that everyone in the bridal party lose twenty pounds or be cut from the roster. The tyrant bride, a marketer in the beauty biz with a lifetime of body issues, ruthlessly dropped the fourth bridesmaid, a childhood friend who was a beautiful size fourteen. Surely Penny would never act like Toots's granddaughter who had flung a sample bouquet of wildflowers at the inexperienced florist, shouting, "Find better-looking nature!" When Frannie described how her newly minted daughter-in-law turned to her in the receiving line and ordered her to move to the other end of the line because she was "ruining the aesthetic" with "her frumpy dress," Alexa had shaken her head. Penny would never say anything like that to anyone, would she?

She might think it, but never say it, Alexa decided.

But there they were at lunch at a bistro in SoHo in what Alexa had envisioned being a festive celebration of the Miracle of the Dresses when the darker aspects of Penny's hyper-organized personality started to emerge. After their inhaling a lunch of grilled salmon and asparagus, coffee was on the way as Penny took her mother through her plans for the wedding. The edge in her daughter's voice took hold as she whipped out her tablet, brought up her PowerPoint, and ran her mother through the details like she was running her through a tour itinerary.

Except the tables were turned. Penny was the boss and Alexa's job was to nod and agree to the task. "Here's what you need to know. First, because we're trying to execute the wedding on an accelerated timeline, there's an availability crunch for me. I don't have a lot of time in my schedule to spearhead this entire plan. My work client, the one with the boutique hotels all over the South, has given me an enormous project. It could make or break my career, Mom, but it means I must focus, focus, focus on that while you focus on the wedding."

While you focus on the wedding? Who did Penny think she was talking to? As if Alexa didn't have a business to run herself. This wasn't how they usually communicated.

"Here are my initial thoughts," Penny said, handing a tablet to Alexa, indicating to her mother that she would page through the electronic presentation that was part mood board, part pitch deck. Alexa stared down at the screen, absorbing both the words and the intent. It was beautifully designed, and for one second, she made a mental note to show the deck to her graphic designer. Maybe all their Odyssey quote documents should use this look and format?

She was starting to get lost in her thoughts when Penny's sharp voice brought her back. "Of course this will need to be refined and refined again. But this is a start for us."

Penny then went on to describe the wedding gimmicks that she and Chase were rejecting: hokey wedding photos setups, matching and mandatory bathrobes for the bridal party, complicated choreography for the couple's entrance and the first dance, tricky baubles to indicate the seating chart, treasure hunt–themed rehearsal dinners, party favors for guests, menu cards and ceremony programs, or any dogs at all. She ran through the list with such conviction it was clear to her mother that Penny had experienced all of these extras in her career as an extreme-wedding guest.

Alexa thought she might be witnessing traumatic recall. Penny's peak sorority life at SMU resulted in a dozen weddings in her twenties. Summers and falls were packed with trips to Dallas or Vail or New Orleans. She had a closetful of pistachio one-shouldered bridesmaid's dresses and pink shorty bathrobes. The hair and makeup costs alone totaled more than the down payment on a luxury car. She'd spent thousands of dollars on trips to Cabo or Nashville to celebrate with her Kappa sisters in an endless stream of bachelorette weekends that all looked the same on social media, despite the changing brides. There'd been gifts galore, in what felt like a never-ending cycle of showers. She'd been to too many to count, including baby showers, with more invitations piling up at home.

Alexa's blood pressure started to creep up as Penny preached. She finished by saying, "What Chase and I want is simplicity. No gimmicks. Do you understand?"

Alexa nodded without a word, hoping her daughter had ordered decaf. "Let me take a look at this list while you . . ." She wanted to say "relax" but sensed that word choice would not be well received. "Enjoy a moment of quiet." Then Alexa bowed down to the tablet and flipped through the deck.

The Wedding of Penelope and Chase: A Love Odyssey

Last Week of December in Montecito (or Santa Barbara if necessary)

Thursday evening rehearsal dinner at casual location with all invited

Friday evening ceremony followed by dinner and dancing

Saturday morning coffee and breakfast burritos at beach

Seventy-five guests max

One attendant each for Penny and Chase

Penny: Sarah (Chase's sister)

Chase: Lloyd (college friend)

Bridesmaid gifts: monogrammed paper pads and notebooks

Groomsman gift: TBD

For Wedding

Eco-friendly a MUST

Natural, Natural, Natural

Simple, Simple, Simple

Intentional, Intentional, Intentional

Environmentally Responsible! No extra printed materials, no dress-up booth or wedding tchotchkes. Absolutely no superfluous signage, paper goods, or stuff that gets thrown in the landfill the next day.

Service at venue

Buffet okay, served dinner preferred

DJ afterward. No cheesy songs. No chicken dance.

Hotel or club preferred if space

Rented private estate also fine

Vibe: Sophisticated Beach

Colors: White, Cream, Silver, Blue

Lighting: Essential! Look: Grecian sunset that fades into a cityscape

Dance floor: investigate smoke for first dance

Food: Mediterranean

Bar: Open

Dress code: California Chic, blue encouraged!

Officiant: Surprise

Alexa absorbed the enormity of the task at hand, from renting a private estate to securing lighting that mimicked a Grecian sunset. How were either of those tasks in the "simple" category? A few days ago, she didn't even want Penny to have a wedding; now she appeared to be overseeing the whole thing. She studied the list for a minute longer than she needed, mainly to let Penny decompress, and then she said, "You need me to plan the entire wedding? This wedding? Where the dress code is 'blue encouraged'?"

"Mom, of course not. What would you know about wedding planning?" Penny snapped, and already Alexa felt hurt. But Penny continued with her tone. "I hired a professional in Montecito. She's a Kappa from UCSB named Madison Meadows. You'll work with her to be my eyes and ears on the ground. But understand that Madison and I will be in constant communication and I'll be making all decisions. You'll visit venues, meet with the caterer—that kind of thing. And you'll need to find me the best florist that we can afford, so ask the Widows. Maybe somebody who doesn't have a full-time business but loves to do weddings. I wish I had paid more attention to centerpieces when I was in high school."

Alexa smiled, mainly with relief. Her daughter hadn't lost her sense of humor yet.

"What are you laughing at? I mean it," Penny said. "Understanding the outrageous price of floral design would have been helpful."

So she had lost her sense of humor, Alexa thought. Damn. She was hoping to open up a conversation about their Athens family attending the wedding. Because as far as Alexa was concerned, if she couldn't have her family at the wedding, she didn't even want to tell them about the wedding. They would never understand a snub like that. But Penny didn't seem open to discussion on this or any topic.

"This is a basic rundown, but I have extensive notes on each line item. I'll send you the complete deck, but I didn't want to overwhelm you at lunch."

That sounded like planning the whole wedding to Alexa, but she said nothing. She was waiting for her daughter to laugh and say, "Just kidding." But Penny wasn't kidding. "You hired a wedding planner?"

"Of course. I need someone like me on the ground to run the wedding the day of the event. Brides don't have time to produce, Mom."

Again, Alexa waited, hoping for the laughter to break out.

But there was nothing on Penny's face to suggest that she was anything but deadly serious about this festive event. "Chase and I agree. We're paring down. This is not going to be some three-day bacchanalia for everybody we went to college with so they can party like it's 1999. This is a grown-up wedding, curated by grown-ups for grown-ups," Penny announced. "No matching dresses. No endless photo sessions. No bottles of wine labeled with our wedding logo. I mean, of course there will be a logo, but we're not going to rebrand the wine, like Katie did. Or give each guest a bottle from the family vineyard like Savannah did. Remember Jillian's wedding? The bridesmaids had to walk down the aisle twice because the wedding video director didn't like our cadence. We had to do a retake in the middle of the ceremony. There won't be any of that! Oh, and there will be one dress and one cake."

At least that was a cost-saver, Alexa thought. And seriously, did brides really have more than one cake?

Penny's voice switched pitch, and she was shaking as she spoke. "I don't want any of that. I don't need the picture-perfect wedding. This is not an Instagram event; it's my life. I want a wedding filled with love and joy. Is that too much to ask?"

Now, it was Penny's turn to cry, but not tears of happiness. Penny was melting down right in front of Alexa. Her mother reached across the table for her daughter's trembling hand. "My dear, you don't have to have any wedding at all. You and Chase can go to City Hall and then we can go out for Chinese food. Isn't that what New Yorkers do?"

Penny couldn't respond, so Alexa continued, "Is this about the wedding? Or the marriage? Maybe this is all going too fast. Maybe slow down. There's no need to rush because of Chase's schedule."

That was exactly the wrong tack. Penny pounced. "It's not Chase's schedule. You're so against marriage. Why is that? Every other girl I know has a mother that is breathing down their neck for them to get married. But you . . . you seem annoyed that I've found a life partner."

"That is not true. Not at all. I am happy for you and Chase. We just bought your dress and mine. You and I are different in one very big way. You've always wanted to be part of something bigger than yourself. The cheerleaders in high school. The sorority. You stay in touch with your old boyfriends and your cousins on Patmos. It's admirable. For me, I prefer to be part of a small group. You know that. And I saw what happened to my mother. She was thrown out of her own family for her life choices. I'm glad she came to Greece and found my father, but I never wanted to be in that position. I like my independence," Alexa finished with a sharp edge in her voice. Penny was thirty years old. She had to own her choices. She didn't get to dump her angst on her mother.

"I'm sorry." Penny had gathered herself, much to Alexa's relief. They were a pair who didn't spar often, especially not in public. "Remember my sorority sister Kelsey who married Cade in that over-the-top wedding in Mexico? I was in the wedding as, like, the tenth bridesmaid. That's what Kelsey did, she ranked the bridesmaids. Well, they're divorcing after three years of marriage. I spent five thousand dollars on that whole fiasco and for what? Three years. And she was the one that had the affair. It's freaked me out."

"I'm sorry to hear that. At least you don't have to invite them to the wedding." Alexa was nothing if not practical.

Now, a genuine laugh. "You got that right. But it has made me think that I don't want to get caught up in all that, Mom. The over-the-top wedding with all the bells and whistles. Those come with so many rules and so much judgment. But I want something that's special, that's mine. And Chase's. I want to be married when we move in together. I want to be his wife. And I want him to be my husband."

That touched Alexa, and she found herself wondering what that sense of belonging must feel like. She'd felt it when she'd looked at baby Penelope, but never for a romantic partner. When she hit thirty and there was a cavalcade of weddings in her social circle and among her cousins, she tried to find that someone special because it seemed like the thing to do. She dated coworkers and friends of friends and guys she met on planes. It was always exciting for a while, but as soon as the relationships ventured into caregiving or compromising her schedule for theirs, she lost interest. In her mind, there always seemed like there was something more interesting to work on than romance—a new project, travel to an exotic land. For a while she got really into scuba diving and that replaced men on her calendar. She went from one wedding to another in London or Athens or Los Angeles, but she never minded going alone. Or leaving with a groomsman for a night of fun. But no one person ever stuck as the person. Her person. Until Penelope. Once she had the baby, she stopped trying to find anyone else because there was no point. She had what she needed: her baby, her work, and her days by the ocean.

The server approached with the espressos and the piece of honey cake that Alexa had ordered.

Penny asked her to clear the rest of the table so they had room to work. "Why don't you bring the check now? I see we're your last customers. We don't want to keep you," she said sweetly. The grateful server hustled off.

There she is. My thoughtful girl.

Penny turned her attention to her mother, who handed her the second fork. The bride-to-be shook her head. "My carbs days are over for the foreseeable future."

And a lightbulb went off in Alexa. Carb deprivation = Bridezilla.

Alexa wasn't going to let the monster in. She was going to regain the top spot in this conversation. And eat this entire piece of honey cake. "Why don't we take these items one at a time and you can tell me how I can be helpful. But first, let's talk budget."

Chapter 11

THE DRESS

The Mother of the Groom

"Look at you! Is that what you're wearing to the wedding? I'm sure Penny would love that," Sarah said as she flopped down on her mother's chaise in the dressing room of the master bedroom. It was the most luxurious part of the Blakeman house, a proper dressing room with ample closet space for two, a makeup table, and an obstructed water view. Sarah had spent hours playing dress-up in here when she was little, watching her mother get ready for a work event or a fundraiser or the theater. She even had her own box of discarded gowns and dresses to use, so she didn't ruin her mother's. Now it was her mother playing dress-up, squeezing herself into her Priscilla of Boston wedding gown, a white lace number complete with capelet. It still fit, sort of. Her weight was about the same, but her body had changed over three decades. She pretended that the zipper was broken, not that her waist had disappeared.

"I wouldn't even joke about that to Penny. I don't think brides have much of a sense of humor. Especially about their wedding," Abigail answered, posing in the mirror for fun. "I still love this dress. Maybe you'll wear it one day."

"As long as you don't mind if I turn it into a field hockey skort."

"Oh, Sarah. That's not funny."

"Apparently nobody has a sense of humor about their wedding, even if it was years ago." Sarah put the veil on, then removed it quickly, noting, "So not me."

"You're right about that." Abigail shook her head and continued, "We didn't take ourselves too seriously back then. Brides today, they want everything to be so special, so unique. Not my generation. We did what our mothers told us to do. We were perfectly happy with the same wedding that everyone else had. The white Tiffany invitations. The Priscilla of Boston dress. Our sisters or prep school friends as bridesmaids in Laura Ashley. We all did our own hair and makeup. Rehearsal dinners were for the wedding party, not everyone we ever knew. The basic country club wedding with a decent band, forgettable food, and lots of booze was fine. And we left for our honeymoon right after the wedding, no Sunday brunch."

"Did you take a covered wagon?" Sarah mocked gently.

But Abigail didn't mind. She knew her wedding was perfect, with the service at her home church in Simsbury and the reception at the country club down the road on a beautiful August day with a pink, green, and white color scheme. She didn't remember fighting with her mother once. They organized the whole event in a weekend. Her two bridesmaids—her favorite cousin, Candace, and her prep school roommate Bernadette, who would later become Aunt B—wore pink floral dresses with pouf sleeves, dyed-to-match pumps, and green gingham headbands. Headbands! George and the groomsmen were in blue blazers, white pants, and green gingham ties. They didn't write their own vows or hire a dance teacher to choreograph a first dance because, of course, they'd gone to dancing school and could fox-trot fine to the Eagles' "Peaceful Easy Feeling." Her father gave a charming toast using quotes from Carole King's *Tapestry* in an attempt to be relevant even though the album was decades old at the time. They spent their wedding night at a B and B on the way to Vermont for the honeymoon. The inn smelled like it had been soaked in tea rose perfume. George sneezed all night. She wouldn't change a thing.

"Couples now want a three-day marathon with all the monogramming and signature cocktails. Even the table numbers must make a statement. I'm not sure all the fuss makes for a better event, never mind a better marriage," Abigail said. "Imagine being stuck with a lifetime supply of monogrammed matchbooks when the divorce happens a year later."

"Somebody had their cup of cynicism this morning. Too much red wine last night?"

Last night, when Abigail and George arrived home, Sarah was up making a late-night omelet and drinking pinot noir. George was thrilled to leave his wife and daughter together in the kitchen and head to bed. The silent treatment on the train ride home was enough punishment for the tent faux pas. Abigail filled Sarah in on the details of the evening and over the course of an hour, they polished off the bottle of wine.

"Not me. Up bright and early doing the flowers for tomorrow. I'm fine," Abigail lied. She was a tad hungover and planned on getting into bed by eight to recover her good mood for the engagement party. "I hope this doesn't spiral out of control. I've spent the last two weeks on every wedding site on the web and I don't understand why on earth every woman at the wedding needs a logoed pashmina. Can't they bring their own wrap?"

"Our generation doesn't own wraps."

"Well, then they should wear clothes with more coverage." Abigail had tut-tutted at the micro-minidresses the Silliman girls had worn to prom. Why had the Empire waist gone out of fashion? It was universally flattering. "I don't understand why the guests' comfort is the host's responsibility, at least in this area. I hope they don't get caught up in all of that."

"Mom, Chase and Penny have great taste. I have no doubt the

wedding will be a classy, if not classic, affair. They have their own style. Well, Penny does anyway. And, come on, Cal leeeeee," she sang, thrilled by the prospect of a California wedding.

"I do wish they were getting married here and not there even though that's not the tradition," Abigail said, wriggling out of the dress and laying it carefully on her bed. She slipped on a T-shirt dress as Sarah watched. They'd always had an easy relationship with each other because there was zero competition between the mother and daughter. Working in a private high school, Abigail had observed so many difficult relationships between the generations of women that usually revolved around who was the prettiest or sexiest, as if mother and daughter were in competition for the same man. That sort of dynamic turned Abigail's stomach. Nobody's mother needed to be sexy. And nobody's teen daughter needed to be either.

Abigail figured that the secret to her relationship with Sarah was mutual respect and the fact that neither wanted to be the other in any way, shape, or form. Honestly, Sarah was a complete mystery to Abigail with her focused athletic life on the field and her easily pleased life off the field. Sarah welcomed all manner of people in all manner of places. Happy as a clam with a beer and clam roll, George once said about his daughter, oblivious to the cannibalistic undertones of the statement. But it was true. Sarah was Sarah in every setting, from debutante ball to backyard barbecue. Chase had described his sister as "part golden retriever," and she was in the best possible way.

And Abigail remained a mystery to Sarah, who would never understand her mother's reverence for tradition, her constant state of stress about propriety, and her tendency to judge first, enjoy second. But nobody's mother on the team had ever cheered louder for their daughter's efforts. She would always be grateful to her parents for being enthusiastic but not over-the-top. Sarah suspected it was because they never really understood the rules of field hockey.

"What do you think of Penny?" Abigail asked carefully, not

making eye contact by rooting through her closet, even though she knew the item she was looking for was right in front of her.

"She's great. Think of all those high-maintenance women who Chase dated in college and after. They were such snobs, with their layered gold necklaces and their houses in the Hamptons. Remember that one, Liesel, who came for Thanksgiving and literally did not lift a finger the entire weekend. She said she was saving her manicure! Oh, but she did bring cupcakes. Cupcakes. For Thanksgiving. What is that? I like Penny. She cleared her own champagne glass and I'm sure she would have hand-washed them all if you had allowed her. She's a doer. Chase said he loves her because she works hard."

"Really? That's what he said?" Sometimes Abigail forgot that her children had their own separate relationship as siblings. The fact that not all their communication ran through her was a surprise. "Well, that's an excellent trait. Her mother seems like a hard worker, too."

Was I a hard worker back when George proposed? Abigail wondered. She had a job, but she never thought of it as a career. The truth was, by the time she met George, she was getting nervous about whether she would ever get married and fulfill her destiny as a suburban mother and pillar of society. She gave notice at work the day after George put a ring on it. And she never thought to question the wisdom of putting her entire financial future into the hands of George Blakeman, a stockbroker and a gentleman. It was only when Abigail started doing the household finances as a favor to George in the stressful days after 9/11 that she understood what a risk she had taken. The importance of maintaining her earning potential and having her own revenue stream dawned on her at age forty-two, when she discovered the financial foundation beneath them was crumbling. An alarm sounded, calling to the pragmatic side of Abigail.

She sprang into action, hoping it wasn't too late for her to revive her career, even though she could barely answer the newfangled phones or understand the advanced software that had emerged in her decade absence from the working world. She took a Make Friends with Your Computer class at the YMCA, dressed it up on her résumé like it was a Harvard MBA. She won that development job at Silliman with unrelenting good manners and false confidence. Abigail came to regret not keeping her hand in the working world, even if it was just a part-time gig during the early years of motherhood. But she vowed to make sure that Sarah didn't make the same mistake. And now Sarah had Penny as a role model as well.

Abigail reached into the closet and pulled out a simple raspberry-pink linen sheath dress that she had scored at the discount store near the senior center. The linen was Italian, her favorite. "Here. I picked this up for you. I thought you might need something new for the engagement party. On sale, and you look so good in sheaths."

It was true. Sarah's tall, muscular physique could pull off the style, and the color was beautiful with her skin tone and sun-streaked brown hair. "Cap sleeves so your field hockey tan doesn't show!"

Another daughter might have balked at having her mother pick out her clothes, but not Sarah. If she had a tail, it would have been wagging. Now it was her turn to play dress-up. Sarah loved when her mother shopped for her, otherwise her entire wardrobe would be T-shirts, gym shorts, and hoodies. She zipped up the dress and spun around for Abigail, who nodded approvingly. "Thank you. I love this color. I invited Taylor and Kelly to stop by tomorrow. I hope you don't mind. They always had the biggest crush on Chase. They want to check out Penny."

"That's fine. There's no food so adding a few more guests won't be a problem."

"There's no food?"

"It's a drinks party. It's very British."

"But we're not British."

"We were once. Hundreds of years ago. And don't you forget it,"

Abigail said, handing Sarah some espadrilles that would lengthen the look of her legs. "These are for you, too."

"I can't wait to meet the British lord. He'll appreciate the fact that we're not serving any food," Sarah said, kicking off her slides and slipping on the beige espadrilles. "These are so sexy."

"I'm hoping your father can take him on a short tour of the neighborhood and show him all the homes built after the redcoats burned the town to the ground during the Revolutionary War."

"That will make him feel at home," Sarah said. "You didn't really say much about the mother last night."

"Well, the mother is very . . ." Abigail hesitated to finish the sentence. Very what? Greek? Intimidating? Surprisingly charismatic? All of the above. She had wanted to get a handle on this woman who had chosen to become a mother but not a wife. To own a business, rather than pour her time into her own home. Choices it would never have occurred to Abigail to make. But she sensed that Alexa wouldn't be easy to truly know. One dinner wasn't going to unlock Alexa. "Very intriguing. A global citizen. Want to help me polish the silver?"

Nobody loved a good "polish sesh" more than Sarah. She found turning the trays from black to bright to be satisfying, like a great massage. "Why do we need to polish the trays if we're not having food?"

"Bernadette is coming. We need to impress her. If Chase is going to run for Congress, he needs her support, so we'll polish the nut bowls and the small trays for the cocktail napkins."

"That you monogrammed. *Chase hearts Penny.* I saw them."

An Etsy find that she had succumbed to during a late-night scrollfest. They did look charming, the white type on the blue napkin. The expedited shipping fee was a splurge, but if Bernadette took the bait, the expense would be worth it. "Again, Aunt B needs to know we're serious contenders for her column. And the mother needs to know we made an effort."

Sarah laughed. "Boom! That's right. Take that, Montecito! Nobody does superfluous monogramming like us Nutmeggers."

"It's not that—"

"It's totally that," Sarah said, whipping out her phone and scrolling for something. "You know what I tell my girls: Healthy competition makes everyone better." She found what she was looking for and held up the phone for Abigail to see. "Pizza? Very Veggie?"

Abigail thought of the carbs, but she decided to let it go for one night. "Sure. Girls' night in." Sarah looked fine in the dress. Maybe her daughter would find somebody someday. Maybe even at the wedding. Wouldn't that be nice?

Chapter 12

THE FAVOR

The Mother of the Bride

"You're still up?"

"Isn't the question are *you* still up?" Alexa asked the familiar voice on the phone. She loved hearing Simon Fox's posh voice on the other end of a call, no matter what time zone she was in. It was eight in New York and her friend was on London time. "It's the middle of the night for you, isn't it?"

"Actually, I got into New York two days ago, so I'm adjusted."

Typical Simon, giving her 90 percent of the details and keeping back some critical information. "Were you trying to avoid me? Or were you attending to your secret life?"

It was a running joke between them since their university days. They had met as first-year students studying economics by day and the London music and club scene by night. They became fast friends early in the term when one night, after too many pints, they discovered they had both lost their mothers at a similar age and were sent to boarding school to grieve. Simon was banished from his bucolic home in Herefordshire to an austere place in Wales, and Alexa was forced from her island paradise to dirty, loud Athens. They both survived, but it was the scars that bonded them and their love of New Wave music. She and Simon remained dear friends, but it would be untrue to say they were only friends.

At certain times, they'd been more than that to each other, much more. The occasional romps in college, the wild night here and there in their late twenties and early thirties when her movie-making schedule crossed over with his music journalism schedule. They could spend a night or two as lovers and leave in the morning as friends. But now in their sixties, with the addition of children and a spouse in their lives, there was none of that heat left. Well, almost none. There were times when a glance from Simon or the sound of him saying her name could generate a flash of desire through Alexa. Still, even after decades of shared experiences with him, she still had the sense that Simon Fox was hiding something.

As for Simon, he loved his effect on her and leaned into their history when appropriate. "You know, the only secret I have left in my life is you and that trip to Glastonbury in eighty-seven."

Oh, she remembered that weekend. Alexa had been in London for work, her first trip back since moving to California, and had a few days to kill between meetings. Simon was still scrambling for regular writing assignments and thought a blockbuster recap of the underfunded music festival might lead to a breakthrough. New Order was headlining so they decided to be goths for the weekend and hit the road. What she remembered was the mud, the dirty tent with no real privacy, and the gallons of cheap retsina they traded for food and clove cigarettes. And the nights, of course. "Do not mention Glastonbury tomorrow around the in-laws-to-be!"

"Pity. From what you've told me, I'm sure they are huge New Order fans. How dull," Simon quipped. "Speaking of dull, I'm trying to secure a distributor here in the States for our hard cider. And our new hard seltzer, sort of a rummy apple soda. Really turning up the British charm in a meeting with alleged mobsters. Did you know the entire beverage distribution system in the US is run by the Mafia out of a warehouse in Brooklyn? Very strange. Anyhow, I've been up to nothing more nefarious than that."

"I don't believe you," Alexa teased.

"If I was here meeting some paramour, would I have asked you to stay with me in the apartment? Or have agreed to go to the country to meet the new in-laws? Of course not! I'd be shacked up with somebody scandalous and have no time for you, my dear confidant." Simon made adultery sound like Shakespeare.

It was true. Alexa had spent many nights in Simon's efficient two-bedroom Gramercy Park apartment, a luxury he bought long ago when he was a music journalist and his life was his own, free from family and family obligations. She was sure a lot of bad behavior had gone down during his trips to New York, Simon entrenched in its music scene, which involved drinking, drugs, and groupies galore even for a journalist. But now he was married with two of his own children. His wife, Hazel, was twenty years his junior, the daughter of a country lawyer and well suited to life on a farm. She had turned their estate, Caston Park, into a destination orchard with a small restaurant, a gift shop, even a glamping area at the far edges of the property. There was merchandise and a revived apple festival in Ledbury, to the delight of the locals, thanks to Hazel. His boys were in boarding school, but closer to home and in a warmer environment than Wales. He was content, fulfilling his obligations to crown and country. His trips to the city that never sleeps were few and far between. And much tamer than in the past.

For years, Alexa had used the apartment whenever she was in New York, whether he was in residence or not. She could have stayed with him on this trip but wanted some space and to be closer to Penny's apartment. Plus, she didn't want to give the new relatives anything to suspect. The dinner had left her with the impression that the Blakemans had a very narrow definition of acceptable behavior. And she needed Simon to be his best self for her real concern: her daughter. "Thank you for coming tomorrow. You'll be a welcome buffer between Penny and me. She's running hot and cold. Today she had a breakdown in a public place over a friend's divorce and the wedding industrial complex. And then later, she told me to calm down when she was describing the exact blue and white place settings that she wants for the venue we haven't secured and probably can't afford. I've barely heard a word about this wedding, and she's already tablescaping, which she informed me is what one does at a reception."

Alexa filled Simon in on all the details from the last thirty-six hours with Princess Penny, including the bit where the bride informed her mother that she should not wear yellow at any official events, because it had never really been her color. "As if I would wear yellow to a holiday wedding. And for the record, I love yellow. Wait until she sees my outfit for the engagement party. I'm losing her, Simon."

"Aren't brides allowed to go off the rails a bit? Isn't wedding planning considered a sanctioned escape from decent behavior?"

"I wouldn't know," Alexa replied dryly.

When Alexa decided it was time to become a mother, she was thirty-five, never married, certainly single, and had recently bought the travel business. While she had plenty of female friends, she didn't have one that could be counted on to talk through this decision without bringing all their personal baggage. At the time, her thirty-something female friends were going through their own tribulations: finding a husband, staying married, conceiving a child, coming to terms with their sexuality or knee-deep in nappies because they had recently given birth and were overwhelmed. And she'd learned the painful lesson that everyone had biases to bring to a conversation about a single woman like her giving birth.

Over the years when Alexa had hinted at single parenthood, her friends had scoffed. Or rolled their eyes. Or, worst of all, lectured her about how incredibly selfish she was being, having a child on her own, without a father in the picture. Especially when there were so many "spare" children around, as if newborns were so plentiful they hung out in parks together, eager to be adopted by single parents. Wait, they all advised. You still have time to find a partner and do it the right way. Alexa knew she didn't want a full-time partner, but she did want a child. And who was to say what constituted the right way? She'd certainly heard enough stories of terrible childhoods or awful fathers or miserable mothers to know that having two parents didn't guarantee a happy life. She was enough for one little baby.

She thought of her mother often during those months and years of decision-making. A young woman whose family was so ashamed of their unmarried, pregnant daughter they shipped her off to a faraway island to give birth. Her mother turned that punishment around and made Patmos, her accepting new husband, and her four children her life. Alexa knew that she didn't want to "avenge" her mother by having a baby on her own, that wasn't the right term, although she did feel anger toward the grandparents she'd never met. She wished she had been old enough to have a conversation with Leni about her choices before the accident. But it never occurred to her as a teenager to speak to her mother about such personal things. But now, in her thirties and feeling an overwhelming need to have a child, she wanted her decision to honor her mother.

She knew what she had to do.

She flew to London and spent a week with Simon on his farm to talk through it with him. He wouldn't have the issues her female friends had, but she learned he had his own issues. His father and brother had died in a train accident the previous year, a tragedy that was all over the news because the number of dead was in the dozens. The estate, which was never meant for him as a second son, became his along with the title and the seat in Parliament. All Simon had wanted to do was to live in London and be a music journalist of some acclaim, but now he was back in Ledbury, tending to the apple and pear orchards, like generations of Foxes had before him. He was lost when Alexa arrived. And the minute Alexa told him about having a baby on her own, he was found.

"Let me be the father," he had begged. "I need some sign of life. I want to give you this. And you'll give me something, too. I don't need to be a couple and I don't think you want to be either. And I know that you don't want to live here on the outskirts of humanity worrying about the bee population, like I do. This is my duty, Alexa. This estate and these people. But I'd love to know that my child was out there in California, free to choose whatever they want to be. Please, Alexa."

It was a nondecision. Of course this was the solution. Maybe it was why she had made the journey in the first place, knowing that this was where their relationship would lead them, after years of dancing around the edges of romance. She and her best friend spent the week eating, drinking, walking through the apple trees, and trying at least once a day to conceive a child. Like it was the most normal situation in the world.

They weren't kids anymore, depending upon the potent fuel of youth, drinking, loud bands, and dark clubs to spark their interactions. Nor were they hardened twentysomethings squeezing in sex between intense work obligations, like it was a high-impact aerobics class. For this week, which Simon kept referring to as the Maculata Conceptionis, a bastardization of his schoolboy Latin and a reflection of his misunderstanding of the Immaculate Conception, they were both conscious and self-conscious of being together. They eased into the daily ritual, trying to find the balance between fertility and fun. All it took was a few glasses of a good white burgundy at lunch, a rainy afternoon, and the call of the pressed Irish linen sheets in Simon's bedroom. They could laugh at the folly of it all and then get down to business, but in between there were moments of such tenderness. Yes, these were two dear friends.

A few weeks later, Alexa learned that she wasn't pregnant. She was disappointed, but Simon was distraught. How could you spend your whole life trying not to get someone pregnant and then fail in your first serious attempt to do so? Alexa made a quick decision before Simon got any crazy idea that they were a couple. A trip to the sperm bank and several home inseminations later, she was pregnant. She knew the baby wasn't Simon's and Simon knew the baby wasn't his, but they acknowledged that he was the spiritual father, the impetus and the inspiration. Without Simon's enthusiastic support, there would have been no Penny. So of course he was Penny's godfather.

Back in the present day, more than thirty years since that week of the Maculata Conceptionis, Alexa had another favor to ask. "Can you do something for me tomorrow?"

"Of course. A toast. Or a proclamation. I'm very good at those, you know. Constantly proclaiming things now that I'm an MP."

"Tell me what you think about Chase. And the family. I want to know your impressions."

"You sound worried. Do you think there are issues?"

"Everything seems to be moving so quickly. And the decisions are so big, life-changing. Marriage, moving, becoming a political wife. Penny has never expressed any interest in a life of public service. Why now? And the fact that the district is heavily Greek, that makes me wonder if this union is about expediency. I feel terrible saying this. You know about these sorts of people. Old money, politics, WASPs. You're them. I want you to tell me what you think of the Blakemans."

"You know I love Penny like my own daughter," Simon said softly, letting the words sink in. He would do as his old friend asked. "I'll uncover what I can tomorrow at the engagement party and report back. Now I've got to run. I'm off to dinner."

Dinner? Alexa was planning on room service and an early night. "There you go. There's that secret life of yours again."

From the Desktop of Dearly Beloveds and Betrotheds

Dear B & Bs . . .

Time to clear out that mailbox! This week, I'm answering your questions about engagement protocols. Are there any other life events where the journey from joy turns to tyranny in so brief a time as from the proposal to the engagement announcement? What starts as a profound moment between two people deciding to share their lives morphs into a nonstop question-and-answer period about everything from the style of your dress to the date you plan to procreate. If you can control the chaos, couples, you might have a chance of enjoying this liminal period between single and married.

Dear Aunt B,

My boyfriend and I got engaged on a super romantic camping trip in Yosemite, far from people and cell service. He dropped to one knee at the foot of El Capitan and then we spent a week in the backcountry, just the two of us. It was perfect. When we arrived home, we stopped by my parents' to announce our engagement and they freaked out. How could we have kept it a secret for a week? My mother was hurt and angry I hadn't driven 100 miles to cell service to call her with the news and my father was furious that my boyfriend hadn't asked for "permission." I'm a thirty-three-year-old woman, not chattel. Now, they are refusing to host the engagement party we suggested. Plus, so much drama. Whyyyyyyyy?

Signed, Melissa from Manhattan

Dear Melissa,

First off, no one owes you a party. Not your parents. Not your friends. Not your neighbors. So, let's put the party planning aside and get to the propriety of the situation. Secondly, is camping ever really "super romantic"? This former Manhattanite is suspicious.

As for asking for your father's permission, yes, it's a throwback, old-timey gesture that originated in the days when women were chattel and marriage was a business deal. And in today's modern family structure with parents of all types and couples of all genders, who is asking for permission from whom? It's a relic of a tradition best left buried.

Let's reframe this moment. It's not about permission so much as it is about inclusion, celebration, and, frankly, buy-in. Lots of couples choose to include their parents, family, and friends in the engagement moment with all of them being "in" on the secret except the one getting the ring. Facebook tells me so. Given that you had a destination engagement with the two of you in a bubble, a big granite bubble, I think your parents are feeling left out. Why don't you acknowledge that with your parents?

And do you want me to tell you that your mother is being ridiculous? Okay: Your mother is being ridiculous. Everyone knows that there is no cell service in national parks. But instead of forcing your parents to throw you a party, why don't you take them out to dinner, just the four of you, and reset this engagement off on the right foot?

Dear Aunt B,

My soon-to-be in-laws hosted an engagement party at their home over the holidays in honor of my fiancé and me. It was festive and well attended. Everyone seemed to be genuinely happy for us, but here's the problem: no gifts. Not one gift. Now we are putting together our guest list and my future mother-in-law wants to include some of the engagement party attendees at the wedding. I told my fiancé I don't want a bunch of freeloaders taking advantage of us again. He's afraid to tell his mother the real reason we've limited her guests. What's the best way to inform her?

Thanks, Chicago Suzee

My dear Chicago Suzee,

Your self-righteousness is . . . what? Courageous? No, it's deplorable!

An engagement party is a small gift-free celebration for a happy couple to acknowledge their commitment to each other and the institution of marriage. It can be hosted by either side of the engaged couple's families. Or, in cases of deficient real estate on the parts of the parents, dear friends. It's a glass of champagne, a toast, and best wishes for the future. Plus, for pure fun, it's a chance for family friends to check out the Bride or Groom.

It's not supermarket sweeps or a lottery payout. Not every event in the wedding cinematic universe is a gift-collecting situation. Even your actual wedding.

Someday, when you are less young and less self-righteous, you'll understand the joy of simply being included in life's lovely moments. You'll understand what being a witness to love means and the importance of those witnesses in the tapestry that is your life. Honestly, to use a haggard phrase that is one hundred percent on-target in this instance, their presence is your present.

Dear Aunt B,

My boyfriend and I became engaged two months ago. We've really enjoyed how happy everyone is for us. Buying us drinks! Treating us to dinner! Sending small gifts. We were in no rush, but now we're really in no rush. Is two years too long for an engagement? We'd like to enjoy this outpouring for a while longer.

Patient Pamela

Dear Pamela . . .

Kudos to you for discovering the spontaneous benefits of betrothal. Celebrating love is contagious. That said, unless there is a military deployment or medical reason for a long engagement, I encourage you to speed up your timeline. Those same people who toast your happiness now will get bored and cynical if you don't fulfill the promise of your engagement within a year, eighteen months at the outside. Momentum is meaningful in matrimony. Keep the ball rolling by picking a date and sharing news as you have it. The good news for you is that you clearly have a tremendous circle of support. Every couple needs that. Don't make them wait too long for the vows.

Big Kiss & Wedding Bliss,
Your Aunt B

Chapter 13

THE ENGAGEMENT PARTY

The Mother of the Groom

"Welcome to Fair Harbor," Abigail said as the bride, groom, mother of the bride, and the impossibly handsome godfather of the bride made their way up the front walk. Sarah and George stood next to her, dressed in exactly what Abigail had instructed them to wear: the raspberry linen sheath for Sarah and the green gingham tie from their wedding plus a blue blazer for George. Abigail, in a Samantha Sung floral-print dress secured through Poshmark, stood at attention, all five feet three inches of her. The Blakemans were ready to receive their guests.

The New York Contingent, as Abigail had been referring to them all day, arrived a half hour early as instructed, so the families could have time to connect before the crowd descended. Chase had assured her that Penny's family always ran on time because they were in the business of getting to the airport early or meeting in the lobby at a specific time, but Abigail had her doubts. She was grateful, and a touch envious, to see the big black town car pull up at the appointed hour. At least she wouldn't have to deal with what she saw as a significant character flaw: tardiness.

The afternoon was warm and slightly humid for June, a teaser for the July weather to come. The heat of the last few days had pushed Abigail's roses to a first bloom, and she couldn't have been happier. Her own dress featured pink roses, and she thought she looked smashing, matching the landscaping. "We're so happy to have you here at our home for this wonderful occasion."

She was laying it on thick, but the presence of an actual British lord thrilled her. Even as a proud Daughter of the American Revolution, she was a sucker for members of the peerage. But first Abigail had to make her way through Penny, Chase, and Alexa. The MOB was dressed in yellow palazzo pants and a matching top with sparkling but sensible sandals and enough gold jewelry to sink a galleon. She had a vintage striped market bag in her hands, which she handed to Abigail.

"Thank you for hosting. Please accept some olive oil and very special honey from my home island in Greece as a token of our appreciation," Alexa claimed in the same sort of forced language that Abigail had used. Then she loosened up. "Our family on Patmos keeps us well supplied, but we only share with people we like because the honey is credited with the amazing longevity of the Diamandis clan. And the olive oil is so pure, I use it on my skin. It's luscious."

Abigail was mesmerized, both by the fact that she was right about Alexa being dipped in olive oil and by her use of the word "luscious" in conversation. Had Abigail ever experienced anything luscious in her entire life? Did the Yankee pot roast at the Sturbridge Inn count as luscious? Snapping back to awareness, she made a mental note to find a signature Fair Harbor product to give to Alexa the next time they met. There must be Fair Harbor salt or mustard or cranberry sauce. Abigail nearly laughed out loud thinking of Alexa rubbing the cranberry sauce all over her skin. She had to get ahold of herself. "How thoughtful of you. I'm looking forward to trying both."

George cut in. "Well, don't slather yourself with honey. You may stick to the couch." There were polite laughs all around, except from his wife, who had the sudden urge to smother him in honey.

Alexa turned to her companion with a broad smile. "May I introduce my dear friend and Penelope's godfather, Simon Fox."

When the handsome man in the sharp blue suit stepped forward with an outstretched hand toward Abigail, to her horror, she almost started to curtsy. George, in an astonishing moment of awareness, grabbed her elbow and pulled her upright.

He had met these British types before on the bridge circuit, the type who charmed you out of your mind at the beginning of the match so that you made careless mistakes before you realized that the British Empire hadn't colonized the globe because they were gentlemen. He wasn't going to let this Brit get in his head. Or undermine his damn drinks party. There would be no class system here.

George believed deeply in the concept that all men were created equal, even though he personally had benefited greatly from the reality that some men were more equal than others. "Great to meet you, Simon. Come in! Let me get you a drink and then we can take a stroll around the neighborhood. Your people burnt down quite a few houses in this town a few hundred years ago. You should see what we've done with the place since then," George boomed.

"Well, I'm sorry to report that I'm not in a position to make reparations, but I do come in friendship," Simon shot back in return, nodding knowingly to Abigail as he followed George to the bar that had been set up on the patio.

The rest of the New York Contingent followed Sarah into the house. Abigail eyed the beautifully wrapped gift in Penny's hands, assuming it was for her. But then she heard Penny say, "Sarah, can I speak with you for a moment? I have something I'd like to ask." And then squeals of delight.

How lovely, Abigail thought. Penny must have asked her to be a bridesmaid. What an unexpected gesture. Abigail knew that Penny had been in a sorority and must have had a dozen women she could have asked. To choose Sarah and to bring a gift was very . . . well-mannered. Old-fashioned. She was pleased that Sarah would have an official role in the wedding. She filed the kindness away for future reference. She heard the voices trail off as Sarah led them out onto the patio.

Abigail stood for a moment, alone on her front porch, holding the bag of olive oil and honey. Showtime.

**

THE PARTY WAS well underway. The patio was filled with thirsty neighbors and friends who had managed to pull themselves together after a day of sailing or golf to toast the happy couple. The lawn was dotted with some of the younger crowd, peers of Chase and Sarah, who arrived in flip-flops and sundresses and still managed to look lovelier than any of the older set, simply because of their youth.

Her generation was represented as well in similar dresses but better shoes. Abigail spotted her former tennis partner Janice chatting up her former garden club ladies. The DAR was represented by Martha, Pru, and Lucinda dressed in various red, white, and blue combinations. Others were paired up by area of acquaintance—the neighbors, the sailors, the bridge players, the lacrosse moms. She was pleased to see that almost everyone who'd RSVP'd yes had shown up, so unusual in today's last-minute-bail culture. The result was a festive summer event on the flagstone patio with lawn rolling down to the water and the harbor beyond with sailboats on moorings. For sure, it was a three-million-dollar view today.

By Abigail's timeline, George was scheduled to do a short toast in ten minutes, followed by another half hour of socializing. She had hired two former students as bartenders and serving help, because someone needed to replenish those warmed nuts and their rates were reasonable. Once the toast ended, guests had a few minutes for another drink and then they'd be on their way home to dig through their own refrigerators for Sunday dinner.

"This looks like a magazine spread, Abigail. What a special home you have. There is nothing like being on the water to make everything beautiful," Alexa said as she joined a grouping that included Abigail, Sarah, and Bernadette, the prep school roommate turned wedding journalist who had not missed a single detail of the party, including the tussie-mussie in the guest bathroom, always her first stop at any event.

"Isn't this the same pink we wore at your wedding?" Bernadette asked Abigail, holding up her glass of rosé and not even bothering to introduce herself to Alexa. She was confident that Alexa had been read in on the guest list by her daughter, so the tone she took with her was conspiratorial, as if they'd been friends for ages. "I was a bridesmaid at Abigail and George's wedding. Pink and green color scheme. Those were the days!" Ironically, Bernadette, a midsize woman with aggressively dyed black hair, impeccable makeup, and skin almost as well aged as Alexa's, thanks to her Italian heritage, was wearing a well-cut kelly green linen dress and chunky gold and pink jewelry. Yes, Alexa thought, Bernadette was still repping pink and green.

On the car ride out from the city, Penny had explained several times who Aunt B was and what it would mean for Penny and Chase's wedding to be featured on her site. Penny used the phrase "jump-start our coupledom," and that concerned her mother. Did they need a wedding site to validate the partnership?

Alexa took in this potential ally with a quick scan. Bernadette reminded her of many of the women from Seven Sisters alumnae groups she'd taken on tour to Mycenae or Oxford: sharp, engaged, and aware of their place in the hierarchy as highly educated white women. The interesting but not quite pretty looks of their youth replaced by the expensive hair maintenance and good tailoring of middle age. Alexa knew how to communicate with the Bernadettes of the world by adopting a warm but informed tone and speaking to them as an equal. Her daughter instructed her be "accommodating," as if Alexa was normally standoffish and her attitude needed work. She turned on her professional charm. "You still look lovely in those colors. I'm Alexa, and you, of course, are Aunt B. I've heard so much about your work. I'm happy to make your acquaintance."

Bernadette nodded in faux humility, accepting homage from her fan.

Thankfully, Sarah stepped in on the conversation. "Mom was trying on her wedding dress yesterday, Bernadette. She can still rock it," she said, much to her mother's chagrin. Abigail was mortified, as if her own daughter had revealed her Valium usage or her shoplifting record from 1981. Trying on the dress had only been a bit of fun, nothing more. "I think she wants Penny to wear it!"

"Oh, no—" Abigail started to object.

"Wants Penny to wear what?" Penny interrupted, stopping her circulating for a moment, then noticing Bernadette in the circle, turned on her public relations voice. "You're Aunt B! I'm such a fan. I love your columns and your site. I've learned so much from you about weddings. Etiquette, human behavior. You should teach a class at the New School! Chase told me that you're old friends with Abigail. Thank you for coming." Penny reached out her hands for the two-handed clutch, understanding that a hug would be too intimate for a media contact who could add an important public relations spin to her wedding.

"Please call me Bernadette. You and Chase make a beautiful couple. My, you and your mother look so much alike. Both Grecian beauties. Any of your father in you at all?" Bernadette said, nodding in Simon Fox's direction.

Abigail knew this was a test. She had given Bernadette the background on Penny's godfather, but clearly, she was getting the same hint of something afoot as Abigail. Simon and Alexa had a palpable chemistry, looking cozier than old friends, more like old lovers. Could they have made some bargain thirty years ago to keep Penny's true parentage to themselves? Abigail vowed to keep an eye on those two.

"Simon is my godfather," Penny said adroitly. "We only share a love of Scrabble and ocean swimming," she added, avoiding the question while passing the propriety pop quiz. "Now, what am I supposed to be wearing?"

"Nothing, dear. I mean, Sarah is mistaken," Abigail said.

"My mom hauled out her wedding dress yesterday. In case you wanted to wear a throwback from the nineties. As your newly appointed bridesmaid, I feel I need to warn you that it has a little cape!"

"Capelet," Bernadette and Abigail corrected at the same time.

"And how hilarious would it be if I wore Bernadette's bridesmaid's dress? So funny. We should do it as a joke anyway. Like at the bachelorette party, which I am now in charge of!" Sarah cackled, truly misreading the room.

"Penny's already found her dress. We had such good luck yesterday, didn't we?" Alexa said, looking at her daughter too late to notice the burning in her eyes.

"We did. Total spur-of-the-moment decision! One of my favorite designers from Athens, Kalliope Moon. We happened by her shop in SoHo and they were having a trunk show," Penny explained a little too desperately.

Alexa stared at her daughter, wondering where this fiction had come from, then she turned to Abigail, who was clearly shocked. Of course, Alexa thought. Abigail expected to be invited to the dress hunt. That's why she was trying on her dress; she was preparing for the invitation. Even Sarah looked a little forlorn to be left out, despite being asked to be a bridesmaid. Alexa felt awful, truly awful. She wanted to bail out Penny, so she used a little language trick. "Yes! Such . . . what's the word that means good luck but is much longer?"

"Serendipity," Abigail answered, not believing for one second this woman didn't know that word.

"Kalliope Moon is quite an up-and-coming designer," Bernadette said. "I heard that sale was a madhouse. I have people everywhere and they said the line was around the corner. Do you know her?"

"Yes, we both do. From Athens," Penny explained. "We've taken clients to her shop when we do tours. It was great luck that Kalliope herself was there to do the fitting."

"And you bought the dress?" pressed the reporter.

That seemed like an odd question, Abigail thought. Bernadette was a journalist, and it was her job to ask tough questions, but at an engagement party?

Penny did not miss a beat. She understood the subtext even if her future mother-in-law didn't. "Oh, yes. I'm not an influencer or looking for trade-outs. I love Kalliope's designs and I'm happy to support her work in any way possible. In fact, my mother found a dress, too."

Abigail felt apoplectic. Her plan was to scour secondhand shops and hope to get lucky while her counterpart was being fitted personally by European designers? Why had they run out of money for this part of their lives, the fun years? All that cash they wasted on Legos and math camp and homecoming limos when they should have been stockpiling money for this exact occasion. "What serendipity indeed!"

Sarah, once again oblivious to her mother's distress, said in a dreamy voice, "Do I get to wear a Kalliope Moon bridesmaid's dress? I've never heard of her, but it's got to be better than that Laura Ashley number Mom made you wear, Aunt B. Actually, I wouldn't mind wearing this," she said, indicating her sheath, which was both too casual and too raspberry.

"You'll be in blue," Penny informed her. The command was another blow to Abigail, who thought she might be consulted about what her adult daughter should wear. Though, it was hard to object to blue. Sarah looked lovely in all shades of blue.

"Care to share any details about your dress, Penny?" Bernadette asked, again in a voice that was far from innocent.

"How would you describe it, Mom?" It was the sweetest tone Penny had taken in days with her.

"Ethereal. Aithérios," Alexa said, taking Penny's hand and squeezing it. "You looked like the beautiful sea. Ómorfí thálasa. Magical, my dear."

Abigail and the others watched as Penny's eyes welled up. Suddenly, Abigail felt ashamed by her disappointment at being excluded from the dress shopping. And by her silent internal rant. She had her own daughter, who loved her mother's expertise in this area. That was enough. She shouldn't be greedy and want more than what Sarah would give her. Penny and Alexa obviously had a deep bond, a connection that she could never breach, nor would she want to. Abigail took a deep breath to take in the moment. She had a chance to make this right, to undo the wrong of her reaction to the engagement. "I'm sure you will be the most beautiful bride. I look forward to being as surprised as my son when you walk down the aisle. How wonderful. You've checked that off your list. Both of you!"

Sarah looked at her in wonderment, shocked at her mother's genuine response.

Bernadette looked at her in astonishment, as if she'd never heard her friend of forty-plus years say anything that sweet.

Alexa looked at her in gratitude, as if she appreciated Abigail rising above her bruised ego at being left out of the dress shopping.

And Penny looked at her with more tears in her eyes and rushed at her with open arms for a hug. "Thank you, Abigail."

Once the embrace had ended, Abigail stood back, feeling victorious. She had said the right thing to her future daughter-in-law, and it felt like a triumph. Hopefully, that made up for the law school remark. She would take the win and walk away, not wanting anything unexpected to shift the perfect vibe at the party right now. "I need to herd George to say a few words. Penny, can you round up Chase? May I invite you all to step closer to the front of the patio? I need to tell Chip the bartender to pass out the champagne. Excuse me."

***

"I ASK YOUR indulgence because I'm going to start my remarks by quoting Aristotle. Especially yours, Penelope. And Alexa." George tipped his head to Penny and her mother, who both smiled and nodded. This was the sort of spotlight for which a man like George Blakeman was uniquely qualified, having grown up in a pretentious family where toasts were common at holidays or special occasions or Tuesday night supper. George carried on the tradition by nabbing prizes for public speaking at school. He often stood at his dining club in college to give a welcome speech. And during his professional life, the partners always let him give a rousing victory hurrah at the annual sales meeting, the only task he was truly superior in executing. For George, any day could be his personal St. Crispin's Day and he was going to savor the moment.

"Abigail, Sarah, and I welcome you to this humble gathering for our star couple, Penny and Chase. Aristotle wrote, 'Love is composed of a single soul inhabiting two bodies.' And now that you've all had a chance to meet Penny and to see our son and his future bride together, you understand why that is the quote I chose to start with. To Penny and her mother, Alexa, we welcome you into our family and we are honored to be connected with yours. Love gives us the extraordinary gift of expanding our world in so many ways. And now we can say that we have family in California and Greece. And you can claim a branch here in Fair Harbor. We're all the bigger for their love. To Chase, your mother and I are proud of all you've accomplished in your work life. But your choice of a life mate in Penny will count as your greatest accomplishment. Well done. So, if you please, lift your glass to Penny and Chase—two bodies, one soul—and their bright future. Yiamas!"

The crowd roared back in various versions of the traditional Greek toast. Abigail beamed at her husband, joining him at the front of the crowd. He surprised her sometimes with his confidence. You would never know from looking at George, in his blue blazer and the green gingham tie from his own wedding, that their world was collapsing around them, both in terms of their personal finances and place in society. Fewer and fewer people cared about the opinions of a man like George Blakeman, too old, too pale, and too privileged. But on this day, he was triumphant as lord of the manor. Even in the presence of a real British lord.

Suddenly there was a blast of three boat horns and the distinct booming of an amplified accented voice. "Ahoy, Blakemans! Can I get a wee hand?"

The entire crowd turned from the triumphant father on the patio to the harbor and began moving en masse toward the water's edge to take in all the commotion. Approaching the dock in an antique Chris-Craft motorboat was the distinct figure of the mayor of New York, Timmo Lynch. He stood in the stern of the boat, tall and thin, dressed in a blue shirt, red pants, and dark sunglasses, bullhorn in hand. His thick head of gray hair was windblown, downright sexy, like the Platonic ideal of a head of hair for a seventy-year-old man. He put down the bullhorn and picked up the line to tie the boat off to the dock, letting the young man at the wheel do the real work of docking the boat.

One of Sarah's friends, who had sailed at Brown, raced down the gangplank to lend a hand. She caught the rope, executed the knot, and the mayor of New York climbed out of the boat, hopped onto the deck, and declared, "Fine day for an engagement party. I come bearing sandwiches because Tony at Santini's Italian market near my place in Northport loves love so much, he insisted on making up a couple of platters when he heard I was bringing the boat over here. Who can help me pass these?"

The famished partygoers burst into applause, as if the mayor were a magician who had completed his grand finale trick of producing subs out of thin air. But Abigail was horrified. Plastic trays? Common white deli napkins? Mortadella? She watched her son abandon his fiancée and his drink to sprint across the lawn to assist his boss. He was still the chief of staff even at his own engagement party.

Abigail scanned the partygoers to take in their expressions. Hadn't it been George's finest hour a second ago? Now all eyes were on Timmo. This was not what she intended. She wasn't a fan of surprises. Or the mayor. She hoped to find sympathetic nods in her direction. But instead, she caught two distinct reactions to the arrival of Hizzoner: Bernadette's mouth agape and Alexa's intent stare. She knew in that moment that Bernadette was on board to cover the wedding. And that Alexa had more life in her than she suspected.

Chapter 14

THE ENGAGEMENT PARTY

The Mother of the Bride

Until the moment when the mayor arrived via boat, Alexa was having a perfectly fine time at the party. It was hardly the social event of the season, but it was a beautiful day in a stunning spot with attractive people and strong drinks. Even though she didn't know any of the guests, these were her people. Well, her clients anyway. As the Odyssey brand grew, her reach extended beyond Montecito and California to other clusters of travelers who could afford a luxury experience, and she had worked with many groups from Connecticut over the years. The faces all ran together but the overall impression was the same: moneyed and well-mannered.

Then the mayor of New York arrived and shook her up. She'd always had a thing for men on boats, no doubt because she grew up on an island. But even during her time in Montecito, when most of the female frothing was aimed at polo players and surfers, Alexa's few long relationships had been with sailors. Fit, energetic, at home on the water and restless on land, which suited her style as well. Granted, the mayor arrived under motor power, not wind power, but he had the look of a man who was comfortable at sea.

Alexa paid attention to politics, because she was an engaged citizen of the world, in her own estimation, but tried not to get sucked into the day-to-day battles of her adopted homeland. She read her local paper, the *Montecito Journal*, which reported extensively on the three R's—restaurants, retail, and real estate, all topics she adored. (Every digital issue started with the words "Good Morning MoJo-ers!", a greeting that became her call to action.) For real news from the real world, Alexa's preferred source was the BBC, as it always had been. Global context counted to her. She remained publicly nonpartisan as far as her clients were concerned; red money or blue money was all the same to her. But her knowledge of New York City politics was limited. She'd seen photos of Timothy Lynch, but not in the bow of an antique Chris-Craft Runabout with windblown hair. He was a very handsome man.

She watched as first Chase dashed to the mayor's side, then a cater waiter to relieve Himself of his sandwiches. Next, Penny made her way to the water's edge to greet her fiancé's boss. Then Abigail and George joined in for handshakes and animated conversation, and then the small group turned to her and waved her over. Simon appeared at her side.

"Shall we?" he said. They had already made the rounds with the Connecticut crowd, tag-teaming introductions, explaining the same personal details repeatedly about her American-born mother, her Greek father, her relocation to Southern California, and her travel company. She let Simon handle the university stories, his role as godfather, and how delighted Penny was to be joining the Blakeman family. They were a winning team who could impress the locals with their Euro-appeal. But what about Timmo Lynch?

"Oh, yes. I'm sure the Irish mayor of New York is dying to meet an English aristocrat."

***

THERE WAS NO doubt that Timmo Lynch had noticed the striking woman in yellow. In a sea of blond and gray heads, both sexes dressed in the colors of the American flag because it was summer in Connecticut, the statuesque brunette in yellow silk stood out. Which was why Alexa had worn the outfit in the first place.

Actually, she wore the yellow to annoy Penny after her warning yesterday. But right after that consideration, she wore it to stand out and serve notice that she, the single mother of the bride, was up to the challenge of the role. She had never even considered the effect it might have on the Irishman.

"Yellow is my favorite color," Timmo Lynch declared as he shook Alexa's hand.

"I don't believe you," Alexa responded. "There's not an Irishman alive who doesn't count green as his favorite color."

"You've got me there. It's my second favorite color then," he confessed with a smile, holding her gaze with the patented bright blue Lynch stare. Alexa held his gaze as well. "It's a pleasure to meet you. You couldn't be anybody else but Penny's mother. Well, I can tell you that Chase's work has been absolute garbage since he's met your daughter and I hope this wedding puts an end to that nonsense."

Chase shook his head. "He's exaggerating."

"And I understand that you and I are in the same business?" the mayor said to Simon without hesitation. Obviously, his chief of staff had briefed him on the party guests as well.

"Both representing our constituents to the best of our ability. Although most of my constituents have four legs and curly hair," Simon said, and Alexa noticed that he slipped into a more localized Northern English accent, not the posh tones of the upper crust as usual. Man of the Sheeple, Lord Simon Fox.

"We wish we had a few more sheep in New York City, don't we, Chase? Everybody I represent seems to have their own opinion. I could use more followers and a few less leaders." Everybody laughed, except Abigail, who was still looking distraught over the unexpected

Italian subs and the lingering guests. "Speaking of work, Chase, can I pull you away just for a second? I won't keep him long, Mother."

Abigail breathed deeply. She had never liked when men referred to her as Mother, like the elderly pediatrician she'd had when her son was born, but especially this man. He was all talk and charm. She didn't buy it. As if Chase had neglected his duties because of Penny. What rubbish. She didn't care if he'd built a billion-dollar business and then executed his office with sky-high approval ratings, she wasn't impressed. "He doesn't need my permission anymore. I must go check on the party favors. Excuse me." And she strode off with purpose, even though party favors didn't exist. *Nuts to go?*

Chase and his boss departed and George looked at Simon. "That must be familiar to you. Everything is politics, even an engagement party. Can I interest you in another drink and a sandwich? I'm famished."

"Yes, please, to both," Simon said, following his host to the other side of the yard, leaving Penny and Alexa alone.

"What was that?" Penny hissed at her mother.

"You mean Chase and his boss?" Alexa asked. "That does seem rude in the middle of a party."

"No, you and Chase's boss. Were you flirting with Timothy Lynch?"

"I've never known how to flirt and I'm certainly not starting now."

"Something was happening there."

"Maybe he really does love yellow."

"Mom, he's Chase's boss." Penny said this as if Alexa had an ongoing issue with hitting on men in inappropriate situations when really the opposite was true. Alexa had spent the last thirty years of her life, as long as Penny was alive, purposely avoiding any questionable men or relationships. She was the most discreet woman in town, the Merry Widows always said, much to their dismay. They wanted to live through her sexual adventures, only to be told by

Alexa, time and time again, that there was nothing to tell. Even if there was.

"Penny, you know he has a reputation as a charmer. He was doing his politician thing with me. I suppose he thinks women, especially women of a certain age, are desperate for attention. He can't help himself. But you have nothing to worry about. I'll never see him again."

"Mom, who do you think is going to marry us? As in, perform the ceremony?"

"You said it was a surprise."

"Mayor Lynch is the surprise. He's coming to the wedding. He insisted. He already has his reservations at the Miramar. Please behave. I can't have any drama," Penny said, again as if her mother's romantic life had been an ongoing soap opera in her daughter's life instead of an afterthought.

Immediately, Alexa recalled the tasteful but billowy sequined caftan she'd put on hold at Kalliope Moon for her mother-of-the-bride dress. That wouldn't do at all now. She was going to need something more formfitting. Maybe even in yellow, even though Penny wanted guests to wear blue. She'd call Monday morning to see what else Kalliope had in her shop. In a blue *green*, she thought with a wicked smile.

Alexa put on her diplomatic voice for reassurance. "How lovely that he and Chase are so close. It will be an honor to have him in Montecito, and I'll call over to Raoul at the Miramar to touch base on Mayor Lynch's visit. We should do brunch there when you come out in a few weeks to scout venues. Sound good?"

Penny nodded. The brunch idea soothed her. "We should go soon. I need some food. I'm so hungry, aren't you?"

***

ALEXA AND SIMON'S exit was sooner than expected. The mayor also had a car waiting, leaving his nephew Gerry to pilot his boat back across the sound to Long Island. He was headed into the city and Penny and Chase were to ride with him. This, Alexa suspected, would be a pattern for the foreseeable future, Penny as third wheel to her fiancé/candidate. In the meantime, the trio were making the rounds with guests again, in what looked suspiciously like the start of Chase's campaign. Lots of handshakes, back slaps, and raucous laughter by groups of men who had separated themselves from their wives and were basking in the glow of Mayor Lynch, even if they resented the New York City taxes taken out of their Wall Street paychecks.

Alexa and Simon said their goodbyes, while the other guests, sated by sandwiches, appeared to be settling in for another round of cocktails.

Poor Abigail, thought Alexa. *She'll never get rid of these people.*

Bernadette spotted her and made a beeline toward Alexa, panting a little as she reached her. "Before you go, I wanted to get your card. I'm looking forward to the event in Montecito. I'll be doing an engagement piece on Penny and Chase and may have follow-up questions. We should stay in touch." It wasn't a suggestion; it was a directive from Aunt B. She would be covering the wedding, launching her daughter and Chase's coupledom, along with his political career. Alexa saw the potential for the whole family to gain. Like the business owner she was, Alexa had stashed a few cards into her clutch. A few other guests, interested in booking travel, hadn't blinked when she slipped her cards into their hands. And Bernadette didn't either.

"Absolutely. Contact me for anything you need," Alexa responded, handing her card to her fellow female hustler. They both understood the assignment. "As far as the ceremony, I'm happy to arrange your accommodations. Montecito can be busy at the holidays, but I have a wonderful circle of friends who have offered guest suites or casitas to wedding travelers. I'd love to put you someplace special." It was true. As soon as the word got out, longtime clients had called with congratulations and offers of housing for family and friends for the event. The sort of old-fashioned kindness the locals prided themselves on.

Bernadette nodded. She, too, understood the currency of connection. "What a generous offer. Put me down for a casita for two. I might even persuade my husband to join me for this one." And then, the vision of pink and green hustled off to secure a sandwich for the ride back to Niantic.

***

At the door, Alexa thanked her hosts and made all kinds of statements about looking forward to the future and how she couldn't wait to see them in December.

Sarah looked at her with a perfect doggy head tilt. "December? You'll see us in July. Penny asked Mom and me to come out and be part of the wedding planning in two weeks. I have the summer off, and Mom can get out of her volunteer gig at the senior center. We're psyched, Cali-bound!" She did the type of dance that indicated one too many Aperol spritzes on an empty stomach. "I can't wait. I've never been to California. I heard UC Santa Barbara has a field hockey pitch overlooking the Pacific. So cool."

Alexa tried to hide her shock. She didn't need the help from these two for a wedding in her town, especially now that her daughter had hired Madison, the wedding planner. And if she had any further questions, the Merry Widows, with their wise counsel and their deep knowledge of florists, caterers, staging companies, dance bands, and glam portable toilets, were all she needed. What was Penny thinking? Was this a makeup for the dress shopping slight? She guessed yes. But what about accommodations for them at the height of the summer tourist season? It would be impossible. Her mind was spinning. Abigail picked up on that.

"It looks like this is news to you?" Abigail said, offering a small bag of warm nuts for the road.

Alexa wasn't going to throw Penny under the bus. Plus, it was important for her to appear one step ahead, not one step behind, on all wedding plans. She'd built her entire professional life on being one step ahead. She didn't trust Abigail yet so she gave a nonanswer. "Penny handed me quite a list yesterday. I haven't been through all the line items, but we welcome your assistance. Bring your bathing suits!" The two mothers exchanged a quick hug. "What a lovely party. Such a beautiful home you have. A very special place. And George, you gave a wonderful toast. You did Aristotle and our family proud."

George puffed up a bit, and Alexa felt a genuine connection for the first time to this man.

Simon added his thanks and said, "I'll see you both again in Montecito in December!"

As Alexa's car pulled away from the curb, she turned to look back at the house and there was Timmo Lynch on the front porch, giving her a tip of his head. As she returned the gesture, a tiny jolt shot through her. Maybe this wedding would have its perks after all.

Simon noticed her spark. "You and the mayor? Quite the pair."

Alexa pulled two Italian subs out of her handbag and offered one to Simon. "Sub?"

"Oh, I couldn't. So many hot nuts, I can barely eat another bite," he joked, taking the sandwich he was offered, along with the extra napkin. "And people say the British have bad food."

"I think we better pre-eat before the rehearsal dinner. I'm afraid it will just be cheese and crackers and a few carrot sticks," Alexa agreed, and now they both were laughing. When they settled, she asked, "What do you think of them, Simon? They'll be such a big part of Penny's life."

"That George is a very solid guy, but I get the sense he lives in a world that's disappearing. A world where bridge and good manners and references to Aristotle have tremendous value. But Chase doesn't live in that world and that's what counts. He's of this time and place. As is his boss. But I liked all of them for different reasons. Penny will be fine, Lex," he said. "And say what you will about the mother, she's an amazing gardener. Did you see those roses? And those hydrangeas? Impressive. A person who can cultivate a garden like that one has something to offer. Be patient."

"Now who's the man who lives in a world that is disappearing?" Alexa said, popping the last of the sub into her mouth.

From the Desktop of Dearly Beloveds and Betrotheds

Aunt B's Engagement of the Month

Penelope Diamandis, Chase Blakeman Engaged to Marry

The afternoon event started with stunning Connecticut coastline views, crisp G&Ts, and Aristotle and ended with the mayor of New York arriving via boat and toasting the couple with good cheer and Italian sandwiches. In between, there were dozens of well-wishers celebrating the engagement of New Yorkers Penelope Diamandis and Chase Ellsworth Blakeman at the Fair Harbor home of Mr. Blakeman's parents, George and Abigail Blakeman. The wedding is planned for late December in Montecito, California, where Ms. Diamandis was raised by her mother, Alexa Diamandis.

The couple met the old-fashioned way—on the corner of Seventy-Sixth Street and Third Avenue in Manhattan. Both early morning runners in Central Park, they had been eyeing each other for months. Mr. Blakeman, a graduate of Fordham University, is the chief of staff for the mayor of New York City, Timothy Lynch. Long hours by the mayor's side meant that his workout time often came before sunrise. Ms. Diamandis, a graduate of Southern Methodist University in Dallas and now a senior account executive at Lynx Communications, a boutique public relations firm specializing in travel, is an early riser as well. The two would often find themselves headed back to their respective Upper East Side apartments at the same time after a loop around the reservoir. One morning, before ducking into a deli for coffee, Mr. Blakeman introduced himself and asked for Ms. Diamandis's number so he could ask her out.

Instead, she gave him her work email and little hope. "He always wore the same T-shirt when he was running. I was worried he didn't know how to do laundry," Ms. Diamandis recalls.

It turns out that Mr. Blakeman had more than one college T-shirt, and his persistence won over the California native. Over the next eleven months, Ms. Diamandis learned the city outside Manhattan while accompanying Mr. Blakeman on the weekends to community events and fairs in the outer boroughs. The two shared subway rides, churros, karaoke contests, and bonding with constituents. "We were a good fit from the start," Mr. Blakeman says. "Penny jumped right into cakewalks and barbecues and whatever might be happening in Queens or Brooklyn or the Bronx. I fell in love with her optimism."

As for Ms. Diamandis, who spent her childhood summers on the island of Patmos in the Aegean Sea and traveled extensively throughout Europe with her mother, who is a travel professional, she said, "With Chase as my tour guide, New York City became my oyster."

Thanks to some help from his boss, Mr. Blakeman dropped to one knee at the top of the Empire State Building while on a prearranged private tour, offering Ms. Diamandis an aquamarine and tourmaline ring from designer Evvie Taylor.

Irish singer-songwriter Dermot Kennedy, a supporter of the mayor, serenaded the duo with his hit single "Kiss Me" while photographer Colin Brookes snapped photos of the newly engaged couple. Afterward, a table at Bemelmans Bar was waiting for them.

"It was the New York moment of all New York moments," Ms. Diamandis said.

"That's how I roll," Mr. Blakeman responded.

Mr. Blakeman's parents are George Winthrop Blakeman, a former partner at Pierce, Fenner, and Smith Brokerage and now a ranked bridge player, and Abigail Ellsworth Blakeman, the former director of development at Silliman School, now retired, of Fair Harbor, Connecticut. The Groom-to-Be is the great-great-great-grandson of Oliver Ellsworth, a founding father of Connecticut and a signer of the Declaration of Independence. The Bride-to-Be is the daughter of Alexa Diamandis, a citizen of both America and Greece, where she was raised on Patmos by her parents, hoteliers Yiorgos and the late Eleni Diamandis. She is the CEO of Odyssey Vacations in Montecito, a luxury travel company.

An intimate California celebration is planned with a honeymoon to follow in the summer in Greece. The Bride will be walked down the aisle by her godfather, Simon Fox, 4th Baron Plumley, a member of the House of Lords. And will the mayor make another surprise appearance? The engaged couple are not saying. But their eyes are shining.

A note from Aunt B: I have known Chase all his life, thanks to my decades-long friendship with his mother. I cover this both as a journalist and as a longtime family friend.

Chapter 15

THE VISIT PREP

The Mother of the Bride

"I can't thank you enough, Ming. I didn't know where I was going to put them," Alexa said as she arrived with an overflowing basket of goods from Pierre Lafond market to place in the guest wing. Water, wine, beer, sunscreen, chocolates, even baseball caps curated by the prevailing purveyor of gourmet food, baked goods, and gifts in Montecito, along with a few prepared meals in case they woke up hungry because of the time difference. Ming's house was a modern single-story oasis on the grounds of one of Montecito's premier golf course communities, Nottingham Forest. Tucked at the end of a cul-de-sac, the home had enough elevation for a view of the Pacific from one window and the Santa Barbara mountains from another.

Ming's late spouse, Bob Cowan, lawyer to the stars and husband number two, had made sure to include in his will that this house was hers for as long as she wanted to live in it, much to the dismay of his adult children, who were hoping to sell the place and split the proceeds. Recently, there'd been some pressure on Ming to move into a smaller home so the boys could "liquidate the asset," as the quasi-legal email from John, the eldest son, said. Periodically, real estate agents showed up at her door to do an assessment at the request of John and James Cowan. While it wasn't in Ming's nature to be petty, she'd recently remodeled the kitchen, an unmistakable signal to her stepsons that she wasn't going anywhere anytime soon.

"This is a masterpiece," Ming said, referring to the basket of goodies. "I like your style. Kill them with kindness and chocolate hazelnut scones."

"I don't know why I'm so nervous. It feels very different to be hosting future in-laws as opposed to normal clients. And really, it's Penny's weekend, not mine. I can't thank you enough for offering your guest wing. I know you said no house gifts, but that's not possible for me. This is for you," Alexa said, handing over a bottle of wine and a pound of coffee to her friend, who lived on both. "Hydration is everything. Shall I bring this around to the guest quarters?" she said, pointing to the basket.

"Just leave it there. Win can do it later." Win was Ming's house manager, a tanned, fortyish surfer who made sure that the property was clean and landscaped, kept the fridge stocked with "Ming food" (wine, cottage cheese, chocolate, and sliced pineapple) and ensured everything was in proper working order. Win didn't perform menial tasks like scrubbing, mowing, and hammering, but he hired people who did. He worked for several widowed women in Nottingham Forest and had quite a reputation for "going the extra mile." Not with Ming, of course, but reportedly with some of the other single, and lonelier, women. "He's coming by to check on everything to make sure we're set. He's opened the wine and put together a cheese platter, too. I don't know what I'd do without him."

Save sixty thousand dollars a year, Alexa thought. But she didn't say anything. Ming was a retired financial planner; she knew what money was worth. If she wanted to spend that amount on an employee like Win so she never had to talk to a service person or go to the grocery store or retrieve her mail, that was her prerogative. She was very busy with her mahjong and the Merry Widows. "I can't thank you and Win enough."

When Alexa had arrived home from the engagement party with the news that the MOG and her daughter were arriving in town for a long weekend in July without lodging, the Merry Widows jumped into action. Ming immediately offered her guest wing, a convenient and tastefully decorated collection of rooms with its own private entrance off the back of the house. Abigail and Sarah could come and go, fix breakfast in the kitchenette, and find their way to the pool all without disturbing Ming. As a bonus, she promised to invite them for a glass of wine upon arrival.

Toots had volunteered to host a dinner one night at her house, another architectural masterpiece called La Mariposa, so they could all get a reading on the Blakemans in a relaxed setting. Roxanne, Frannie, and Mitsy would also be attendance, as if dining together on a weekend night were the most natural thing in the world. Which it wasn't, because that was social time, the nights of the week when these society stalwarts put on their festive outfits and opened their wallets. But summer was not the time for fundraisers, and by some miracle the whole group was home.

Just then, Alexa's phone rang. It was Penny. She looked at Ming, who pointed out to the patio, indicating that she could talk privately there. Ming knew business and wasn't offended. Alexa slid the door open and stepped out onto the flagstone. "Hello, dear. Are you on the plane?"

***

"I can't come. I have too much work."

"I don't understand. Aren't you in the air?"

"No, I should be. But I'm at the office and I'll be here all weekend. The client, that hotel chain I told you about, they want to expand the curated gift-box program I worked on last year. And they want me in charge. I can't say no, Mom, even though we should have started the process months ago. It took so much energy to do one hotel last year. Now they want me to do four in the same amount of time. This is a huge opportunity and I need to be in Bentonville, Arkansas, on Monday."

Last holiday season, Penny had a breakthrough moment at work that she had proudly shared with her mother. Their client, a boutique hotel chain with ten properties in the South, wanted to promote their connection to local makers and creators to lure travel pros, editors, influencers, and ultimately the paying public to their redesigned and rebranded country inns. The client chose Savannah as destination number one and Penny spent weeks there, finding the perfect knitters, tinsmiths, weavers, gourmet food purveyors, and watercolorists with products to sell and stories to tell. The boxes themselves were works of art, becoming a coveted item among the travel in crowd. Penny and her crew spent equal amounts of time shooting, writing, and posting about the artisans for social media. The project was considered a real success by her agency and her client. The media pickup was impressive. The featured makers became minor stars, and the hotel bookings for the year rose almost immediately.

It was a win for client and community, the kind of work that felt beyond satisfying. It was Penny's future. She saw the project as her route to partnership in the firm. She wanted to be known for taking an idea that could have been ho-hum and creating something special and memorable. She carried that momentum into other projects that year.

But now, there was a tension in Penny's voice that Alexa recognized from the toughest days of her own career, the days when it felt like she had to solve every problem by herself. Like right after 9/11, when she watched her business plummet. Or during the global financial crisis, when clients stayed home in droves, licking their own financial wounds while she struggled to keep the business afloat after buying out her partner. Or all the agonizing days of the pandemic, when she had to pivot from booking luxury cruises to scouting home rentals in Montana for clients who needed to get out of town because their palatial California homes were too suffocating. To Alexa, Penny sounded like she had on so many phone calls, like a working woman whose future depended upon pulling everything together in the next forty-eight hours. A world on your shoulders and yours alone.

"Arkansas? I hear only good things about Bentonville. So, what can I do? How can I make this easier for you?" That was a phrase Alexa had learned from her own mother when she was dealing with some tourist who had lost a passport or missed the ferry. *How can I make this easier for you?* No one wanted to accept help, but people welcomed ease. "Tell me what you need."

Penny started to cry. "I don't know if I can do this, Mom."

"Do what?"

"All of it. Work, plan a wedding, be the supportive spouse on the campaign trail. I feel so much pressure to get everything exactly right." And there it was: the burden of being a perfectionist. Anything less than exactly right was a failure. "I love Chase, I do. But I feel like this campaign is already taking over our lives and it hasn't even officially started." Another sob could be heard. Penny went on to remind her mother that because she was marrying a public servant and not a high-paid lobbyist, she needed to hold her own in the income department.

Alexa paused a second. Now she felt the pressure. She needed to get this right or this phone call might be the moment that Penny realized her mother didn't fully support her life plan. "You need to take your tasks one at a time. I know you can do that. If work is this weekend's priority, then work. I'll cover for you here. It's going into buildings and taking photos. Of course I can do that. And taste the cake? Happy to do that. You can come out in October and nail down all the final details. As for Chase . . ."

And here, Alexa faltered. Her relationship history didn't put her in the Advice Givers Hall of Fame. When the going got tough or intimate or even slightly inconvenient to her work schedule, Alexa bailed. But Penny was different. Penny dug in and made it work. She stayed with her completely inadequate, in Alexa's opinion, college boyfriend for far too long. Five years! Despite his lack of ambition and love of beer pong.

But Chase, he seemed like a good match for her striving daughter, despite the Queens move. Alexa attempted to finish her sentence with wise words. "You are a team and you need to be in constant communication with each other. He needs to know what you're feeling and you need to know what he is thinking. Because men don't feel." She said the last line to get a laugh out of Penny.

It didn't. "Thanks, Mom. You're right. One task at a time."

"Is everything else okay, dear?"

"I'm sure Chase's mother will be furious. I'm not sure she likes me." For Penny, who had been universally liked her entire life, especially by adults, who appreciated her ability to not ask tedious questions because she already knew the answers, this was a shocking revelation. Because of Alexa's status, she had no history with mothers-in-law. This was all new territory. "I think she really expected Chase to marry someone like her. You know, New England–y. She doesn't quite know what to make of me."

Alexa thought about her own family, where all males were kings, loved by their mothers despite having no discernible skills or ambitions. It was the Greek way. She'd seen her aunts and grandmother fawn over their adult sons like they were little boys. To Alexa, Abigail Blakeman seemed on edge about more than just her son's choice of wife. She seemed anxious about every part of her life, as if she were gripping too tightly to a fantasy instead of embracing her reality. Chase represented the Blakeman family's last stab at entitled success before their downward mobility engulfed them all. Penny must threaten that legacy, with her single mother and her Greek/Californian background. Also, Alexa suspected, with her style, her ambition, and her confidence. Abigail was probably a touch jealous of her son's fiancée.

But Alexa was determined to win Abigail over, if only for Penny's sake. It was the least she could do. "Her only son is getting married. It's not you, it's her. Should I turn on my patented Diamandis charm offensive?"

"Thank you! Get the Widows in on it, too. And keep pouring the wine."

"Don't worry. The Widows never run out of wine. And I bought some beer for the sister. She seems like the beer type."

Penny laughed finally. Some of the stress was draining from her voice. "She's totally the beer type. Thank you, Mom. I appreciate this so, so much. I'm so glad you're on top of this."

Alexa was proud of herself. A huge part of her job was mitigating the issues that arose when a group of strangers traveled together to a foreign country, all of them harboring their own (out of control) expectations. De-escalation was her forte. But Penny was so self-sufficient, Alexa rarely had to use her techniques on her. The crisis now over, Penny needed details. "Tell me about your plans. What are you doing? Where are you going? I'm so proud of you. You're going to smash this."

***

"Is EVERYTHING ALL right?" Ming asked when Alexa stepped back into the house after her phone call.

"She's not coming. Penny. She's not on the plane. She has too much work!"

"Oh, what a shame. You've done so much planning and scheduling. All those venues and florists and cake makers. And my cheese platter. You and I can eat it," Ming said, opening the door of the fridge.

"We'll need the cheese platter. The mother is coming. And the sister. Just not the bride."

"What?" Ming said, shutting the fridge again.

"The Blakemans will be here, but Penny will not." Alexa pulled up a chair at the breakfast bar and launched into an explanation. "Remember her client, the boutique hotel in Savannah that she did those special gift boxes for last year? She sent us an extra for the holiday gift exchange?"

"Oh, yes. I picked it! That delicious face oil and the bourbon peach jam. I could have eaten that with a spoon." Ming, who had a legendary sweet tooth among the Merry Widows, wasn't lying about the jam. It was that good. But Alexa felt the need to soften the truth of Penny's situation. Someone in Ming's tax bracket wouldn't really understand the financial pressure Penny felt, so Alexa skipped to the details.

"Well, the client loved it so much, they want her to create boxes for four more locations and send out to hundreds more media and celebrities for the holidays. She was in a minor panic two weeks ago when we went dress shopping and the project was in the pitch stage. And now it's a major panic because it's a go. First, her assistant quit, and then the new assistant quit. Apparently, talking on the phone was too stressful for Gen Z. They didn't want to call suppliers and fulfillment companies. Or call the hotels to set the fam trips up," Alexa explained, using the travel business lingo that she and Penny knew so well. "Fam" equaled familiarization, and hotels or tourism bureaus often invited top agents to experience their hotels or cities for free in hopes that they would recommend them to clients. "Penny is working all weekend to set everything up for the next two weeks. On Monday, she goes to Charleston, New Orleans, Magnolia Springs, and somewhere in Arkansas. I can't recall exactly where, but she's not coming here. Ricky's picking up Chase's mother and sister at LAX."

Ricky was a regular driver for the Merry Widows, taking them to Los Angeles International Airport two hours up the road so they could avoid flying out of the small, underserved Santa Barbara Airport, which always meant a connection in Salt Lake City or Denver. When her trip fell apart, Penny arranged for Ricky to do the pickup because she wouldn't wish the rental car lot at LAX on her worst enemy. And certainly not on her future mother-in-law. He charged a premium for late notice, even though the patronage of Odyssey Vacations had probably put both his kids through college.

"So thoughtful of Penny to arrange a car for them," Ming said, as if booking a driver were complicated. Because Ming did so few of her own quotidian tasks, she had no idea how little effort it took to open an app on your phone and get a car. Or food. Or turn on the lights of your home before you arrived. The woman who had advised millionaires about their money marveled at the mundane.

In the meantime, the enormity of what Alexa had promised her daughter dawned on her: a mile-long to-do list and two soon-to-be in-laws arriving with attitudes. "What am I going to do with the two of them all weekend?"

Ming laughed. "You're a tour guide with a wedding to plan. I'm sure you'll be able to keep them busy for three days."

Chapter 16

THE APPALLING CALL

The Mother of the Groom

"What do you mean she's not coming? It's her wedding. She needs to pick the venue, not us," Abigail said, putting the call on speakerphone so Sarah could hear Chase, too. "We're on our way to the airport. Your father's driving us. And now she's going to cancel?"

Chase's voice came through loud and clear, even though the car was so old it didn't even have a wireless connection. "Mom, it's work and it's important to her. And it's important to us. This is a big opportunity and she doesn't want to blow it."

"And your wedding isn't a big opportunity?" Abigail snapped back, more annoyed now than ever that the couple couldn't be persuaded to have the wedding in Fair Harbor instead of this California nonsense. She knew having the wedding in the groom's hometown instead of the bride's was not traditional, but she was hoping the smashing success of the engagement party and the press coverage would make them see the light. Why not an easy, elegant East Coast event? What could be more traditional than that? But no, Penny would not be swayed and now this mess! *She's the one insisting on California and now we have pick the soulless venue from a list without her,* Abigail seethed. "I'm not sure I understand Penny's priorities."

Chase was silent on the other end of the phone for a moment, gathering his thoughts. Then he answered his mother as if she were an annoying journalist who'd asked the same question five times hoping for a different response. "Mom, Penny and I both prioritize work. I'm in public service, that means it's likely she will be the primary breadwinner in our family. We are partners in this enterprise, equal partners. So, if she needs to work this weekend, she needs to work this weekend. I'm working, too, as a matter of fact. Headed out to Long Island for a planning session with the mayor. Work is important to both of us."

The Blakemans let that statement settle. There was that implication again that his parents had not only chosen a different path, but the incorrect path. George turned to his wife and could see she was starting to build up a head of steam. He gave her a one-handed "settle down" gesture.

They'd had this conversation before when Chase or Sarah had made comments about how they'd never be able to buy a house because their parents' generation had sucked up all the wealth. But, their children boasted, they were going to change the paradigm! They believed themselves to be so much smarter than their parents, as if all the opportunities they thought they deserved for their own children would be delivered in a beautifully wrapped package, thanks to their deliberate, enlightened choices to share household chores with their spouses and buy their kids nongendered toys.

But Abigail and George, being older, wiser, and much less convinced about the New World Order, knew that the hard choices about money and parenthood and doing work you believed in versus work that made a decent living were right around the corner for their kids, not decades away. Economic reality came at you fast and it was exhausting. What seemed like a good idea at thirty was a terrible reality at forty and an unsustainable trap at fifty. But the couple held their tongues because they believed there was a time and a place for a conversation like this and it was not while stuck in traffic on the Whitestone Bridge.

George extended an olive branch. "We believe in work, too, son. What can we do to be helpful?"

This trip was Penny's idea, Abigail mouthed at George. It was costing them a small fortune in airfare, fresh hair highlights, a few new wardrobe items, and one Hydrafacial because she needed to look her best when she met the Merry Widows, whom she'd heard so much about. She'd even been suspicious about the offer to stay at Ming's house, until she looked at the hotel situation in Montecito and realized that the only available rooms were the ones she could never afford. When the offer to stay with Ming was extended, Abigail was relieved and then paranoid. Did Alexa suspect that their financial situation was so dire?

Now Chase was insinuating that Penny needed to work because he had no family money. That was what he was implying, wasn't it? And what was it with this new generation of men and their "equal partnership" stance? The minute Penny gave birth, the scale would tip in one direction for the next eighteen years. He'd flee public service for a private company paycheck minutes after the baby arrived. Did he know the cost of day care?

Chase ticked off his notes like he was debriefing an advance team. "Penny has sent you all the details on the venues for the wedding and the rehearsal dinner and the schedule for the site visits. Madison the wedding planner will pick you up on Saturday morning. Of course Penny has looped in her own mother so you're not in charge of anything, but just another set of eyes. Also, she wanted me to make sure and let you know that because our family is hosting the rehearsal dinner, anywhere you choose is fine with her."

Abigail rolled her eyes and muted the phone so she could say to George, "I don't believe that 'anywhere we choose' is fine with her."

Wisely, he didn't respond. She unmuted.

Chase continued, "And, Sarah, can you take lots of photos and videos and get those to her ASAP? Doesn't need to be real time, but she can go over those on her flight on Monday. And their regular driver will pick you up at LAX, so you don't have to worry about a rental car. Sarah, she'll text you the details on the pickup."

Again with the cars! And why was Sarah in charge of everything all of a sudden? Didn't Penny trust her? Abigail was beyond annoyed. Why were they even getting on the plane? Sarah could see her mother's face and waved a cautionary finger at her, before answering her brother. "Sounds great, Chase. I'm happy to do that. Also, I contacted Lloyd so I'll see him at some point. Tell Penny to have a good work trip. Don't worry about Montecito! Mom and I will represent. No problem." Sarah stared hard at her mother, indicating that she should talk next. And be nice.

"Yes, tell Penny not to worry. We're looking forward to being as helpful as possible. Safe travels to her. She should text us if she thinks of anything else," Abigail cooed with conviction, more to assuage Sarah than Chase.

"Thanks, Mom. I mean it. I really appreciate you doing this for us."

That simple sentiment soothed Abigail. She so rarely got thanks from her family. Strangers at the grocery store, clients at the senior center, even former Silliman parents she might bump into at church all said thank you to her for some small gesture she afforded them. But her own family, especially Chase, rarely acknowledged her in that way. "Of course, Chase. Happy to help."

"We're pulling into JFK, son. We'll sign off now. Your mother and your sister are all set. Safe travels to Penny," George closed and ended the call. He turned to his wife and said in a faux-sympathetic tone, "You almost lost it, but you hung on."

What do you know about hanging on? Abigail wanted to burst out in admonition but held her tongue. George breezed through the world despite their circumstances, while she could barely sleep at night, worried about their finances and their future. How could he not see the bind they were in? He wasn't going three thousand miles to go look at second-tier clubs and barbecue joints for the rehearsal dinner they couldn't afford. But she didn't like to fight in front of the children, even if the child in question was twenty-seven. So instead, she answered, "Chase is a very supportive partner. I hope Penny returns the favor."

She stared out the window at the airport signs. "We're at Terminal Six, George. Oh, and Sarah, who is Lloyd?"

**

ABIGAIL BLAKEMAN WAS a proud daughter of New England. She believed in clapboard white houses, pewter over silver, mashed root vegetables on Thanksgiving, and all that was Colonial. But even she had to admit that Montecito was drop-dead gorgeous. She hadn't been all that impressed with what Southern California had to offer on the drive from the airport until the full expanse of the Pacific Ocean came into view about ninety minutes up Highway 101 at the curve at Rincon Beach. The stunning scale and scope of the California coast became clear. She took in the huge waves, the wide beach, and dozens, maybe hundreds, of surfers dotting the water. It almost took her breath away. Almost.

The last half hour of the trip took them past houses pitched out over the ocean or climbing up mountainsides. They drove past polo fields and beach clubs and citrus groves. As they wove their way through the streets of the town itself, she admired charming cottages, low-slung midcentury moderns, and Mediterranean estates peeking out behind high walls and long crushed-granite drives. The village shops looked inviting, chic, authentic. And the flowers and the foliage! It was like being in another world, maybe even another millennium, ancient and unexpected. From birds-of-paradise to sage bushes bigger than a car. The olive trees! The lemons! The enormous prickly pears! Roses and bougainvillea everywhere. She wanted to remain unimpressed but couldn't.

In her only previous trip to California, more than two decades ago, Abigail had stayed in downtown San Diego for work and found it appalling. Everything about it seemed engineered for naval ships and conferences. She barely left the hotel because she had no real need. Who needed to explore a town filled with Fuddruckers? But this part of the Golden State seemed to live up to the hype, even though she would never admit she was the type to care about hype. One look at a stone-capped stucco wall overhung by brilliant pink bougainvillea and Abigail was sold. She wanted to move right in with the royalty, the celebrities, the barons of business and Hollywood. If the Old Guard would have her.

"How beautiful," she said to no one in particular.

"The most beautiful," Ricky answered with conviction.

Sarah had spent the bulk of the two-hour drive entertaining herself with fun facts about Montecito that she gleaned from her phone. How she could look at that tiny screen and be in a car at the same time perplexed Abigail. She could get car sick changing the radio. But not Sarah, who stayed glued to her device, shouting out facts periodically. *The town of Montecito is an unincorporated area in Santa Barbara County. It's not exactly part of the city of Santa Barbara, but the two towns share resources like schools. It's home to ten thousand or so people, from billionaires to immigrants, retirees to ranchers, royals to movie stars. Dogs are pampered, horses are welcome, and beware the coyotes. The area has survived drought, fires, and a terrible mud and rain event in 2018 that killed dozens. The ocean is on one side, the mountains on the other. But everyone agrees, there's no place better.*

Sarah continued to shout out the facts, now at a more rapid pace: *There is a nearby zoo and botanical gardens! The Mission was founded about the same time as the American Revolution! Julia Child was a treasured resident!* The details got smaller and smaller as the car got closer and closer. *Best tacos are at East Beach! Lotusland is open to the public! Full Moon Soundbath!* Finally, as the Lexus pulled through the gates of Nottingham Forest, an elite enclave for golfers and the people who loved them, Sarah announced, "Wow, the Zestimate on the house we're going to is almost six million dollars!"

As the car turned onto the final street, Abigail marveled at the number. "Six million dollars! Does it even have a view of the ocean? It has a view of . . . a cul-de-sac."

But she knew she'd take Ming's house in a second over any golf course–adjacent condo that she and George could afford in South Carolina.

Sarah buzzed down the car window and stuck her head out to feel the breeze, then popped back in to declare, "This place is awesome."

When the car pulled up to Ming's house, Sarah's head was back out the window, taking in the exquisite surroundings of Nottingham Forest. Abigail collected herself before exiting the black Lexus sedan and urged Sarah to do the same. "First impressions, dear."

Sarah popped out of the car, jumped up and down to loosen her limbs and take in a deep breath of the rosemary and lavender–tinged air, the scent of the Mediterranean that defined the Montecito landscape. Abigail got out more slowly and smoothed her clothes, also breathing deeply as she took in her surroundings. Ming's garden was a masterpiece of native plants, thanks to a talented designer and her team of landscapers. As a gardener, Abigail approved. But as the mother of the groom, she had one thought: *I can't compete.*

***

ALEXA SIGNALED TO Ricky to bring the luggage up to the front of the house. She waited to greet her guests until Ricky said goodbye. It was a habit she formed over the years, thanks to her professional experience. Let the settling happen first, she told her trip leaders.

Don't try to communicate with clients who are worried about their luggage. Wait until they are focused on you and your message, she would advise.

"Welcome to Montecito," Alexa announced to the visitors and then gave them each a hug. Abigail was in an all-navy ensemble including a raincoat and a pashmina, as if she were going to the Pacific Northwest in November, not a California beach town in the summer. Sarah looked like she had to get to practice immediately upon arrival, in sweats, slides, and shades. They were an odd mother-daughter pairing. She couldn't see any of Abigail in Sarah and vice versa. While Alexa despised the "mini-me" comparisons she and Penny were subject to, she was grateful that her DNA won out over the sperm donor's, as crass as that sounded. But Abigail and Sarah seemed to share no physical attributes or personality traits at all. Abigail was petite, fair-skinned, and operated at high levels of self-awareness that veered into social anxiety. Sarah was solid and athletic, with tanned skin, streaky brown hair, and a loud voice. Maybe as she got to know the mother and daughter better, she'd find the overlap between the two of them.

Alexa put on her tour guide voice and fake smile because the next seventy-two hours were all on her. "We're going to have a busy weekend, aren't we? It's a shame about Penny's work, but we'll carry on in her absence," Alexa announced like a loyal mother. She was not going to question her daughter's decision in front of the Blakemans, even though she questioned it plenty in private. "Let's get you settled and then we'll make plans. I hope Ricky drove safely and didn't talk too much. Sometimes I tell him I have a migraine coming on so he'll be quiet. Win, the house manager, will bring your luggage to the guest wing. Please, come in, I'll introduce you to your host, Ming."

"This house is amazing," Sarah said.

"How lovely to have so much help," Abigail observed.

Chapter 17

PALTROWED

The Mother of the Groom

A short time later, after a property tour from Ming and a recital of the guest house amenities from Win, Abigail, now refreshed and minus the extra layers of clothing, accepted a glass of wine and tucked into the cheese plate on the patio overlooking the garden with a sliver of a view of the ocean in the distance. She was hungry and tired from travel, but started to unwind as she watched her daughter backstroke in the lap pool. Maybe this would be a relaxing weekend, getting to know Alexa and her life here. Why was she so stressed? She thought of Bernadette's advice: *None of this is on you, Mother of the Groom.* This should be fun, after all. *Lean in, Abby.* That's what she called herself when she resorted to personal pep talks.

Alexa seemed so much less intimidating on her home turf in linen pants and her hair up in a ponytail. She had been terrifying at the engagement party with the British lord on her arm and the mayor checking her out. Alexa was off the swagger charts and guests afterward mentioned how much she looked like Anjelica Huston and what great genes Chase's baby would inherit. Abigail wanted to snap back that the other half of Penny's genes were a mystery but held her tongue.

Today, on this sunny day in this sunny place, Alexa looked approachable, accepting. She didn't look worried that the bride had abandoned them, so why should Abigail worry? The decision-making was on the mother of the bride. All Abigail had to do was find a casual spot for the rehearsal dinner and pray that the wedding venue didn't need a tent.

The local sauvignon blanc and the warm breezes were doing all the right things to Abigail's mood. By the second glass, she had convinced herself that it was easier with Penny out of the picture. No bride drama. Just mature women making mature decisions.

Alexa returned to the patio with a carafe of water and more wine. "A gentle reminder to hydrate. It's dry here, even if it's not blazing hot. I'm always telling my clients to drink more water when we travel." She set a glass of ice water in front of Abigail.

"Thank you," Abigail responded. "Do you live in this same area?"

"No. I'm not a golfer," Alexa explained, even though they both knew that the subtext was more about money than golf. But Alexa, unlike Abigail, wasn't embarrassed to talk finances. "Thirty-five years ago, when I decided to settle here, I had enough savings to buy a condo and a travel business, thanks to my film production job. I found a renovated place in a lovely old building near the beach. The older woman moving out loved traveling to Greece and sold it to me under market."

"The Greeks must have a word for that!" Abigail said.

"Yes, moira. Fate, destiny. It's small, but Penny and I don't need much space. Over the years, I thought about selling the condo and buying a bigger house, but the prices got more and more out of reach. And truly, we travel so much, it didn't seem worth the headache. I didn't anticipate the summer rental market. I could have made a fortune renting the place out all summer and paid for the rest of the year."

"Who knew?" Abigail said, remaining unconvinced that there was really a rental market here. Didn't the rich people in California already live on the beach?

"I met a couple from New York who rent here now because he said the Hamptons was too noisy with all the hedge trimmers and helicopters," Alexa said.

"Imagine." And Abigail couldn't because the truth was she'd never been to the Hamptons. When you lived on the water in Connecticut, why travel to be on the water on Long Island?

"When I bought here, Montecito was a small, sleepy town. Filled with real people, who had lived here for generations or wanted to build that kind of life for their family. But once the town got Paltrowed, as they say, the values changed, both the real estate values and other values. But, where I live, not much has changed. I know my neighbors. We watch out for each other and share herbs from our gardens and citrus from our trees. My street remains simple, like the town used to be. I walk to Butterfly Beach, where I swim or watch the sunset. It's lovely. Small, but lovely."

"It must remind you of home," Abigail said, trying for the first time to break through the polite professional exterior of Alexa Diamandis to get to something personal.

"Yes, the best parts of Patmos. The blue water, the blue sky, the beauty. The heat that comes from the ground up into your bones. The fragrance in the air. It's why I stayed here all those years ago when I could have moved to Los Angeles. Montecito represents both the familiar and the possibilities. Still."

Abigail nodded. She was comfortable with the familiar, but not so much with the possibilities.

Ming joined them, dressed for another activity beyond lounging at home. She was headed to the clubhouse for Thursday Night

Bingo. She poured a short glass of wine and lifted her glass in a toast. "We're so glad to meet you, Abigail! And to welcome you to town. On behalf of the Merry Widows, we want you to know how much we love Penny and we know that you'll love having her in your family. We can't wait to meet Chase. Cheers to them both."

Abigail lifted her glass. She was struck by the graciousness of both these women. Alexa had to be nice to her, but Ming was a revelation. She had to admit to herself that she thought polished manners ceased to exist west of the Mississippi. She expected this part of the world to be a lot more casual, bohemian, on the verge of uncouth. The kind of place where wine was served in jelly jars and everyone stood around in the kitchen eating food with their hands. But that was not the case at all. These women lived up to her exacting standards: a cocktail napkin for every glass.

"Now that I'm here, I'm looking forward to the weekend. Thank you for hosting Sarah and me. It's very generous of you. When Penny invited us, I didn't understand the burden in terms of hotels. And tomorrow night, another friend of yours has invited us to dinner? Very kind."

Penny had sent a minute-by-minute schedule for Friday and Saturday, most of which was wedding related, but there were a few slots for meals. Friday night was dinner at Toots's house, which sounded intriguing. "This is a treat for me. Don't tell my husband that this is really a vacation!" Abigail confessed. The more she divulged, the more relaxed she felt.

"I'm off," Sarah announced loudly. During the conversation she had slipped out of the pool and into the guest wing, and now wore the raspberry sheath dress from the engagement party. Her wet hair was wrapped up in a bun and she wore silver hoop earrings. A swipe of lip gloss and mascara highlighted her features. Her young skin was tan and dewy. She looked, Abigail thought, quite pretty.

"Where are you off to?" Ming asked with delight.

"My brother's friend Lloyd is coming to pick me up and show me the town. Will he be able to get past the gate? I didn't know about the gate when we set this up."

"I'll ring down. What's his full name?" Ming asked.

"Lloyd Chandra."

"And is this a date?" Ming asked playfully.

"No. He was my brother's roommate at Fordham. I've only met him once, at Thanksgiving years ago. But he's a scientist and works at UCSB now. Chase connected us. We've been texting back and forth for a few weeks. He's the best man at the wedding."

Again, Abigail was surprised that her children had any contact with each other outside of her sphere of influence. And that Sarah was ditching her without warning. But she was shocked that Lloyd was the best man. Chase hadn't mentioned him in years. She blurted out, "He's the best man? I had no idea."

Sarah shook her head. "Gotta keep up, Mom."

Abigail made eye contact with Alexa, who gave her a sympathetic smile. "Well, as the mother of the groom, I'm finding it's hard to keep up and stay out of the way at the same time."

"He and Chase talk all the time. Lloyd's in New York a bunch for work. He's raising money for some kind of startup for his research. We mainly talk about, you know, music and *Game of Thrones*. We're both into that." Abigail realized she had no follow-up question to the revelation that her daughter could keep up a conversation about *Game of Thrones* for weeks with anyone. Sarah had never mentioned that TV show to her.

Ming made a quick call to the gatehouse and then turned back to Sarah. "That color looks lovely on you, my dear. Wait here. I have something for you."

As she left, Alexa explained, "She's a giver. And an over-shopper. So take whatever she gives you or else the offers won't stop! Shh, don't tell her I said that."

Ming returned with a raspberry and gold wrap that looked beautiful with Sarah's dress. "I bought this in Hong Kong. It can get chilly here at night. No humidity. The gold sets off your lovely skin. It's not my color at all. Please, keep it." Abigail watched as Ming wrapped her daughter in the fabric and watched her bloom under its cover.

"This is gorgeous," Sarah said, studying her reflection in the window as she ran her hands over the smooth silk and gold embroidery. Her usual fabric choice was fleece. "Thank you so much."

"Truly my pleasure to give it to someone who appreciates it," Ming said, studying her guest. She smoothed her hand over Sarah's shoulder and down her arm in a warm gesture. "Young skin. Treasure it."

Just then Win escorted a handsome young man onto the patio. Abigail was stunned. "Lloyd?" she sputtered.

"Lloyd!" Sarah shouted.

The Lloyd who had spent his first college Thanksgiving in Fair Harbor was a tall, skinny kid with terrible skin and long hair. This Lloyd Chandra looked like he'd been treated to the male makeover that maturity and money bring—thicker, fitter, and a decent haircut. He seemed energetic, comfortable in his surroundings. He rushed to give Sarah a thorough hug, as if it had been a long time coming. Sarah blushed deeply. Abigail couldn't take her eyes off the young couple who had materialized out of nothing right in front of her.

As if sensing her shock, Lloyd pulled himself away from his friend's sister and strode over to Abigail with an outstretched hand. "Hello, Mrs. Blakeman. It's great to see you again."

"Please, call me Abigail. What a pleasure to see you again." Now Abigail understood Chase's choice. And her daughter's. A scientist and entrepreneur with that handsome face! He looked like a movie star with his dark sunglasses, expensive T-shirt, and linen shorts. He'd certainly be a star in Aunt B's write-up of the wedding. Next to Chase, of course.

Introductions were made all around with chitchat and a drill-down by Ming, ever the wealth management expert, on his financial status. "You run a lab at UCSB? And do you share in all the IP that comes out of the lab?" Her inquisition took place less than five minutes into his visit, and he held up well. Yes to both questions, and his field of expertise was diabetes research, specifically bioidentical insulin. The startup would be the beginnings of monetization of his research. Ming told him that she'd like to hear more about his work one day, ending by saying, "I know people. And they know people."

"Thank you. I'll be in touch," Lloyd said. Then he turned to Sarah with a gleam in his eye. "Shall we get going? We have to make it to the sunset spot. And then the best tacos in town."

"East Beach?" Sarah asked.

"Yes, how did you know?" Lloyd gasped, as if he had no idea that Yelp existed. He was now putty in Sarah's hand. "You're going to love it here."

"I already do," Sarah said without any guile.

"Here," Ming said, handing Sarah a parking pass. "Show this to the gate attendant when you come back in tonight. If you come back in tonight." Both Sarah and Lloyd blushed. And so did Abigail.

***

"What am I smelling? Jasmine?"

"Yes, it's night-blooming jasmine season. Intoxicating, yes?" Alexa asked.

Abigail agreed, although maybe because she was slightly intoxicated. The third glass of wine had gotten to her and she had had to speak slowly not to slur in front of Alexa. Ming was off at the clubhouse and Sarah had gone galivanting. It was the MOB and the MOG and a diminished cheese platter. Basically, two complete strangers and only the salami left between them. She tried and failed to stifle a yawn. "I apologize. Air travel is exhausting these days. I don't know how you do it."

"Lots of water and audiobooks," Alexa answered. "Might I suggest an early night? I know you're three hours ahead and you must be tired. We could go out to dinner if you wish, but there are salads and meals in your guest kitchen in case you want to stay in."

Abigail thought two things: She wants to go home, and *I will be asleep in ten minutes*. Both of which were fine. "I think it's an early night for me. Thank you for everything. You've gone above and beyond, especially with all the gifts in our room. Very thoughtful."

"We have an early start in the a.m. Our first site visit is at nine in the morning at a women's club here in town. It's nice on the outside, but a little run-down on the inside. Penny said it's available and affordable, so we'll start there. Then a private home that I don't think will work at all, but Penny wants us to see it. And finally, the winery in the afternoon. Fingers crossed on the winery, the best choice by far."

Abigail nodded. *See,* she thought, *I'm in charge of nothing.*

"And the wedding coordinator will pick us up here. I'll text you when we're on our way."

First the car from the airport and now a wedding coordinator. Chase had mentioned one during the car conversation, but Abigail hadn't absorbed the information. She was too annoyed to ask follow-up questions. But this was a point of connection for the two mothers. "Tell me about the wedding coordinator." Abigail managed the short sentence without mishap.

"She's a sorority sister of Penny's who is trying to break into the business. She does corporate events but wants to transition to weddings. So, we're her first official client. But Penny said we must have one so we will have one." For the first time, weariness with the bride crept into Alexa's tone.

The wine emboldened Abigail. "Bet you're glad you never had a wedding."

Alexa chuckled and answered without hesitation. "Every. Single. Day."

From the Desktop of Dearly Beloveds and Betrotheds

Your Aunt B's Guide to Wedding Venues

Dear B & Bs . . .

Let's face it, the second the word "venue" comes out of your mouth, the price tag for the event you're planning goes up fifty percent. Everyday events, like birthday parties or graduation celebrations, don't need a venue. They need houses or restaurants or public parks with good picnic tables. But a wedding needs a venue these days, with extras that vary from a temporary greenhouse-inspired wedding chapel to an outdoor kitchen run off a generator, so let's look at your options and my opinions.

The Bride's Home
Sure, the venue is free—until you need to replace the entire electrical system to accommodate the caterer's request or re-landscape the backyard to match the Bride's color scheme. Still, there is a lot to be said for a home wedding. Hosting a wedding where the bride grew up provides a warm, personal backdrop and a welcome understated tone. The size of the home dictates the number of guests in a way that is helpful to whoever is paying for the wedding. Most of us don't have houses that can accommodate two hundred and fifty guests. But we can tent the backyard for one hundred family and friends. (My favorite-size wedding.) If you can swing this, I love a home wedding. And bonus, after the guests have gone, your house will be in its best shape in years.

Somebody Else's Home
An increasingly popular venue choice: a spectacular rental house that can accommodate large events in a desirable des-

tination. Like your home, only much, much better. I've covered rental home weddings in Cape Cod, Jackson Hole, and Austin as well as other trendy locations. Costs vary, but don't expect bargains and do expect to secure at least a year in advance for some choice locations. Bonus, family can stay in the rental house. Don't think of it as a cost savings, because these places can rent for fifty thousand plus for the weekend. But at least there's someplace to stash Grandma or other guests who might not be as mobile. Said with love always.

Country Clubs/Private Clubs

A venerable standby for a reason: The experienced event staff makes the wedding a plug-and-play situation. The menu choices are limited to what the kitchen offers. The best table layout is already established. The staff knows how to get guests in, served, dancing, and out in a well-regulated manner. Personalization limited to table decor, flowers, and first-dance song, but it will be a smooth, lovely, expensive event. Note: Many private clubs have a no-jeans policy. Make sure your vendors and guests are aware of it. I've witnessed the FOB lend the wedding photographer a suit minutes before the ceremony.

Local Hotels or Destination Resorts

Like private clubs, hotels and resorts in the wedding biz know how to get the job done. They churn and burn big weddings, and some do it very, very well. At a top-notch hotel, you can feel like your event is unique, thanks to planning pros who know the best way to execute every aspect of the day, from the best spot for a "first look" photo to where to stage the sparkler gauntlet. Again, limited possibilities for personalization but endless possibilities to spend lots of money. Passed drinks before the ceremony! Specialty cocktails in the receiving line! Martini bars!

Pre-ceremony coffee cart! Midnight burger bar after a full dinner and dancing! Late-night s'mores by the firepit as an after-party! Cha-CHING, cha-CHING. Still, happy guests and a short trip back to their rooms for the parents of the bride and groom.

Museums, Libraries, Concert Halls, and Other Prestigious Locations

This is rarefied air here. And your Aunt B knows that while all her readers have impeccable taste, they do not all have impossibly large bank balances. No shame in not having the budget for a six-figure venue fee. Yes, I said six figures and a seat on the board to get married at the Met or the Art Institute or the Huntington. Let's face it, if you are in the million-dollar-wedding category, you stopped reading this column when I mentioned the tired martini bar in the above paragraph.

Wineries

Hit-or-miss location for me. Some of the loveliest weddings I've ever been to have occurred at stunning vineyards with a rustic elegant feel in Paso Robles, upstate New York, and the Willamette Valley in Oregon. Also, some of the hottest/wettest/coldest/smokiest weddings I've ever attended have been at vineyards, which are subject to the elements in a way that hotel or home ceremonies are not. On a perfect day, it's a perfect place. But beware the weather and the fire season and make a Plan B. (And a Plan Bee because someone will get stung. I guarantee it.) Ditto this for farms, ranches, and orchards. So much dust.

Chapter 18

VENUE HUNTING

The Mother of the Bride
The Mother of the Groom

"Good morning, Ms. Diamandis! I'm Madison Meadows. I've heard so much about you!" said the young woman in the pink dress holding an iPad standing at her front door. "I'm so excited to be working on this wedding!" The last few words were sung rather than said. Alexa was suspicious of all this enthusiasm. Energy was one thing, but this was something else.

"Please, call me Alexa. Penny has told me all about you as well. It's wonderful that the two of you connected through that sorority even though you've never met. Really extraordinary." Penny had explained that she found Madison through her sorority directory.

"We Kappas stick together," Madison declared, opening the passenger-side door of her Prius. "Even though she went to SMU and I went to UCSB, we're sisters."

That was a concept Alexa struggled to understand, but she

smiled warmly as if she did. "Do you know how to get to Nottingham Forest?"

"Oh, yes. And Penny sent me the addressess, so sit back and relax."

If there was anything less likely to make Alexa relax than someone telling her to relax, she couldn't name it. "Thank you."

***

"WHERE'S SARAH?" ALEXA asked as the mother of the groom slid into the car, wearing a navy-blue cotton day dress, white sweater over her shoulders, and simple white sneakers. Abigail looked put together but tired. Alexa had learned long ago not to ask travelers how they slept. Of course they slept poorly. Dwelling on it would only make the issue linger for them and for the questioner. Nobody needed that. Plus, she assumed that Abigail had a bit of a wine headache. She was a little sloppy last night and was clearly not hydrating enough. But again, never something Alexa would acknowledge. After years of practice, she knew how to nudge the hungover traveler to get moving. "One iced coffee for you. It's a special brew with cinnamon and just a touch of sugar. It's magic."

Abigail accepted the beverage with gratitude. She'd already had her hot coffee, but the icy-cold brew felt energizing in her hands, never mind going down her throat. It was cold, sweet, and spicy. "Sarah is out with Lloyd. They are scoping out a special spot for the rehearsal dinner. Some surf club that Lloyd belongs to which sounds . . . quirky."

Abigail struggled to sound positive in front of the wedding planner and the MOB. Did Alexa somehow know that Sarah hadn't come home last night after her tacos-at-sunset date? Abigail had been abandoned by her daughter in shameless fashion: a short text at midnight informing her mother that she was staying at Lloyd's because "the sound of the ocean from his bedroom is awesome." Had

Sarah forgotten that she was her mother, not her college roommate? The truth was that she wanted her daughter to share details about her life with her in a way that she could never have shared with her own mother. That felt like a breakthrough in terms of mother-daughter relations. Like many young women of her generation and class, Abigail spent years deceiving her parents about her sex life, concocting bogus trips with girlfriends or work conferences when she was really with a boyfriend. Shacked up, they use to say. But now it was all out in the open, sometimes under the same roof, and occasionally, Abigail felt that some details were too much. She wasn't nearly as open-minded as she pretended to be. Still, she texted her daughter back in a wine haze, "Please be here for venue search."

But there had been a follow-up text with a photo of Sarah's coffee cup from the patio of Lloyd's seaside condo and the words "Coffee First! Then doing our own scouting. Surf Club! Possible rehearsal dinner place. Stand by!" and then a string of emojis that were meaningless to Abigail. *They do what they want*, she thought, *not what I ask*.

Adding to her discomfort was the image of holding a rehearsal dinner at a surf club, whatever that was, instead of a proper country club. She couldn't wrap her throbbing head around what that might look like at all, except an image of those Gidget movies from long ago with a creepy older guy character named Moondoggie in a straw hat. Abigail concentrated on her iced coffee, hoping to zone out of the conversation.

But Madison Meadows had other plans.

"Amazing!" Madison said because she was the sort of girl who used "amazing" as a catch-all for every rejoinder, every adjective, every adverb. "Is it the Padaro Surf Club? That would be an amazing place for your rehearsal dinner. It's super exclusive and has the beachiest vibe but super chic. Like, très, très chic. And totally chill with a beach bonfire and big blankets and a bartender that makes the most amazing margaritas and palomas. Is it Padaro? Do you know?"

Abigail checked her texts. "It is."

"Amazing. They should grab it if it's available. Like right now!" Then Madison realized she was ordering the client around and pulled back a bit. "My gosh, Mrs. Blakeman. I'm so sorry. It's only that it's a very special venue and perfect for the casual intimate rehearsal dinner that Penny described. *Beach Chic. Cali Greek. Patmos on the Pacific.* Even in December, we can make that work." Madison was speaking so quickly now, the words were ping-ponging around Abigail's head. "They can accommodate dinner for twenty and then others could arrive later for the bonfire and s'mores on the beach. In my other job, which is more corporate than weddings, we did a sixtieth birthday party at PSC and it was amazing. Sorry, PSC equals Padaro Surf Club. Can you ask your daughter to take photos? It's private and only members can reserve the clubhouse, meaning that someone like me can't even get in to scout it. The members pay a fortune to store their boards there and have their famous breakfast burritos after their morning surf. But to rent the clubhouse for the night is very reasonable. Because, duh, no one surfs at night. And they do an amazing taco bar, with grilled-shrimp cocktails first and tres leches cake for dessert. Elevated! But very California."

"Oh! How wonderful. What did you call it? Cali Chic? Beach Greek?" Abigail flushed with pride. Somehow Sarah and her wanton ways had led them straight to an exclusive club for their event that lived up to Penny and Chase's elusive standards. And, honestly, how much could tacos cost? What luck this Lloyd had turned out to be. "I certainly will have Sarah take photos! And put that date on hold if you think it's . . . amazing."

"I do. Alexa, what do you think?"

Alexa was a big believer in checking things off the list, no matter what list she might be working. Getting the wedding venue and the rehearsal dinner spot secured in a single day would be a triumph. And it wasn't her job to tell Abigail that the grilled-lobster tacos probably cost more than filet mignon at the best steakhouse in town. She had clients that liked to whisper such fun facts in her ear when she was informing them of the cost of certain luxury resorts in the Caribbean. As in, "We pay twenty-five dollars a taco for the lobster ones at Padaro. I think we can afford the cost of a rum punch at Jade Mountain."

So, Alexa kept her mouth shut and responded with enthusiasm. "I think Penny and Chase would love to have the rehearsal dinner there. It's a Montecito classic. Not something you can find anywhere else. Penny in particular would be thrilled. That's her favorite beach," Alexa said, trying not to give away her secret connection to the PSC and the evenings she'd sampled the lobster tacos and the palomas.

Her mind drifted back twenty years to the handsome surfer she'd dated, and her neck got warm. Her only surfer, for the record. A fall fling that involved bonfires and more on the beach. She wondered whatever happened to Peter "Pedro" Merriweather, real estate scion and water rat. Probably married and divorced by now. But they had some fun while it lasted. "Madison is right. It has a great vibe."

"I'll text Sarah right now," Abigail said, thrilled at the development. Her headache was clearing and she felt wide awake now. This town, maybe even the iced coffee, seemed to be working some magic on her. Wait until she told Aunt B the rehearsal dinner was at an exclusive surf shack. Forget Patmos on the Pacific. More like Gidget on the Gold Coast! American Riviera Retro! No doubt the venue was column-worthy.

Madison pulled the car into the parking lot for the Montecito Women's Club. Compared to an on-the-beach clubhouse, this location looked tired and unremarkable. There was zero enthusiasm in the Prius.

"Let's make this quick," Alexa said.

"Agreed," said the wedding coordinator.

***

THERE WILL BE no miracles today, Alexa thought. The sad, basic women's club was an immediate no. There weren't enough flowers and white lights in the world to bring the once-venerable 1920s building back up to standards. Even the admin giving them the tour remarked on how tragic it was that all the members were so old now that no one wanted to pay for the repairs. "Honestly, we're looking for a buyer if you know anyone. It's registered historic, so it can't be torn down for condos. Or turned into a med-spa."

"Better suited for a charity rummage sale than a wedding," Abigail remarked. "What a shame."

Alexa nodded. "The photos on the website must be of some other club!"

Strike two was the private home of a former *Baywatch* cast member. Another fine example of deferred maintenance, the house was an eighties mini-mansion that seemed to defy every zoning law in town. The place looked like a cross between an overbuilt Moorish palace and a dentist office. The grounds were drab and the kitchen was too small for the caterer, so the cost to build an outdoor kitchen would be prohibitive. It did have plenty of parking in an area that used to be a tennis court. Still, it was simply too ugly to bear.

"This is a hard no. I don't have to see the upstairs," Alexa said, ending the tour without fanfare.

The trio piled back in the Prius and made their way up through the mountains to wine country and the vineyard that was going to save the day. Madison distributed boxed lunches and beverages to her clients, informing them that it was a forty-five-minute drive to wine country. "But it's amazing. So totally worth the schlep. For the wedding, we'll rent buses."

Alexa and Abigail spent the time eating chicken salad sandwiches and fruit cups, saving small talk for the ride home.

***

"THIS IS UNACCEPTABLE," Maddie said in her big-girl voice. "I called yesterday afternoon to confirm this appointment. How could the venue be booked?"

"I'm sorry. The booking came in this morning. A bride from Chicago. I tried to call you to save you the trip, but there's not much cell service on the drive. I left a message.. . ." The events person from Los Olivos Vineyards let her voice trail off. She was inexperienced and, despite her apology, rather unapologetic. She took the first legit reservation and the deposit that came with it for a night in December during a slow week. Minutes before their arrival at the charming spot with the perfect barn, the permanent tent over the dance floor, and enough grapevines to please the average wine taster but not so many as to fool everybody into believing that Los Olivos was anything more than a for-show vineyard, a bride-to-be from Chicago had beaten them to the punch. "The bride hasn't even seen the place, but she said there was nothing else left in town, except the women's club. Which is . . . not top-tier."

"This is not top-tier. We should have been given first right of refusal seeing that we were on our way here." Madison was working up a head of steam but staying on the right side of polite. Barely.

Alexa stepped in. She had been through too much in life to be undervalued by the events coordinator at a fake winery. "It's not even a real vineyard. I don't think it would have worked anyway. Good luck to the bride from Chicago. This place will be a muddy mess when the December rains hit."

Turning to poor Madison, Alexa reassured her. "Let's head back down the mountain to real civilization. I have a few thoughts on places much better suited for our purposes." And then with a nod to Brittany or Kelsy or whatever might be the name of the young woman in the inappropriate polka-dot minidress, she headed back to the car.

***

"Is this a disaster?" Abigail spoke first once they got back to the car.

"No." Alexa and Madison spoke at once.

"We can regroup. We will find a spot that's not the women's club. I'm thinking some out-of-the-box place for the wedding. Someplace uniquely Montecito. Like the Padaro Surf Club, but inside for seventy-five people and a ceremony," said Madison with false confidence.

"Agreed. I'll reach out to my local contacts. There must be someplace we're missing. We need a day to come up with it," Alexa added, energized by the incompetency of the winery employee. Now she finally felt invested in this task. This was her Penny, her wedding. "Can you call Penny? For some reason, she really had her heart set on that fake vineyard. And I don't think I can break it to her."

"Of course I'll call. That's my job. But not until we're down the mountain. I'll drop you both at home. I know you have a dinner tonight and you probably want to rest, Mrs. Blakeman. A little jet lag may be setting in. I'll head back to the office and get to work on alternatives before I call Penny. Everything will work out," Madison concluded, giving herself the pep talk that Alexa often used with clients.

Everything will work out.

Abigail sat in the back of the car, eating her oatmeal chocolate chip cookie from the box lunch and saying nothing. These two accomplished women seemed afraid of Penny, she thought. And it made her smile. That and the fact that she had secured a rehearsal dinner spot with ease. She felt a tiny bit smug. And exhausted.

***

"And here she is!" Ming announced as Sarah finally arrived home nearly a full day after her Not a Date began, in a new set of UCSB shorts and a matching tee, fresh sweatshirt wrapped around her waist. She held a Trader Joe's paper bag in her hand, presumably holding the raspberry dress and the shawl inside. Ming and Abigail lay out by the pool. Abigail recovering from the venue site visits and Ming doing the *New York Times* crossword puzzle and filling her houseguest in on the local gossip like the dress code policy change at the clubhouse allowing denim on the property during the day ("And so begins the decline . . ."). Sarah's arrival signaled a change in tone and beverages, and Ming wanted all the details in the hour they had before Alexa arrived to take them to dinner. "Don't say a thing. I want all the details. But for that we need gin and tonics. I'll text Mariah."

Mariah was the weekend housekeeper, and she arrived in moments with three cocktails with plenty of ice, and lime from the backyard tree, on a silver tray. By that time, Sarah had flopped down on a lounge chair, looking to her mother like the cat who ate the canary. Or whatever the vegan version of that expression might be.

"Tell us everything," Ming encouraged, handing Sarah a glass.

"That was the best twenty-four hours of my life," she said without hesitation, and then became self-conscious that her mother was there. Texting her saucy details to declare her independence was one thing, but describing them in person was another, so she pivoted. "Except the time UConn made it to the field hockey final four and we beat Princeton in overtime. That was a great day, too."

But a breathless Ming, who was asking all the questions that Abigail would never dream of asking her children, was determined to get the details out of Sarah, who had been completely wrong about the Not a Date bit. "Start from the beginning. What did he smell like?"

"Ming!" the Blakeman women said at the same time.

"Well, he was very handsome. I just was wondering." And they all laughed.

"Like coconut," Sarah confessed, and then opened up after another sip of her drink. "He was in date mode the minute we got to the car. He had flowers, a straw hat, and sunscreen for me!" Sarah, who was more accustomed to young men whose idea of romance was grabbing her a beer out of the cooler, was overwhelmed by Lloyd's maturity. "His car was immaculate."

"That says a lot about a man. My late husband's Porsche was pristine. If you know what I mean," Ming gushed.

They didn't. But Sarah went on with the details, Ming added commentary, and Abigail practiced self-restraint. Normally not a fan of personal details revealed in public, she wanted to know what had happened between her daughter and this sudden suitor.

Sarah told them that first he took her to the university campus and they toured his lab. ("He's letting you right into his world! That's a wonderful sign!") Then to the beach, where they swam in the Pacific, bought tacos at the beachside stand, and watched the sunset. ("Very spiritual. Water, heat, corn.") Then they bought shrimp and fish at the market and he made her dinner at his place, a three-bedroom condo within walking distance of the beach that he'd recently remodeled. ("Ocean view! He's a keeper.")

And then Sarah explained away their night together in the politest terms. "We'd had some wine. So we didn't think driving was a good idea."

Abigail jumped in. "Very sensible. And I appreciated the text. You did the right thing." She had no interest in hearing the nitty-gritty of what happened after the wine.

"Yes, you did the right thing," Ming agreed with a wink and a lilt in her voice.

In the morning, they headed to the PSC, where Lloyd took to the water and Sarah ran on the beach. Afterward came the famed breakfast burritos, followed by a day at the zoo, where they held hands the whole time. "Mom, it's not just animals. It's the most beautiful botanical gardens, too. Imagine Connecticut, but totally different flora and fauna. You would love it."

Abigail smiled at her daughter, for this gentle reminder of the interest they shared. They had spent so many mornings together out with the roses at Fair Harbor when she was little and through her teen years, working side by side trimming, weeding, feeding. Those were happy days. "Maybe I can get there on our visit. If not now, at the wedding for sure. It sounds like you had a very lovely date."

"It was perfect," Sarah said, glowing. The grown-up glow of a woman who'd met her match, not a schoolgirl with a crush.

Sarah put down her drink and rose to change for dinner. "I hope you don't mind. He's picking me up in the morning for the farmers market and then a drive to nearby Ojai. Apparently, the field hockey team at a prep school there needs a coach." And with that, she floated out of the room.

"What fun! A romance happening right in front of our eyes!" Ming gushed.

"Yes, what fun," Abigail lied, her head about to explode. One day in the state and Sarah was entertaining new job possibilities. What was happening to her children? First, Chase moving to Queens and now Sarah considering a cross-country relocation! Abigail had to take back control, first of her emotions and then of her family. Sarah couldn't leave her, too.

Ming turned to Abigail. "There's nothing like that feeling, is there? When I met my second husband, I knew from the very first minute we would be together. And we would be happy. And we were."

"Nothing like it," Abigail said, recalling the early days of her romance with George from so long ago. It was possibility and probability all rolled up into one. She was so grateful to have found someone who understood her and appreciated her. She knew he felt the same. From that very first night, they were connected, meant to be, on a path that would guide them the rest of their days. For better or worse, they had vowed. (Though lately, the scale seemed to be tipped toward "for worse" until they could sell that house.) Despite her current worries, Abigail wanted her daughter to have that kind of connection, too. But couldn't it be with someone in Connecticut?

Chapter 19

THE MIRACLE OF LA MARIPOSA

The Mother of the Bride

It was golden hour in Montecito, that moment between day and night when the sun turned from hot to warm, the sky turned from blue to pink, and the locals turned from iced tea to cocktails. In other words, the perfect time to arrive at the iron gates of La Mariposa, the estate of Toots and (the late) Bix Bixby. It was a showstopper, a Spanish Colonial Revival home designed by noted California architect George Washington Smith, surrounded by lush grounds that included world-class gardens, a pool and a pavilion, and a tennis court where Pete Sampras used to train on occasion. When Bix acquired the house in the eighties, it needed TLC and an infusion of cash that dwarfed the closing price. Toots took on the TLC piece and Bix wrote the checks. Her decorating style was an eclectic take on "more is more." There was no pattern that Toots couldn't mix with animal prints. Wallpaper ruled. The good antiques mingled with modest pieces from Crate & Barrel. Art covered every wall. But somehow it all worked because Toots had wonderful taste and a sure eye. A decade later, when the property was finally restored to its former grandeur inside and out, the couple opened their house to a few select charities a year, offering to host their fundraising galas. The invitation itself guaranteed the crowd; Toots and Bix encouraged generosity in terms of donations. The nonprofit community was eternally grateful to the Bixbys for their leadership.

But when Bix died, the magic of the house died with him. Toots maintained the property and entertained family and friends, but the public largesse ended. It wasn't that she grew stingy, but she never quite recovered from losing the love of her life. She had waited fifty years to find a man who made her feel the way Bix made her feel: cherished, respected, and loved. She had always been reserved, on the edge of the party, but he brought her right into the middle of everything for the twenty years they had together. Without him, she returned to observing over partaking. But tonight, it would be a small group, the Merry Widows and the Blakemans, mingling for the first time, and Toots was determined to rise to the occasion.

Alexa and Ming had filled Abigail and Sarah in on the backstory on the way over, driven by Ricky. Alexa had positioned herself in the front seat, so that she could turn to see Abigail's face when the splendor of La Mariposa revealed itself. Now Alexa witnessed the stunned look on the visitor's face and was satisfied. She wouldn't trust anyone who was blasé about seeing this estate for the first time. She thought about what Lord Simon Fox, no stranger to grand houses, had said about Abigail and her gardening prowess. So it was no surprise, as the car slowly rounded a sharp corner and the house and lavender gardens came into view, that Abigail gasped.

"This is extraordinary," she said. "Stunning."

***

THE REST OF the Merry Widows welcomed Abigail like a long-lost friend and Sarah like their own daughter. Alexa was touched, and she rarely felt touched. She had expected a more standoffish greeting, possibly on the side of cold and suspicious after the Widows had heard about Chase's plans to force Penny to move to Queens. Frannie, who couldn't hear well and assumed no one else could either, was always loud, a trait most people mistook for boisterous and friendly. The volume of her greeting startled Abigail. And that got a big laugh out of all the women.

After that, Toots, Roxanne, and Mitsy went out of their way to be convivial, maybe to coax more information out of the visitor when her guard was down. Regardless of the reason, the women circled Abigail with good cheer and another beautiful gift basket filled with Montecito products that she'd never be able to shove in her carry-on. Alexa made a mental note to offer to mail them when they got in the car to go home.

"I can't seem to stop gaping at your beautiful house and gardens," Abigail said, accepting a glass of white wine from Mignette, the server for the evening, who lived on the property and acted as a server/chauffeur/meal-delivery service. On nights when the private chef was off, it was always takeaway from Tre Lune. Tonight's menu was a selection of coastal seafood, the special house salad, and the special house pasta. The usual for Toots. Abigail accepted a skewer of grilled scallops and exclaimed, "These look amazing!"

"Sarah, have you been enjoying your stay?" Roxanne asked, eschewing the skewers like she did almost every other morsel of food offered in her direction. She was determined to not slide soft and paunchy into life post-sixty and post-spouse.

"I would say so. Tell them about Lloyd, Sarah!" Ming interjected with such enthusiasm that Alexa cringed a bit. She waited to see if she would have to rescue Sarah, but she handled the query like a pro, used to communicating with parents from her coaching duties. She filled in the Widows about Lloyd, much to their delight.

Alexa was relieved. There was no judgment, only joy at the story of the scientist and the field hockey coach and their "immediate and epic" connection. Abigail, who Alexa suspected liked to keep the family's private life private, seemed to be enjoying the interaction, which pleased Alexa. She wondered if Abigail had a circle of friends like the Widows. She hadn't seen any evidence at the engagement party, only clusters of two or three women together. Maybe the female camaraderie was what Abigail needed more than anything. She was more relaxed now than Alexa had seen her in their short acquaintance.

And Ming seemed to be enjoying her status as Sarah's confidant. "He runs a lab at UCSB. Works on diabetes research. I'm going to do some follow-up," Ming announced, then seeing Abigail's questioning face, she explained. "We have an informal investment club. We love biotech. I want to see if there are investment opportunities there, that's all. He seemed like a fine young man."

The whole crew laughed. And then filed away the information because Ming had made them all a few bucks in the past with her tips.

After a round of refills, they settled into their chairs on the courtyard patio that overlooked the pool, surrounded by more lavender and olive trees, a view no one ever tired of. Toots, who looked festive that evening in a kelly-green beaded caftan, patted Abigail's hand. "If you have time, you must come back one morning for a proper tour of the gardens. I understand you're quite the gardener. Mornings are perfect for a stroll." And then she looked straight at Alexa. "I know, gardens aren't your thing. You can take a swim in the pool while Abigail and I wander."

"We may have another whole round of venue visits," Alexa said, and then went on to describe the disappointing day while the Widows expressed sympathy.

It was Mitsy who spoke up first, as she often did, confident that her opinion was the correct opinion. "We can't let our Penny get married in that women's club. She deserves so much better. Remember that rainy day in London when she managed to get us into tea at the Goring and then have Tina Brown join us to dish about Diana? All at the last minute? We owe her." Mitsy was a royals enthusiast.

She was drawn to anyone in a crown and had run into Montecito's own British royalty at Lost Horizon Bookstore one afternoon. The encounter gave her dinner party material for a year. Alexa didn't have the heart to add there was a substantial tip to the staff at the Goring and the promise of a beach rental in Montecito for Ms. Brown for an hour of her time. It had been a highlight of the trip, and the Widows assumed Penny had created the moment out of thin air and magic.

"Or the time in Pompeii when she secured that handsome Italian archaeologist to tour us around and then he insisted we go to dinner at his grandmother's house afterward? Wasn't that the most charming evening?" Roxanne added. The others nodded, amused. No one had the audacity to remind Roxanne that it was only she who had enjoyed the archaeologist's private attention that night. They were a loyal bunch.

"Well, nothing was more Penny than the summer she lived with me. I never would have made it through that first year after Bix's death without her," Toots said with tears in her eyes. Toots was big fun until she was big sad. She could pull off both moods with authenticity. The group fell silent. But then Toots brightened. "What am I thinking? Penny must have her wedding here! Of course!"

Sarah jumped up out of her seat and made a whooping noise. Abigail pulled her down, waiting for Alexa's reaction.

"Oh, Toots. It's over the holidays. We couldn't put you out like that," Alexa said automatically, although one tiny piece of her was sure that they could put her out like that, even over the holidays. La Mariposa was the answer to her prayers. A minute ago, the idea had never occurred to her. But now that the words had been spoken out loud, Alexa needed it to happen. This was a special, private spot with an authentic connection to Penny and her life here. It was grand but intimate and personal. Toots's house made the estate of the former *Baywatch* star look like a tricked-out toolshed. Penny would be thrilled to become Mrs. Chase Blakeman in this historic home. Alexa felt like a maker of dreams.

"You wouldn't be putting me out. I'm here all alone! The children go to Sun Valley for Christmas and New Year's. They only come here in the summer now. Or when I'm out of town with you all," Toots explained, mainly to Abigail. The rest of the Merry Widows knew that Toots had never had children herself, but she had stayed close to her stepdaughters and their families since her husband's death. That said, the relationship had changed over the years to one of preference over obligation, with visits at off times of the year, not the major holidays. They still had their biological mother, with whom they were close, and the casual relationship served both sides. And, in this case, it served Alexa and Penny, as the house would be open over New Year's.

"It's me and Mignette rattling around this place at the holidays. I would be honored if Penny and Chase were married here. You know the pavilion easily seats a hundred. Maybe a few less with a setup for the ceremony. You could tent the patio for the dance floor. We've done that lots of time in the past. How about the stage we put up for the opera gala? A night of Puccini. Magical. There's a catering kitchen out there that we used last Thanksgiving for a big dinner, so everything still works. And hookups for Star Waggons. We even have tables and chairs stored away, though they haven't been used in years. You'll need a valet, but they can park cars on the tennis court. And my assistant Delilah can help with any detail management vis-à-vis La Mariposa. And, Abigail, I'd be pleased to offer the main house to you and your family for your stay. I'll move to the guesthouse for the week. Or maybe a hotel. Definitely a hotel. That sounds fun!"

The rest of the Merry Widows started to buzz, as if Toots's gesture had awoken them from their slumber. This mighty crew of women had years of expertise in throwing events, large and small, festive and fancy. They had chaired fundraisers and hosted lavish holiday get-togethers. They had raised hundreds of thousands of dollars for their charities of choice and donated time, talents, even the dated clothes out of their closets to others. Furthermore, they had planned their own daughters' weddings and been to dozens of others. Alexa had been too busy organizing their vacations to learn how to give her expertise away for free as a volunteer. They couldn't let Toots be the only one to rally. They were the people they were waiting for.

It was Mitsy who got the ball rolling, regretting that she hadn't taken a leadership role. She was Toots's best friend, but she didn't like to feel inferior in the generosity department. "Now that the location is settled, the Widows have so much more to contribute," she announced in her imperious voice. "All the flowers could come from our gardens. Winter roses, lavender, olive, rosemary, dried hydrangeas. The blue ones to go with the theme. It could be stunning!" Mitsy was usually too reserved to be excited, but her sense of noblesse oblige won out. Flowers for the people. "I'm not going anywhere for the holidays. My daughters informed me they wanted to take their families to Mexico and made it very clear they didn't want me to tag along, as if I would. And my former daughter-in-law Helen will be in New York City. My grandson Aiden is there, and he's in some sort of off-Broadway production of *A Christmas Carol*, which is so dreary," she said, clearly as an excuse to not fly across the country. "Travel over the holidays is for people who can't go in February. I'd be honored to supervise the cutting and gathering from my friends' gardens, if you hire someone to do the arranging. And all the work on the wedding weekend."

"My niece and her husband own that winery in Paso Robles. It's a fairly decent wine," Frannie shouted. "I'm sure I can get them a deal!"

"I'm happy to offer up my cottage for any overflow guests. I think staying in a hotel sounds fun. What a treat," Roxanne offered. Her "cottage" near the beach slept ten and was walking distance to the rehearsal dinner venue. Immediately, Alexa thought of her own family, the ones Penny was sure wouldn't want to travel from Greece, but the ones Alexa was pretty sure would. Roxanne's place was perfect.

"And I may regret this if the invitation list grows, but I have lovely handwriting. I can address the invitations. Provided I'm given enough advance notice," Ming announced in a tone that suggested this was a gift of tremendous value, that of her own personal time.

"Oh, all of you. You're too much." Alexa was overwhelmed by the offers. She thought of the decade of friendship with these women, how they had grown to admire and trust each other over the years. Six women who'd made their own choices in life. Their friendship had been a gift to Alexa, an anchor in a town where most people thought of her as hired help. And clearly, it had been a gift to them, too. "I can't answer for Penny, but I can't imagine why she would say no. This is an extraordinary gesture. Abigail, do you think Chase would like to get married here? Your thoughts?"

Abigail could barely speak. She had come to Montecito with a terrible attitude, and at every turn she'd been won over by the light, the sun, the landscape, and the people. And by the stunning sensation that she had won. Won! Sure, they'd have to pay for the tented dance floor, but their accommodations would be free! She could even forgive George his errant promise if this worked out. Her mind immediately went to the midnight-blue chiffon dress with the crystal embellishments she'd had her eye on at the resale store in Connecticut. She should have bought it when she had the chance, but she hesitated and it was gone when she went back for it. Damn. It would have looked perfect in this elegant home.

And imagine the photos and the write-up in Aunt B's column! Her son, the future congressman, being married to his lovely and accomplished wife at a storied California home to the daughter of a successful businesswoman and, quite possibly, a British lord. With the mayor of New York officiating! It would be the talk of Fair

Harbor and beyond. Her former friends, the ones who had dropped her when she could no longer afford the birthday dinners and charity donations, would be sorry they weren't on the invitation list. She knew that was petty, but she couldn't help it. "I can't imagine a more perfect setting!"

"Yes!" Sarah jumped up again, this time to the delight of her mother. "A wedding at a house called The Butterfly. Think of the logo! You ladies are very cool. Teamwork makes the dream work." Usually, Sarah's coach-y slogans were conversation enders, but this time she nailed it, thought Abigail.

The rest of the Widows clapped. Toots told Mignette to bring the Veuve. And Alexa and Abigail embraced like they'd achieved world peace.

***

AFTER THE TEAM had been toasted, the champagne downed, and so much ad hoc party planning had happened that Ming, with the excellent penmanship, took notes, Alexa's phone rang. The screen flashed her daughter's photo. "It's Penny on FaceTime. Let's tell her about the miracle!"

She hit the button to accept and then turned the phone around to bear witness to the group of women who were planning Penny's wedding like it was an Amish barn raising. (If said barn was worth three thousand dollars a square foot and featured a tiled pool from the 1920s.) "Look who's here! We have exciting news."

The Widows waved, Abigail blew a kiss, and Sarah found another excuse to jump up off the couch. It seemed like all seven women began to talk at once. The decibel-level alert went off on Alexa's watch.

But Penny didn't reciprocate with enthusiasm. Instead, her voice was sharp, not sunny. "Mom, turn the phone around. Please. Mom? Turn the phone around."

Alexa felt a lightness of being from all the good energy in the room and it took her a second to hear the distress in her daughter's voice. Finally, she did as she was told. That's when she saw Penny for real. She looked devastated. "What's the matter? Are you crying?"

Penny was crying. "It's off, Mom. The wedding's off. And it's all my fault. And yours."

Chapter 20

THE CALL-OFF CALL

The Mother of the Bride

Alexa excused herself from the others and found a quiet spot in the library. She positioned the phone so she could sit at the desk and focus on her daughter. Penny's face was a mess, streaked and wet, like she was eleven years old and hadn't been invited to Mallory Marquart's birthday party because she lived in the "poor section" of town. Alexa used the same tone of voice now that she used then, gentle but firm. "Penny, Penny. What do you mean the wedding's off?"

"We got into a huge fight. I had to work, he had to work. I felt terrible bailing on the trip home this weekend and I took it out on Chase. And he tried to calm me down, but I . . . I don't know, Mom. I don't know what happened. We're both under so much pressure with my work and his campaign and the future of democracy. If I hear that stump speech one more time! So then I said terrible things about being dragged around to all these stupid fundraising events, about having no shared goals and that he was more interested in his campaign than our wedding. And then he said that he was, in fact, more interested in fundraising because I could handle the wedding. How hard could planning a wedding be? You've already been to so many and you always come home with a list of complaints, he said. That made me mad because he was right. I do not need another cheap bathrobe with the word 'bridesmaid' on the back. And then I questioned his commitment to me and he said I was the one with the commitment problem. And you know what? He's right about that, too. I don't know how to be in a marriage. How would I know that? Who would I have learned that from? Not you. What does a lifetime commitment even look like if we can't do the simple task of planning a wedding together? It's too much. I can't do this." She ended the monologue with a sob.

Alexa waited a second before answering. Hiding in Penny's explanation were some hard truths about Alexa's life, at least her life with her daughter. She hoped Penny didn't mean it the way it sounded, but Alexa had to allow for the possibility that she did. When Alexa decided to have a baby and be a mother on her own, she spent nine months trying to anticipate every hard question her daughter might have and every negative comment that people might toss at her. And she'd spent the last thirty years fending off the naysayers and surrounding Penny with love, positive role models, and extended family. She thought she'd done everything right, but apparently not. Now, it seemed, her decision to stay single and be a permanent party of one had consequences. She couldn't decide whether to lash out or apologize, so she did neither. Better not to make this about her at the moment. *Better angels, right?* "Did you truly call the engagement off? Or is this exaggerated language? I'm not sure I understand."

"I guess we did. He said we should take a pause and reassess. That's what he said, Mom, like I was some strategy for how to get more voters on board with a policy issue. Pause and reassess. I lost it and fired back that I don't need a pause. I don't think this is going to work."

"And then what happened?"

"Then the fucking mayor called. Like always." Penny shouted

this so loudly, she was sure Mignette, who Alexa assumed was positioned outside the door taking notes, could hear it clear as a bell.

With the background conversation about commitment running through her brain and the mayor on her mind, Alexa blurted out, "This isn't about not having a father, is it?"

"Oh my god, Mom. No. I'm thirty years old. I've made peace with my daddy issues. Online therapy was invented for me."

The resentment in Penny's voice indicated that maybe the Zooms hadn't been entirely successful, but Alexa moved on. "I'm sorry you're going through all this. But do you really want Chase out of your life for good? You two seemed so happy a few weeks ago. Maybe it's stress."

"Why does everyone keep saying that?" Penny snapped, answering her own question.

"Because you don't seem like yourself," Alexa offered gently.

"I am one hundred percent myself. This is me. I have high expectations for myself and other people," Penny said in what sounded like a quote from an online personality test. "I don't know if I can accommodate another person's needs into my life. You didn't."

Alexa was taken aback. The therapy was not working. Tread lightly, tread lightly. "I accommodated your needs. Always."

Now it was Penny's turn for self-reflection. There was a long pause and some deep breaths. "Of course. I meant a romantic partner. I think everything will be easier if I'm only in charge of myself."

"Penny, I can't tell you what to do with your life. This is a huge decision and it's yours to make. I made the decision a long time ago to remain independent in terms of my romantic relationships. It's what worked for me and what I wanted. But there are times when I wish I had a partner. Like when I see a good relationship between two people who understand and respect each other. Like you and Chase. Let me say this: If you think a future with Chase means too much compromise, then you are doing the right thing for you. But if you see this as a job versus a partner question, remember there are a million jobs out there. But only one Chase."

That may have been the most romantic statement Alexa had ever made. She didn't want to let Penny in on the fact that this was the rationale she'd used when deciding to become a mother. A job was a job was a job. But a baby would be hers, only hers. That's why it was easy to let Hollywood go and stay rooted in Montecito and be a mom. She guessed that Penny could feel the same way about a man like Chase, if she'd let herself off the hook in terms of work.

"You think I did the wrong thing?" Penny's voice was sharp again.

"I think it's worth taking a deep breath. And asking yourself some hard questions."

"So, pausing and reassessing. Like Chase said."

"I am speaking to you as your mother and as a woman who has made some tough decisions over the years, the decades. And I have a few regrets," Alexa said quietly. "Not many. But a few. But never about my decision to become a mother."

There was silence from Penny, then a question. "What was the exciting news? Before I told you about the breakup. What were you going to say?"

Alexa rolled the dice. "We have a wonderful option for the wedding. Toots has offered her house. La Mariposa. Mitsy will provide the flowers for your floral designer. Frannie can get a deal on the wine. Ming can address the envelopes and Roxanne can house overflow guests. Everybody wants to be a part of your wedding, Penny. What do you think of that?"

A fresh round of sobs broke out. "I think it's too late."

Chapter 21

THE BLOW-OFF CALL

The Mother of the Groom

While the Merry Widows did their best to comfort Alexa after she revealed the details of the conversation with Penny, Abigail snuck off to the library to call Chase. He picked up after four calls in four minutes. Abigail wasted no time with pleasantries when a wedding with high-value press coverage was at stake. "What did you do?"

Chase must have expected the attitude because he wasn't fazed at all. "Mom, I told you, I'm working this weekend."

"I understand. But Penny just called Alexa and told her that the wedding is off. Off! And we've only just nailed down a beautiful historic home for the ceremony and reception. It's stunning. A showstopper. It's a house called La Mariposa, The Butterfly. Imagine the logo! Plus, we've nailed down the flowers and the wine and the guest housing. The rehearsal dinner at a fancy surf club. I mean, who even knew those existed? It's all set. You can't call this off," Abigail told her son, as if securing a once-in-a-lifetime wedding venue trumped all, even his personal happiness.

"I can't go into this right now. I promise you, the wedding will go on. Penny's just having a freak-out, that's all," Chase answered before assuring a colleague that he'd be off in a second.

Abigail bristled. Penny was an accomplished young woman raised by a mother who was cool under pressure. She didn't seem like the type to "freak out," a turn of phrase that even high school kids knew not to use anymore. Maybe Penny had cause for concern. Abigail flashed back to her son's declaration during the conversation in the car en route to the airport about their partnership and all that blah, blah, blah about handling their relationship as fully equal adults. Chase had certainly made a short trip from that approach to his fiancée "freaking out."

She had to call him on it. "Please give Penny more credit than that. Perhaps she has reasons to be concerned and cautious. You didn't contribute to her doubts with this campaign? Or this move to Queens? No woman wants her concerns to be dismissed as 'freaking out,'" the mother of the groom said on behalf of all women. Suddenly, surprisingly, she was Team Penny.

"Penny has been with me every step of the way. She was part of the discussion vis-à-vis our futures. This has nothing to do with Queens or the campaign, both of which she suggested and supported from the start. It's the wedding industrial complex that's causing her concerns, Mom. Not me. She's been to all those giant, over-the-top weddings with fourteen bridesmaids and white doves and branded matchbooks or cocktail napkins or whatever the hell else they can put their initials on. She feels the pressure to keep up even though that's not our style. She's getting sucked in. That's a better phrase. *Sucked in.* Anyway, Mom, this is a short detour. I'm sure it will all work out. At least, I hope it does."

"You hope? That's not very encouraging." Despite what her son had just said about the business of weddings, she was thinking of the personalized wine labels that Frannie had promised and the mothers' tea that Ming thought would be a lovely event to add to the weekend. And Mitsy's description of the arch of gathered roses and rosemary over the ceremony space that would echo some temple in Greece. Maybe Penny didn't think she wanted all that, but now Abigail did. She wanted it all and her grilled-lobster tacos. "How are you going to make this right?"

Chase didn't spare a second for his mother's fantasies. "I'm in the middle of a planning session. I'll call you next week. You're flying Monday, so I'll call you Tuesday."

"What are we supposed to do in Montecito?" she asked in an artificially mopey voice to convey heartache.

"Sit by the pool and drink some wine," he responded without hesitation.

How did he know? Abigail thought. Had Sarah said something? Or Lloyd? "I don't know what you're referring to," she said.

"I've gotta go. Don't worry, Mom. This will all be fine." And Chase hung up before Abigail could even sign off.

How will this be fine? she thought before silently correcting herself. *How can I make this fine?*

She knew the answer: by doing what she did best.

Abigail was at her most effective when she worked behind the scenes, using her good judgment and good manners and not getting swallowed up by negative thoughts or her own biases. She'd learned about unconscious biases in a mandatory human resources training at her former place of employment, Silliman School. At first, she resisted implementing the training, feeling put upon as if the entire staff training exercise was aimed at Abigail and her so-called "snobbery." (Paige, the librarian, felt that Abigail snubbed her once in the dairy section at Stew Leonard's because she went to public school back in the day. "Nonsense," she told her boss when questioned about the off-site incident. "The only reason she got into Yale was because she went to public school. How could I hold that against her?")

But it was when she took the job at the Black Rock Senior Center that she started to understand the concept. Everybody there was not like her. She was the outlier in terms of race, background, or education. She watched how her young boss treated everyone with the same level of respect and authenticity and started to mimic her behavior. She found that opening up her mind had opened up her world. And that, to her surprise, she enjoyed herself among these interesting, fun, smart people who worked and played at the BRSC. Like she was starting to enjoy Alexa and the Merry Widows, who also had a dialect of their own.

"Abby, open your eyes and use what's in front of you," she said out loud to herself. Now she had to look at her own biases against Penny—not from Connecticut, not from a family known to them, not blond—and reexamine them. The answer to fixing the situation was probably hiding in plain sight.

When she first met George all those decades ago, she felt an immediate comfort level with him because they spoke the same language, a particular Connecticut/New York/New Jersey dialect of prep schools and private clubs and Main Line colleges (Bryn Mawr for her, Haverford for him.) The crossover of mutual friends and connections and fashion sense created a safety net under their relationship. What could go wrong with so much in common? They felt secure in the knowledge that they would make a good pair.

It was only deeper into their marriage that Abigail realized that the similarity of their backgrounds resulted in the same faults, like an unwillingness to talk openly about money or sex or really anything that was slightly uncomfortable or risky. She and George both valued discretion, but where was the fun in that? She once tried introducing scented candles in the bedroom for their Saturday night nooky and it was too much for her husband, both the light and the scent. They went back to an unscented, lights-off interaction.

She learned that being married to George meant standing one step behind him so she had a view from the rear. She worked in the background, taking over the bills, making the hard choices about paring down their expenses and presenting her decisions to George as if they were the norm, the right thing to do so she didn't hurt his pride. In exchange, he carried on with the appearance of success, wore the ties she picked out and mixed her drinks like he always had. The charade worked for them, and she didn't want to change a thing about George or herself, really. Not that she could now anyway. But did she really want that limited kind of relationship for her children and their partners? Choosing comfortable and familiar over world-expanding?

No, she had to admit, she didn't. Look at the blossoming of Sarah with this new beau who didn't fit the Fairfield County mold! And hearing all the praise about Penny on her home turf made Abigail realize that she was complementary to Chase in every way he needed: global perspective, genuinely thoughtful of others, and possessed of an understanding of how money worked in the real world. (Granted, she had grown up on "the wrong side of the tracks" in Montecito, but it was always the wrong side of the tracks somewhere! She and George had shielded their kids from their money issues and now they were paying for a tent they couldn't afford. If the wedding went on, that is.)

As she ran her palm along the hand-carved library shelves and the leather-bound books, the MOG realized something: Penny was a great match for her son. And Abigail was going to use all her new tools and her connections to make sure the Blakeman-Diamandis wedding happened.

Chapter 22

THE CONVERSATION,

The Mother of the Bride
The Mother of the Groom

The scene was the same as the night before, two women with a cheese plate between them on the patio at Ming's house. The dinner at Toots's had ended quickly after the announcement of the broken engagement. Ming and Sarah had both retired to their rooms for the night, but Alexa and Abigail agreed to a drink and some food before turning in. There were things to be said beyond the ears of the Widows. Last night, they struggled for conversation because it seemed they had nothing in common and nothing to say to each other beyond the logistics of the weekend. But tonight, they shared one critical element: a child with a broken heart.

Abigail was still in shock to hear that Penny had called off the wedding. It wasn't Abigail's fault that Alexa had left the phone on speaker. Her hearing was one of her best features. It allowed her to eavesdrop on some of Penny's call the other night. Until Mignette gave her a stern look and gently shut the door into the other room. Still, Abigail had heard her former future daughter-in-law say "so much pressure" and "not enough shared goals." Not enough shared goals! Since the day of the engagement, Chase had been all about partnership. And he assured her after the breakup that Penny was in full agreement with their plans. He used "vis-à- vis" to convey his conviction! What had changed?

She was disappointed that her own son couldn't make it right in a white knight sort of way. Why didn't he call off this ill-conceived political career and reconcile with Penny? Add to that the sheer tragedy that the magical wedding at La Mariposa would never happen and she may never see her new friends, the Merry Widows, again. She poured herself another glass of red wine, just a half this time. She didn't want to be up all night with wine brain.

Alexa knew she had to take the plunge first in this conversation. After all, it was her child that called off the engagement. "I think this may be my fault."

"Why would you think that? You're three thousand miles away," Abigail answered immediately, not wanting to give away how much of the mother-daughter conversation she had overheard.

"Because Penny said so." Alexa laughed ruefully. "She said that I wasn't a good role model for committed relationships. That she had never seen one. And maybe she's right."

"My mother used to scoff at all those psychologists in the seventies who came to prominence because, quote, they always blame the mother. And she was right!" Abigail added another splash of wine to her half glass. "Whatever Penny's going through, I don't believe it's a straight line from your decision to raise a child on your own to her decision to call off the wedding. You've surrounded yourself with loving relationships in your friends and family and Simon. That's plenty of role modeling."

Alexa was genuinely touched at the show of support. Abigail was right. There was a circle of love around them both. "Thank you. That's kind of you to say."

"We all tried our best to raise children into healthy grown adults. I worked in a high school for twenty years. I saw all kinds of families, and the common denominator in the great kids was a loving family. And I use that in the broadest sense of the word 'family.' From what I've seen over two days, you've created that here."

"Thank you. And so have you. Getting to know you all has been a pleasure." Alexa spoke the words like they would never see each other after tomorrow.

And maybe they wouldn't, so Abigail took a big swing. "Why did you decide to have a child on your own? If you don't mind my asking."

Alexa did mind a bit, but she did understand why Abigail might be curious. Her grandchildren would have been related to a man with a lab number, not a name. "I had love to give and I wanted to give that to a child." Alexa told Abigail about her mother and the accident and the lonely years afterward. She explained how her mother's family had shunned her when she was pregnant, so her mother's parents went out of their way to show support to her even though her decisions were nontraditional. "I felt like I could give a child a beautiful life, even if it was only the two of us."

"I'm so sorry you've been through all this. How terrible to lose your mother at that age. And Penny's father? Is there contact?"

This was way beyond the bounds, but it was too late now. The question was out there. "Penny's father is a sperm donor. Whose family did not come over on the *Mayflower*."

"Touché!" Abigail said, acknowledging Alexa's victory in the retort. Then she turned serious again. "You must miss your father and the rest of your family."

"I do and I don't. Please understand, my father and my brothers are wonderful men, but they haven't always understood me. And I haven't lived with them in almost fifty years, since I was sent to boarding school. I think it made my decision easier for my family to support, because Penny and I are a continent away most of the year," Alexa explained. "For all I know, my father tells people in Greece that I have a husband who never leaves the States. That's why I stayed in California, so I didn't have to curtail my life to fit the expectations of others."

There was a flash of discomfort in Abigail's expression, as if Alexa had identified an issue that hit close to home for the MOG. Perhaps she shouldn't have used the word "curtail"? She quickly turned the topic. "Penny's let Big Wedding undermine her usual optimism and energy. I hope Chase can be patient."

"Nobody's forcing her to do a wedding like a magazine spread," Abigail said because she couldn't hold her opinions back. And then she noticed the look of horror on Alexa's face. *Oh, dear.* She tried to salvage her comment with some generalizations. "Do bridal magazines even exist anymore? Or is it social media that drove them to the brink? Young women need to calm down."

Alexa barked a laugh because Abigail had a point. "The nonstop comparisons can't be helpful. It's a whole new level of self-exploration with these girls today. We all have insecurities. But you're right. I hope Penny takes a few deep breaths and reconciles with Chase. Like tomorrow."

Just a splash more wine for Abigail and then she corked the bottle and put it on the side table. "I'm sure Chase played a part in this. The campaign, the move. That's a lot on a relationship. And men, even this new generation of men, can be clueless about the effect of their actions on another person."

Now it was Alexa's turn. "Oh, yes. I see that all the time in my friends' marriages. It's like they have two calendars, one for his schedule and one for the rest of the family's schedule. But his is always on top. Time-wise anyway."

Abigail laughed. "I love it when George travels for bridge tournaments. I can just do what I want when I want. It's . . . luscious. I imagine your whole life is like that."

Alexa let that sink in. No, of course it wasn't, for a single mother and business owner in the hospitality trade. But it was late in the evening and she didn't want to push back when they'd opened new ground. "Most of the time, I guess it is. I fill it with work. But I get to be selfish about my time in a way that you don't."

"I think about how little George and I really knew about each other when we got married. We were in our midthirties so we knew we were ready, but that doesn't mean we knew each other. We liked the idea of each other, the familiarity of each other, but it took a good decade to really understand the person I was married to."

"Was it a shocker? When George finally revealed himself?"

The image of George revealing himself (or the wine) made Abigail howl with laughter. "George revealing himself. I'm going to assume that's a lost-in-translation thing!"

Then Alexa laughed but tried to banish the image of George in a daring position with nothing but a gingham tie on. It was too much. All at once, she felt the weight of everything on her shoulders. Penny. The broken engagement. The disappointment of the Blakemans. It was exhausting, bearing the burden of expectations.

Then her phone pinged. It was a message from Ricky. "Ricky's here. I asked him to pick me up."

"That was good thinking," Abigail said, swallowing the last of her wine. She did admire Alexa's executive functioning skills. "So, what should we do tomorrow, then?"

"Let's figure that out in the morning. I think we both need a good night's sleep."

Alexa stood, as did Abigail. There was a hug between the women, like they'd been through something they couldn't quite explain. Tomorrow would tell.

Chapter 23

THE STRATEGY

The Mother of the Bride
The Mother of the Groom

As Alexa stormed up the front walk of Ming's house the morning after the cancellation, Abigail looked out the window and knew something was happening. Alexa looked like a woman on fire: fiercely determined and, honestly, smoking hot in an unexpected white jumpsuit with a deep V neckline. She could really pull off almost any look with her height, Abigail admitted to herself, regretting she hadn't packed more resort wear and less navy blue. The knock on the front door pulled her back to the business at hand, undoing the wedding. Isn't that why Madison Meadows had arrived at ten on the dot, summoned by Alexa? They had a wedding to unplan.

Abigail, coffee in hand, opened the front door, informing everyone in the house who might be interested, "Alexa has arrived!"

Quick greetings were exchanged by the assembled team, which included Ming, Sarah, and Madison.

"I've been up most of the night and I've made a decision," Alexa announced. "We are not canceling the wedding. I don't care what my daughter said on that call last night. Or the fact that she isn't returning any of my texts right now. Yes, we need to give them the time and space to work this out. But we cancel nothing."

Abigail could almost hear Alexa's voice say, "Do you understand?" even though she didn't actually say it. So did the wedding coordinator, because the look on Madison Meadows's face read one part terror and two parts "Amazing!"

Ming burst into a round of applause. "That is how you plan a wedding!"

The line made no sense, like the throwaway tagline on an action-movie poster, but Ming really sold it and it riled up the team.

"I'm all in," Abigail declared, a phrase she usually only used to indicate her dedication to neighborhood beautification projects.

"Go, MOB. Go, MOG," Sarah singsonged while doing her best running man.

"Tell me what you need, Ms. Diamandis. I'm at your disposal. We'll plan the wedding like it's . . . actually going to be a wedding," Madison vowed, clearly picking the intentions of the woman paying her fee over the intentions of the bride.

In the last twelve hours, Madison had suffered professional whiplash, thanks to a sob-filled voicemail from Penny informing her the wedding was off and an early morning email from Alexa telling her the ceremony was on. The email included information about La Mariposa, the involvement of the Widows, and a carefully constructed to-do list to execute in the next thirty-six hours. She immediately Google Earthed Toots's house and knew her destiny. Once she saw the splendor and envisioned the wedding as Alexa had described it, there was no way she was dropping this event from her portfolio. If it happened, she wanted to be there for it.

"Here's what I think," Alexa said, beckoning the crew and pulling a medium-size whiteboard out of her bag. "We go full steam ahead on the ceremony and reception at Toots's house. Madison, you got the to-do list, what do you have for us?"

On cue, Madison fired up her tablet and started taking the assembled crowd through some visuals. "I'm executing the to-do list as instructed, Ms. Diamandis. Since today is Saturday, we're going to check a lot off the list because Sunday in the summer in Montecito is rosé all day for wedding vendors. We got a little lucky because our floral designer had a Thursday night gig, so she's open today. In one hour, we'll meet with Flowers by Flora. She's newish to the area, originally from Carmel, but she's already done small events for a few local influencers and . . ." And here Madison lowered her voice and swiped her screen to reveal a fairylike red-headed creature clutching a wicker basket, standing next to Gwyneth. "You-know-who. A moonrise ceremony. Look at the depth of the shades of white in these arrangements. All the colors of the moon. Amazing!"

Abigail studied the image closely and nodded. The baskets were loose and natural but filled with style. "Stunning. Sophisticated."

"Greek!" Alexa added. "I mean, like the wildflowers poking through the cracks in the ancient stones of Patmos." They all thought she might cry.

Madison put her hand to her heart. "I'm glad you feel that way about her. Because she feels that way about this wedding. When I told her about the Merry Widows providing 'found florals' and 'gathered greens,' she said that kind of organic sourcing made for a rich bouquet and a fantastic Instagram post. Plus, foraging is very of the moment. Also, she'd be honored to work with such acclaimed local gardeners, who are part of such a beautiful community of crones."

"'Crones' is a strong word," Ming said sharply. "We prefer 'wise women.'"

"Of course. Understood. Amazing. After our meeting with Flora, it's cake time. Room for Cake, who promise to incorporate blue buttercream and a butterfly motif into the design of the display." (The butterflies were Toots's idea and the Widows agreed it would be charming.) "Cake meadows, no relation to me, Madison Meadows, are very popular now. I suggest a trio of flavors hidden amid the blooms and butterflies. One lemon olive oil, one chocolate, and one coconut." Madison swiped to a photo of a tiered cake hidden among a three-dimensional floral wreath, so really the best of a wedding and the worst of a funeral in one concept. It was a no from Alexa, but Madison's enthusiasm was so endearing, she didn't want to shoot her down right away.

"I'm not so sure about the meadow concept. Penny didn't want too many trends incorporated. But let's keep an open mind and taste that cake, shall we?" Alexa said in her warmest tone of the morning.

"Great. Finally, in the late afternoon, we'll meet with Zina the caterer for some preliminary ideas and to establish a budget. Her specialty is Greek and Mediterranean. She's a personal friend of Penny's so this could get tricky?" From the question mark in her voice, it was clear that she didn't want the bride to find out about the meeting with Zina.

Despite Abigail's misgivings on ethnic food at the wedding, she wanted to be a team player. "We'll tell Zina that we have Penny's best interests at heart and to keep the tasting on the down-low. We can order dinner to go from her to make our time worthwhile. My treat. If that's all right with you, Ming?" Abigail offered, and her host accepted.

"If we can nail all this down today, we can work on linens and rentals tomorrow," Madison promised.

Alexa nodded. She liked this Madison, and she'd already decided to save her from a career planning weddings and offer her a job in the travel business, but not until January. "We proceed as if this is a blip in the planning. A minor blip! Madison says we have until the first of November to cancel before losing most of the deposits. And, if I pay for a cake for a wedding that never happens, I'll eat it myself," Alexa vowed. Again, the "Do you understand!" was implied.

Hearing Alexa use her imperious Anjelica Huston voice, Abigail knew exactly how she pulled off travel miracles for her clients. It was like she was willing the couple to re-engage and keeping the plans in place was her secret weapon.

Chapter 24

THE PARTING

The Mother of the Groom

There was a palpable sense of purpose as Abigail, Alexa, and the others parted ways on Monday morning. The weekend of secret wedding planning, tasting, scheming, and mouthwatering Mediterranean mezze had forged a bond between Alexa and Abigail and by extension to all the Merry Widows, who pledged support of their efforts. The wedding would go on, even if the bride had other ideas.

Only Sarah was crying like a lovesick teenager, having said goodbye to Lloyd the previous night. Ming, representing the Merry Widows, who had been depressed about the sudden implosion of what had been shaping up to be a very festive holiday wedding, not to mention the departure of her new friend Abigail, with whom she shared a love of David Austin roses, landscape painting, and household help, rallied some positive energy to support Sarah. Secretly, Ming felt like the fairy godmother of Sarah and Lloyd's relationship, a role that gave her hope and made her feel young, a welcome commodity these days. She patted Sarah's back, wrapped in the gifted raspberry silk, while Ricky put the bags in the trunk of the black sedan. "Call or text me any time. If you need me to do a drive-by of his condo, I will. I'm here for you."

Alexa, in her signature velour tracksuit, stood with Abigail, back in her multilayered navy travel outfit. "Be in touch. Tell me what you learn from Chase when you speak to him. I'll do the same with Penny. We need to give them time to realize their mistake. We can't rush them. It's better if they fix this themselves. But if not, we formulate a plan before we lose those deposits," Alexa whispered to Abigail. As every mom knew, guilt was the mother of all motivators. And Penny had shoveled a load of it on Alexa.

"I'll start a Google Doc," Abigail whispered back, as if this were some sort of top-secret communication tool. "We share what we know and work from there."

"Don't leave us out!" said Ming, who unlike Frannie, must have hearing like a bat. "The Widows want in."

Sarah cracked a small smile. "I like it. Operation Butterfly is in play."

And with that, Ricky whisked the MOG and the SOG to LAX. And the Montecito contingent did what they did best: They went to lunch to work out the details.

Chapter 25

THE PICKUP

The Mother of the Groom

Abigail had not stopped talking to George since the minute he picked her up from the airport in the old Mercedes. Abigail missed the smell of Ricky's new Lexus, but she was glad to see her husband, if only to have a new set of ears. Sarah had proven to be a terrible travel companion, alternating between sleeping and ignoring her on the five-hour flight home. But George was eager to hear the many details about the Montecito trip, as if he had really missed his wife and found her to be the most interesting woman in the world, asking follow-up questions to all her commentary. The conversation started and ended with the shocking news about the wedding, of course.

"And we were right in the middle of celebrating when Penny called and dropped the bomb! Well, Alexa immediately went into the other room to speak privately, but you know, my good hearing. I heard Penny say that Alexa had been a terrible role model for her. Didn't I, Sarah?" Abigail looked to her daughter for confirmation. She was in the back seat, earbuds in and texting furiously, presumably to Lloyd or about Lloyd. "Have you heard from Chase? I spoke to him a few days ago but he was in the middle of work and, well, you know how that goes with him."

"I haven't. I'm sure this is a simple misunderstanding, and they'll get it sorted out," George replied, not taking his eyes off the road. Driving through Stamford on I-95 at rush hour was his personal Le Mans. "It's a shame. I secured a good deal on a tent rental with a company out of Ventura. Hate for that discount to go to waste."

"You didn't . . ."

"I did. You know Antonio who runs the pro shop at the club? His cousin lives out there. Works for a big events company, if you can believe that. He said he'd set me up a tent at half price. See? I told you it was no big deal."

Abigail shot him a look. He did one thing and expected praise after all she'd done to hold their lives together? "Well, Alexa said we should keep moving forward with plans. No cancellations, so don't give Antonio's cousin the bad news yet."

"Sounds like you and Alexa reached a détente."

"Not a détente. That would imply there was hostility, and there wasn't. We didn't know each other, that was all. The assumption that two women should automatically become friends simply because they share gender is outdated, George. But now that I know her a bit better, I like her. A lot. There's a lot to admire in her. We work well together."

George sniffed a bit. "I apologize for bringing the assumptions of the patriarchy down on you."

Abigail laughed. She did enjoy his stuffy sense of humor, even after all these years. And his command of language. He may not have been the financial superstar spouse that other women possessed, but his manners and charm occasionally won the day.

Her time in California had convinced her of one thing: She had to come clean with George about everything, from her fear about their financial future to the truth about her gig at the senior center, a job that she discovered she loved once she was away from it for a few days. After watching how the Widows connected with one another and how quickly Sarah and Lloyd had bonded, Abigail was inspired to be more open in her relationships. Full disclosure was her new personal motto. Tiny resentments had compounded to create major stumbling blocks in Abigail's life. But no more! She wanted to make their next few decades a model marriage and vowed to recommit to her George. Balding, bridge-playing George. Maybe she'd even reintroduce the scented candles.

Staring at him now, she even felt a touch of warmth throughout her whole body. How could that be? Spontaneous desire rarely made an appearance these days. Maybe the wine on the plane, she thought. She hoped Sarah would head straight to bed with her heartache and headphones. Maybe she and George could do the same minus the heartache. "Apology accepted." She gave his thigh a light squeeze while tossing him her sauciest look. He took his eyes off the road for a few seconds to take her in with enthusiasm.

All of a sudden, Alexa popped into her head. Strong, lonely Alexa. Abigail knew in that instant that she wouldn't trade George for all the independence in the world. (If there was such a metric.) She couldn't imagine navigating the last third of her time on this earth on her own, and she certainly didn't want to face her remaining days as a singleton. He wasn't perfect, but he was hers. She thought back to the conversation she'd had with Alexa in Ming's living room about schedules and obligations. Sure, she loved it when George went away, but she should have added that she loved when he came home. Or, in this case, when she came home. They might not have known the essence of each other when they married, but they did now.

She thought about the picket fence they had built along the front of their house on Water Street shortly after they moved in, their first expenditure from the house maintenance trust. George said he wanted a proper entrance to their home, a statement that you were entering the Blakeman domain. George spent hours talking to woodworkers and driving all over the state taking photos in pursuit of designing a historically accurate fence with the correct finials to adorn the posts. Abigail was mostly concerned that the fence would be sturdy and stay true to form so she could grow roses along the top rail. When the work was done, they both got what they wanted, a handsome historically accurate fence that supported the blooms and created a grand entrance. Abigail ensured the posts were indestructible by sourcing galvanized steel that mimicked wood. George found a master craftsman to create the finials of his dreams.

And that was them, really. Abigail was the solid foundation and George was the decorative finish. She needed to talk to him about their future. But first, she'd light that candle in the bedroom and see what happened.

Chapter 26

CARDS ON THE TABLE

The Mother of the Groom

"I'm not volunteering at the senior center. I'm working at the senior center. And I like it. A lot."

George studied his wife of thirty-one years as if she'd been overtaken by aliens. This was the big confession she had warned him about? The one she'd promised over breakfast would be happening after golf? He'd barely made a putt all round, worried about this moment. And this was it. "Oh, thank God. I thought you were having an affair with that Silver Sneakers Pilates instructor you're always going on and on about. Rodolpho. I thought that's why you were spending so much time there. What a relief! It's just a job!"

"Rodolpho is a former Broadway dancer who teaches chair Pilates. He's gay, George," Abigail replied, her emotions going from anxiety to annoyance. "I thought you might be more concerned I'd been stashing the money in my own slush find so I can maintain the lifestyle I'm accustomed to. A secret bank account for highlights, facials, decent clothes, laser hair removal. And not just for my benefit. Where do you think that Brooks Brothers blazer you wore at the engagement party came from? Or Sarah's new sheath? The Goodwill on Post Road, thanks to my money. But I've been deceptive, George." She put down her iced tea dramatically and stared out at the harbor view, hoping for a Brontë heroine moment.

George wrapped his arms around her, hoping for his own hero's moment. "No, you've been proactive. You've kept us afloat, Abby. I know that. So you're pocketing some spare change to keep up appearances, literally. By shopping at the Goodwill! Imagine that. Your Yankee ancestors would be proud. As am I. You deserve more than I can give you," George admitted, but still with a twinge of condescension toward Abigail's contribution. She wriggled out of his arms and turned to face him.

"'Kept us afloat' is one way of putting it, George. Implementing and maintaining austerity measures is another. I don't want to spend the rest of my life resentful that we don't have a second home or a new Mercedes or a retirement filled with cruises and spa weeks planned. I'm trying to be positive and my job at the senior center has helped. It's made me feel useful and alive. Maybe that's why you assumed I was having an affair." She rarely joked about sex, but this time her insinuation broke the tension. She didn't want to be defensive and he didn't want to antagonize. "But I think we need to acknowledge our situation, George. And make real plans based on real data like our bank accounts, so you don't promise anyone any more tents and I don't feel guilty about earning my own money and spending it on our wedding clothes. We need to be open and honest. Which is not really our style."

"I'm sorry I've failed you—" George started.

"Stop with that. The pity party is over."

"You didn't count on downward mobility."

"I didn't, but life happens. For richer, for poorer. I meant it," Abigail countered. "You haven't failed, but I don't want to pretend anymore. The misdirection is exhausting. I don't mind putting up a front with the neighbors, but I can't with you anymore. Agreed?"

"Agreed," George said softly. "I can't either. I don't want to pretend to make all the decisions."

"Let me make us lunch and we can talk about what we want the next ten years of our life to look like in theory. And then we're going to sit down with our financials and talk about how that's going to happen." Abigail turned and headed back toward the kitchen, not giving George an opportunity to dodge an afternoon of radical financial honesty.

"Are you going to make the good tuna fish sandwiches?"

"Is that what you'd like?"

"You can't go wrong with tuna fish," George said, repeating one of his personal aphorisms that he used every time the subject of lunch came up. "Hey, how much money have you made at that fancy job of yours?"

"More than spare change, George," Abigail said, thinking about the night before and her candlelit reflection in the mirror. It had given her confidence. She did a little twirl in her skort and fitted T-shirt. "Enough to look this good."

From the Desktop of Dearly Beloveds and Betrotheds

Dear B & Bs . . .

In over three decades of professional wedding-going, your Aunt B has only received a handful of calls and cards informing her that the wedding in question has been canceled. As the recipient of this information, I've experienced a sort of hollow sadness, a grand celebration jettisoned in favor of staying at home on the couch. But for the (once) happy couple, canceling your wedding must feel like a ton of bricks dropped on your head as you walk past a construction site: all at once painful, unforeseen, and humiliating.

That said, it really can be for the best. My goal today is to give you some practical guidelines for the immediate future in the wake of a cancellation. After you take care of business, the emotional aftermath is up to you.

- Take a few days to decide if this is truly what both of you want. Weddings are stressful and can take a toll on even the most even-keeled individuals. No need to cancel everything if this is simply a glitch in the fabric of your future. Yes, I am giving you permission to have cold feet, call it off, change your mind, and call it back on.

- Remember that calling off a wedding is easier and cheaper than divorce. Harsh, but true. If this is really the end of the road for your relationship, then end it now. There is nothing noble about going through with a wedding if you know the marriage is doomed. Even your mother's scorn is easier to endure than a divorce attorney's wrath.

- Behave like grown-ups. If it's a no-go, you need to work together to call off the vendors, the guests, your relatives, and your wedding party. So, as hard as it might be to be civil, given the circumstances, you need to be civil for a few more days.

- Resist the need to overexplain. Ninety-eight percent of the people in your life don't need all the dirty details, even if they are dying to know them, but they need a shred of information. Use a simple explainer: We've decided that marriage is not the right path for us. Thank you for your support as we move forward separately.

- Repurpose those vendors! Want to save the deposit and do something to celebrate (or at least ease the pain) of your newly single life? Keep the photographer and do a shoot with you and your dog living the good life. (Yes, I did suggest a photo shoot with your dog because even Aunt B loves dogs.) Take that honeymoon with your two best friends, who would love to go on a cruise down the Danube, thank you for asking. Throw yourself a dance party with that booked deejay and some cheap wine and beer. Don't keep your wedding date, of course. But do put those deposits to work.

- Nobody wants tainted wedding gifts back, so don't sweat this task. Return the gifts you can. Donate the engraved items to Habitat for Humanity. Or save a few to smash in the privacy of your own backyard.

- Take time to grieve. I'm sorry that your wedding plans didn't come to fruition. The loss of an engagement is a true loss. You will need a moment, and I hope that you can find some solace in the fact that you did a very brave thing.

Big Kiss (even without the Wedding Bliss),
Your Aunt B

Part Two

FALL

Chapter 27

THE ONE THAT GOT AWAY

The Mother of the Bride

Six weeks! Six weeks! Penny had been ghosting her for six weeks. Her own mother! After the original call at La Mariposa, Alexa hadn't been able to reach her daughter by phone at all and had received only a handful of texts. Penny had announced that she was "going offline" to "disassociate from relationships and focus on work," but Alexa didn't think she really meant it, not with her anyway. She couldn't remember a day since the advent of smartphones when Penny hadn't at least sent her a funny meme or heart emoji, a daily reminder that they would always be a team. But six weeks and counting without a decent phone conversation, barely even a text. Around week three, Penny responded to a text inquiring about her health with "Am OK. Need space." She added a rocket ship emoji for emphasis.

Space! How much more space did her daughter need? Her annoyance in weeks one and two turned to true heartbreak by weeks three and four and nonstop worrying by week five. Now at week six, she turned to the internet to search "signs of depression," "Can calling off a wedding lead to a medical condition?" and "Is it common for thirty-year-old daughters to resent their mothers?" The internet provided many theories but few answers, and Alexa used work to distract her from the fact that Penny had abandoned her.

Alexa had led three trips to Southern Italy in the last month for groups of families and friends celebrating birthdays, anniversaries, and reunions. Even though she remained parked in Italy while the groups flew in and out, it was still a nonstop pace. She was starting to feel her age when these tours ran back to back and she was trekking the familiar streets of Palermo or Taormina with groups of first-timers who asked the same questions over and over again. She needed to cultivate some new trip leaders who could take her place on the tours while she stayed stationary for the summer on Patmos, running the business off her laptop in the lobby of the family's hotel.

Despite the fatigue and cranky knees, she was thankful that it had been a successful summer for Odyssey Vacations, without any major fiascos. "Every trip without a broken hip on those ancient cobblestoned streets is a miracle," she always told her staff. But despite the distance, all Alexa could think about when she closed her tired eyes at night was Penny and Chase's canceled wedding.

According to Abigail—who was using Sarah as her primary source—Chase had barely divulged any information except that the two of them were still not back together, by mutual agreement. They "decided to decide" about next steps once Penny had completed her work project and Chase had gotten the mayor and the city through the UN General Assembly. By Abigail's calculation, that would be later in September. But as each week ticked by, Abigail evolved from hopeful to hope-adjacent to nearly completely without hope, texting to Alexa, "I'm going to have to let Aunt B know by the end of September. She's making travel plans soon. I don't want to lead her on any longer."

The Merry Widows checked in from their summer retreats in Maine and Whidbey Island, filling the group text chain with questions and pitching ideas to reunite the young couple. Toots was convinced that this would require an all-hands weekend in New York to work their magic in person. She was formulating a plan to hitch a ride on her stepson's corporate jet. ("The empty seats are just sitting there.") Alexa knew there was a germ of an idea there, but what could they do that wouldn't be labeled entrapment?

"You say entrapment like it's a bad thing," Ming texted back.

And the clock ticked louder.

Back in Montecito and aware that final deposits would be required in a few weeks, Alexa had tried to work, but it was no use. She was deflated, and jet lag was catching up to her. She knocked off early, went home, and poured herself an afternoon glass of wine, something she never did. Then she sought counsel.

"Is it my fault?" Alexa asked Simon Fox. She was once again at the island in her cozy kitchen on Zoom. It was nighttime in England and Alexa felt a touch guilty that she was interrupting his couple time with Hazel, but she needed his perspective. No one knew her like Simon and no one who knew her had spent as much one-on-one time with Penny. "Was I a selfish parent who never taught her about loving relationships?"

"Were those her exact words?"

"Very close."

"That doesn't even sound like Penny. I've never seen any large-scale resentment in her that would make her lash out at you like this. I'm not saying it doesn't come from somewhere, but I don't believe you're the cause. She understands the choices you made. We've had that conversation." Simon was succinct and to the point, as if briefing his constituents.

Penny's lengthy stays at Simon's orchards must had led to plenty of time for deep talks. Still, it surprised her to hear Simon reveal the content of their conversations with words like "large-scale resentment." Alexa had to ask, "Is there small-scale resentment?"

He avoided answering the question by responding, "You said she nearly had a panic attack after the dress fitting. Could it be as simple as nerves?"

"She was panicked about the wedding itself but not the groom, not the concept of commitment. She had a long list of things she didn't want to do, like first-look photos. But overall she seemed very secure in her choice to get married, no matter how she felt about the wedding itself."

"I'm not even going to ask what a first-look photo is."

"It's the photographer's way of ruining the only interesting moment in a wedding, when the groom sees the bride for the first time. Now, it's a staged photo op at a secondary location."

"Ah, sounds performative. My least favorite kind of behavior," Simon declared. "It's a shame, really. I like Chase. I thought they complemented each other well. I've been on the phone with him quite a bit lately and I've been impressed."

"You have? Why? How?" Alexa deliberately poured another half glass of wine off camera, as if Simon would care.

"Remember when the mayor showed up at the party? Well, he slipped me his card and said if I ever needed anything to call. I had a couple of questions about that distributor in Brooklyn I'd been working with and needed to smooth out some sales permit issues. New York State has their own hard cider business so I was getting some pushback as an import. I thought the mayor might have some thoughts on who I should petition. We had a good long conversation, then he handed me off to Chase to close the deal."

"And you didn't tell me?"

"It's business. Beverage distribution in the State of New York doesn't seem to be your thing."

"How about my possible future son-in-law calling off the wedding? That's my thing."

Simon shook his head. "I don't think we exchanged more than five words about that." He paused and then said, "But maybe I should have."

"What does that mean?"

"Normally, my British self wouldn't get involved in someone else's relationship. Too personal. But Chase reminds me of me. He feels strongly about his community, about service. And I like to think I have the same edge he has. At least I used to. Remember, I was ambitious once. I don't want him to regret not pursuing Penny hard enough. She could become the one that got away if he doesn't do something soon."

"That is the most romantic thing I've ever heard you say. And I'm Greek so I know emotions."

"Do you remember that girl Vanessa I was with in my late twenties? Dark hair, the red lipstick?"

"I was so jealous. Of her. Not you. She was so confident. And she had that great leather jacket. And that car! I liked her." An image popped into her head of the three of them in Vanessa's Austin Mini Metro zipping around London in the eighties. Vanessa could smoke and drive a stick shift at the same time. Those were the days.

"Well, I was doing the music writing in London and sure I was going to break through any minute. And she was a journalist in world affairs. I was crazy about her. We weren't together that long, but there was something there. Then she got this big opportunity at the *Times* desk in Hong Kong and we split. We both wanted to establish our careers before we committed, so she went to Hong Kong and I stayed in London. And that was it. But the day she left, she came to say goodbye to me. My mates were at my place watching football. It was awkward. I blew it. And instead of walking her downstairs to say a proper goodbye and tell her how I felt, I just waved from the couch and watched her leave. Like a wanker."

"And she was the one that got away?"

He nodded.

"Oh, what a relief. I thought I was the one that got away."

"No, you were the one that stuck around because we hadn't made it messy. Well, not too messy."

"Do you think she feels the same way? That you were the one that got away?"

Simon thought for a minute. "That's the imaginary conversation

I have with myself when I'm out walking the orchards. That we see each other at a coffee shop or in a dimly lit hotel bar and revisit that day. I've convinced myself that Vanessa knows what I know . . . that we could have had something."

Poor Hazel, Alexa thought. *Does she know her husband is still dreaming about a woman he slept with forty years ago?* Probably. Hazel was a very practical sort, more concerned about drainage in the orchards than spicing up the bedroom. Alexa always had the sense that Simon and Hazel's marriage was more of a real estate deal than a love match. Her family owned the property next door and had proper money; he had a title and most of his hair left. They were companionable together, but they never sizzled, not even in the early days. Everybody made accommodations, Alexa knew, and she suspected that Simon and Hazel had agreed to their own arrangement. She would never ask him directly because they still had boundaries and because he respected Hazel even if he no longer desired her. So back to the topic at hand. "What does this have to do with Chase and Penny?"

"He needs someone to tell him to get off the couch and walk the girl down to her car. Metaphorically speaking. He needs a nudge. One that may change the course of his life. You know as well as I do, work is not a substitute for a relationship. It's why you have Penny. And I married Hazel twenty years after I let Vanessa leave."

That and the land. "I can't tell Chase what to do."

"No, you can't. But the mayor can," Simon retorted. "And you can work on Penny. Something has rattled her. You should fly to New York and find out what it is. Perhaps she's not pining. Maybe she's thriving. She's a grown woman. She's allowed to change her mind. Remember when you were thirty? You were managing million-dollar budgets on sets all over the world. She's as capable as you. She may know exactly what she's doing. Maybe she really doesn't want to live in Queens. Or be a political wife. It's not for the faint of heart. Even my wife, who barely registers my time in London, isn't keen on attending any formal events. And, you weren't exactly on board with this whole thing, as I recall, so Penny's throwing you under the bus a bit."

"That's exactly what I feel like. Like I've been hit by a bus." Alexa felt a heaviness in her whole body. "I feel like my own choices are coming home to roost. What if I somehow ruined her for marriage?"

"You brought Penny into this world with love and intention. That's the most any parent can do," Simon said, visibly yawning.

Alexa felt tears prick in her eyes. She sometimes did wish Simon were Penny's secret father. "Thank you, Simon. Lots of love."

"To you too." And the screen blinked off.

Alexa had been trying for weeks not to let Penny's grievances bury her. Maybe Simon was right. This was her chance. She could get Chase off the couch. And she had the Merry Widows, with a corporate jet in the wings, waiting for their assignment. Abigail, too, who'd been adding thoughts and observations to her Google Doc like it was high-level oppo research: *Chase looks thin. Chase came out to the house for Labor Day weekend for no good reason. Chase told Lloyd he regrets not sending flowers the day after the fight.*

It was time to act.

She opened the drawer in her kitchen where she kept all the cards of service people who had fixed her appliances or installed a new garage door opener or washed her windows. The men who had come into her life to perform the tasks she didn't want or know how to do and then disappeared. Next to those cards was the one she had tucked away after the engagement party in Connecticut.

The card read *Timothy Lynch*, and then a private cell phone number. "If I can ever be of service," he'd said with a wink, slipping it into her hand as she passed him on the way out the door.

The card stock was heavy and the printing clean and sharp. Alexa took another sip of wine and dialed the mayor's number. It was time to intervene. Operation Butterfly was a go.

Chapter 28

OPERATION BUTTERFLY

The Mother of the Groom

The ruse was on. It was a sparkling September day, a snap in the air as if fall had decided to start that morning. Abigail could feel a frisson of excitement and intrigue as she and Sarah awaited the arrival of the private jet. Inside were the Merry Widows, Lloyd Chandra, and the corporate CEO stepson-in-law of Toots, a middle-aged man named Trey who spent the entire flight grilling the group on their plans, adding his own commentary and strategy and saying things like "Flood the zone" and "Fish where the fishes are."

The Connecticut duo waited on the tarmac as they watched the plane land, like billionaires in a movie, an exhilarating experience. Abigail sat in the passenger seat of the van that Sarah had commandeered from the coach of a club lacrosse team in Fair Harbor. It wasn't the luxury Mercedes coach that the Montecito contingent was accustomed to boarding on their travels, but it was clean, odor-free, and stocked with kombucha and snacks.

Sarah was behind the wheel. The next destination was Manhattan, where the Merry Widows would stay for the weekend. Operation Butterfly was underway, a multiborough plan that involved a mayor, an English lord, and the sculptor Isamu Noguchi, plus a cadre of wealthy widows from California, a handful of Daughters of the American Revolution from Connecticut, and the staff of the senior center—all in service of love.

The plan, conceived by the MOG and the MOB, was to lure Penny and Chase to the Noguchi Museum in Queens for a romantic tête-à-tête that would lead to a reconciliation and then the restoration of the wedding date. Abigail and Alexa had picked the museum in Queens on purpose, a symbolic offering of support for their new life together in a new place. Even if that place was Queens.

It was Toots who insisted the Widows be part of the plan, acting as shills to get Penny on board. Penny had been told that this was a sanctioned MW Trip and that the group was on an art weekend in New York. Even though she was still ghosting her mother, she agreed to accompany them to the museum for what she had been told was a private tour of the collection with dinner afterward. (Penny couldn't say no to Toots.)

Mayor Lynch, who concocted a fake fundraiser, would be the lure for Chase. He also secured the location but didn't disclose his methodology. (Abigail suspected a hefty donation but couldn't verify.) The food, music, and visuals were in the hands of the DAR and the team from the Black Rock Senior Center, whose skill set included the talents of a concert cellist, a floral designer, an electrician, and a couple of competitive ballroom dancers. Abigail had drawn them into the planning, much to their delight. Sarah and Lloyd would be on hand to act as servers. George would be the driver for the Connecticut crew, boasting about his foresight in renting a minivan like he was a winning America's Cup tactician.

The operation was risky and could backfire spectacularly. Alexa's spotty and charged communication with Penny was distressing, but Toots had been in regular communication, ostensibly about a possible PR project for a nonprofit she funded. Her real goal was to assess Penny's mental state, which Toots, not a doctor, assessed as "broken and down but not out."

But it was scientist Lloyd who convinced Sarah, who convinced Abigail, that the relationship was salvageable. "He's ready to be vulnerable," Lloyd had told Sarah, who told Abigail, who scoffed and admitted that she had to learn another level of acceptance for the quirks of Gen Z cuspers. But for some reason, she trusted Lloyd. He was a man of science, and if he felt like this was a worthwhile endeavor, then so it was. Broken and Down but Not Out, meet Ready to Be Vulnerable.

Honestly, the whole thing was so preposterous that it might be the most fun Abigail had ever had in her adult life, beating out planting one thousand tulip bulbs in front of the Fair Hope Town Hall for the town's three hundredth birthday. Was this even more improbable than her junior year abroad in Florence and her romance with Arturo? Possibly. She looked at Sarah, who was wearing one of the Operation Butterfly hats she had made for the weekend, and said, "Are we ready?"

"Hell, yeah," Sarah roared. "LFG!"

"I don't know what that means," Abigail responded, wrenching the van's door open and carefully maneuvering down to the ground so she didn't break anything.

Toots, Ming, Roxanne, Mitsy, and Frannie piled out of the plane wearing a compendium of high-priced fleece travel sets and stylish European comfort sneakers, looking like a cadre of aging secret agents/spa-goers. They greeted the Blakeman women with hugs and good wishes. Lloyd rolled out a minute later, waving goodbye to his new buddy Trey who climbed into a waiting black Escalade. Then he planted a big kiss on Sarah's lips.

"This is going to be so much fun. We've been rehearsing our parts on the plane ride," Ming announced to a sea of nodding heads.

"Oh, and Lloyd asked me to be on the board of his new company. It's been a very productive trip already." The Widows were raring to go.

Alexa followed, dressed in another of her seemingly endless supply of stunning silk ensembles because her mission was different from the Widows'. She had to pay homage to Hizzoner. She double kissed Abigail. "I can't believe we're doing this. Are we crazy?"

"Yes. I think we might be," Abigail said as a black town car pulled up alongside the jet on the tarmac. "You look gorgeous. Looks like your car is here. I guess the mayor wants you all to himself. Are you picking him up at the office on the way to his place?"

"That's the plan. Or, I should say, his plan. My plan is to confirm all the details and be in my hotel room by nine. Wish me luck!" Not one person within earshot believed Alexa. Surely, the mayor was involved in this scheme for reasons that included the dark-haired goddess who stood before them in elegant Athenian ready-to-wear.

"We want all the details," Frannie bellowed.

"Every. Single. One," Mitsy echoed, but at a lower volume.

Alexa slipped into the back of the car and waved to her crew. "See you tomorrow!"

Once Coach Sarah and Lloyd stopped making out, she instructed the Widows, "Load up, ladies! You, too, Lloyd!" Then she high-fived all the women as they boarded the van. "Let's remember, ladies, teamwork makes the dream work!"

Chapter 29

DINNER WITH TIMMO

The Mother of the Bride

"I was expecting a drafty dining room in Gracie Mansion."

"I only pretend I live there. I host events, staff parties there. I even sleep there on occasion. But you're right. It is drafty, and old. And I had enough old, drafty housing growing up in Galway. This place is more my style. Can I get you a drink?" the mayor of New York asked Alexa as he loosened his tie and headed to the bar cart.

She nodded. "I'll have what you're having."

He nodded. "An old-fashioned it is."

There was measuring, shaking, and pouring while Alexa watched. She had certainly been in the presence of powerful men before. Greece was a small country and, thanks to her well-connected uncles, she was part of the elite, running in the same circles as politicians, shipping magnates, and art dealers in Athens and on the islands. Over the years, she'd been entertained by mayors, ministers, and presidents in other countries. Her luxury tours included embassy visits and mixing with sports stars and business titans. But Timmo Lynch had a certain humility that most men in a similar position didn't even bother to feign. He looked at home in his own apartment, as if he really did make himself an old-fashioned every night after a long day at the office. He wasn't waiting for his staff to rescue him. In fact, there was no staff there at all. He handed her the drink and a cocktail napkin, then lifted his own beverage. "Sláinte."

"Cheers," Alexa said, taking a small sip of the balanced drink. Perfect. "Thank you. I'm impressed by your bartending skills."

"Once a bartender, always a bartender. It's my fallback job."

"In case International Man of Influence falls through? You seemed to be a star at the UN." Since the engagement party, Alexa found herself searching his name once or twice a week and following him on social media. He had made a powerful speech on the ethics of globalization at the UN General Assembly last week.

"I could be canceled any minute," he replied.

Politics was too tricky for her to weigh in on that statement, so she circled back to his domestic skills. "Don't tell me you cook, too."

"I won't because I'd be lying. My chef, Beatrice, left us something in the kitchen. I'm guessing salmon because that's about the only thing my doctor lets me eat these days," he said wistfully. Then he gestured to the living room. "Please, make yourself at home. I'm going to change out of this suit if you don't mind." He nodded and proceeded down the hallway.

She didn't mind at all, although she thought he looked very dashing in his navy suit and purple and green tie. But she was happy to have a little time alone to check out the apartment. Especially the photos, which seemed to feature the same blonde over and over again. But then she realized he probably had security cameras everywhere, so instead she glanced around the room in a vague, nonthreatening way, like a normal houseguest and not a woman casing the joint.

The modern condominium in Chelsea where the mayor had lived before he ascended to the office and where he intended to finish out his days in the Big Apple was a sophisticated mix of glass, views, and abstract art with a Celtic color palette of greens, blues, grays, and more grays. Layered textures ranged from sleek marble countertops to cozy wool throws. Some designer had the good sense to stop at the edge of maximal and saved Timothy Lynch from too much of a good thing. The open living room led out onto a patio high above the Hudson River. A table for two had been set outside under some heat lamps, taking advantage of the September sunset.

The living area and kitchen were three times the size of Simon's entire pied-à-terre on the other side of Manhattan. This was the kind of New York crash pad that Alexa could get used to. But first, she had a job to do.

***

As PREDICTED, THERE was salmon. But there was also wine and non-stop conversation, a combination the two of them seemed to relish. They talked about their home countries, their decisions to emigrate, what they missed and what they didn't. They talked about leaving family behind and how that impacted their family relationships. Alexa divulged that her three brothers treated her like a fourteen-year-old when she returned home and still rolled their eyes about the fact that she'd had a baby "from a turkey baster," a joke that was never funny. Timmo explained that the blonde in all the photos was his "beloved" sister Peggy, still in Galway, who announced her intention to visit New York City every time the press reported that he'd be out of town and then left a thank-you note with a new photo as a lark. "She uses me for guest quarters and good seats. She loves Broadway."

They talked about starting their businesses, the good years and the bad, the nonstop pressure and the rewards. And they brushed up against the fact that both of them had never married and why that might be. Could it really be as simple as they didn't have the time for a relationship when they were younger, and by the time their lives slowed down a bit, they were too stuck in their ways? Was that the whole truth?

For dessert, Timmo served Alexa a lemony pudding cup on a silver tray. It was light and tart. Alexa scraped the dish clean while her host laughed at her. "Do you want to chew the glass? I believe there's an extra one in the fridge if you'd like it."

"It's the lemon. I love all things lemon. My heritage," she explained, putting down the small Waterford bowl. "I'll stop at one, but please let Beatrice know how happy she made me."

"I'll tell her. And I'll remember that, the bit about lemons," he said, splitting the last of the wine between their two glasses. "But of course, I couldn't forget because you were wearing lemon yellow at the party when I first saw you. And you were a sight to see."

The first hint of flirtation in their evening caught her off guard. She averted her eyes from his, which wasn't her style.

"Have I embarrassed you?" he asked softly. "Mentioning the party?"

"No. Not at all. It was a remarkable day. I mean, when you arrived on that beautiful boat with . . . those sandwiches," she said with a smile. "I hadn't realized how hungry I was until you arrived."

That line got a rise out of the Irishman.

She saw an opening. "Not to change the subject too abruptly, from food to our Romeo and Juliet, but I want to get to the task at hand."

"The fact that we're scheming to force a young couple to marry when they can't seem to make up their own minds," Timmo said.

"Is it scheming? Or is it creating the environment where they discover the truth about how they really feel?" Alexa countered.

"Somebody has made a living in the making-dreams-come-true business." He stood up and collected the plates. Again, the small domestic acts looked authentic to him. "I hope that Chase and Penny appreciate our planning. I will say, Chase has not been himself since the split. And that's not malarkey this time."

"My sources tell me that Penny is tense and miserable. She's avoiding my calls still and texting the bare minimum number of words to respond to my questions, but she's committed to being at the museum tomorrow."

"So has Chase. He claims his whole weekend is free."

"Penny too. Which is why I think forcing them together one time is the right thing to do. They are miserable. We have nothing to lose." She followed him into the kitchen.

He put the plates in the sink, wiping his hands on a towel afterward. "By the way, I leave the washing up for the housekeeper in the morning, in case you think I'm too good to be true."

She matched his energy. "You read my mind. I was thinking that you must be the perfect man. But I'm relieved you have a single flaw."

"So, to the task at hand . . ." He pulled out his phone and found a pair of readers in a drawer. "Here's the information my assistant Tanesha sent me. She said this is the best assignment she's worked on during my administration. Good to know that among my staff, romance is a higher priority than affordable housing," Timmo joked. He read off his device, "'The museum will shut down at six, so you can move your people in to do the setup in the sculpture garden. The regular guards will be there as well as a few members of the museum staff to make sure'—and I'm quoting here—'the crazy ladies from California don't steal anything.' She confirms that the abundant sushi platter from the restaurant where they had their first date will be delivered on ice by six thirty."

"How did you, or Tanesha, pull all this off?"

"Believe it or not, I am a well-liked powerful man and people do things for me. In turn, I do things for them. And when all else fails, I pay people. Out of my own account. That sushi isn't free, you know."

"I'll cover the sushi."

"Not on your life. This whole incident will make a very humanizing chapter in my memoir, which I am pitching now. My monster advance will cover the sushi."

"As long as your motivations are pure."

"As the driven snow. Chase and I will arrive by car at seven. I told him this fundraiser was for a cause very personal to me, but I didn't want it on the books. And he had to come so I'd have someone to talk to and an excuse to leave early. When we get there, I'll bluster about and take a call or two to kill some time until I get the all clear from Tanesha that everything is set up. I'm to pretend that I may have the wrong address or the date, that's why the museum is empty. This will be my finest acting, I promise. We'll head to the garden to pretend to do one last check for the fundraiser, where I assume you and your Widows will be waiting."

"Oh, no! My group is supposed to be VIP tourists there for an after-hours tour and reception. We arrive at six forty-five and go directly to the galleries upstairs to stay out of view until you and Chase are in position. We've hired a Noguchi expert to give us a walk through the museum so Penny doesn't get suspicious right off the bat. And before that, we're doing a historical tour of Queens, so it's clear that we are all in on Queens."

"I know I'm the mayor and I have to say this, but I like Queens. It reminds me of the city I grew up in, with real neighborhoods and gossip and a sense of connection. Plus, some pretty swanky high-rises now. I think you'll like it if you give it a chance."

"I'm on board with Queens. It was just such a shock. I'm probably related to half the borough. Obviously, you know it's very Greek. I made a conscious decision not to live there when I settled in this country, seeing California as a fresh alternative to the old ways. Now, ironically, Penny may end up there. But if this all works out, I welcome Queens. I'm rooting for it, in fact."

"Very wise."

"It's Chase's parents and their team who are in charge of transforming the small patio in the sculpture garden into what Abigail calls 'a dreamscape.' There's a whole lacrosse team van of volunteers coming in from Connecticut. There's a cello player and ballroom dancers and an electrician who is a magician with little white lights.

You get Chase to the garden and tell him the real reason he's there. Then we follow with Penny. And we all disappear. You're welcome to join us at a bistro in the neighborhood afterward. I reserved a private room for our post-Noguchi party."

"Have you thought about what might happen if this doesn't work?"

"The world will go on. But there will be one less happy couple in it."

"Yes, poor Penny and Chase."

"I'm talking about me and Abigail."

"I don't think she cares for me," the mayor admitted as he leaned back against the marble countertop.

"I don't think she does either," Alexa confirmed. "But this act of charity may change her mind." Then, to change the subject, she looked around the kitchen. "This island is bigger than my entire kitchen in Montecito."

"But you can walk to the beach. As I recall, Penny told me you're an open-water swimmer. There's your trade-off. Swimming in the Hudson is not the same as the Pacific."

"I love the Pacific, but it's not the Aegean." Her mind flashed to the clean, clear aquamarine waters off Patmos where she'd learned to swim. She missed her home island sometimes.

"Nothing is like the Aegean," Timmo said.

The mayor's move toward Alexa was so smooth, it took her by surprise. They were talking about the ocean, and she was thinking that the color of his eyes was like the Aegean, and then he was standing next to her. He was close enough so one of his hands rested on the counter, while the other slipped around her waist. She wasn't flustered, only ready. She had been imagining a moment like this since their first encounter. He jolted her system into gear that day in Fair Harbor, and she wanted more than clever conversation. She placed her hand on his chest, not to ward him off but to reassure him.

"Yes?" he asked.

"Yes," she said.

The kiss was light and playful. He was good at this. Then there was much more as he leaned into her and she leaned into him, the pressure and the pleasure increasing. Judging by his reaction, she was good at this, too. Their kisses tasted like lemon.

He pulled away slowly, a satisfied smile on his face. "You know, I'm going to have some time on my hands after the first of the year," he said, alluding to the end of his term. "Maybe you will, too, after we pull off this wedding?"

"We're a 'we' now, are we?"

"As Americans like to say, we both have skin in the game. You want a son-in-law and I want a candidate. We are going to make that happen." He traced his hand across her breastbone and down her arm, over her hip.

She smoothed his hair. "I like your confidence. About the wedding."

"And about your schedule in January?"

"How about we start with tonight? And see where it goes."

***

THE NEXT MORNING, Alexa marched into the hotel lobby, dragging her Rimowa roller bag behind her, the result of having gone straight from the plane to dinner and never getting over to the hotel to check in. She was grateful to have a change of clothes and her own toothbrush with her this morning. She had been dropped off at this modest tourist hotel in Midtown by the mayor of the greatest city in the world on his way to a breakfast meeting with the secretary of labor. (At least, that's what Timmo Lynch had reminded her when they parted.) She hoped she had enough time to get to her room, change, and return to the lobby before the nine o'clock meetup. She figured the time change was in her favor and most of her companions would just be waking up.

But no. The Merry Widows were camped out in the breakfast room, which faced the front door of the hotel. *Were they waiting for her?*

"We see you!" Frannie bellowed and waved, so Alexa had no choice but to join them even though she wanted to head to her room, deep moisturize her face, and go down an internet rabbit hole of everyone that Timmo Lynch had ever dated in his seventy years on the planet. But all that would have to wait.

Standing tall and proud, Alexa called, "I see you, too!"

They made room at their table and Mitsy summoned over the server. "What can I buy you?" she said, taking control of the situation. (Mitsy was proving to be surprisingly adept at spycraft for an eighty-year-old philanthropist. She was a timeline master, kept everyone on schedule, and had a keen understanding of protocol. Plus, she understood that the primary mission of the Widows was to provide cover. She was the one who had chosen the hotel for its low profile and average tourist clientele. "We can't stay in our usual place. We need to make Penny think this really was a last-minute trip and this is all we could secure," Mitsy had argued as she instructed Alexa to make the reservations.) Enveloped in tweed and cashmere with a swipe of Black Honey Almost Lipstick in place, Mitsy was the opposite of average. And the first to ask the question they all were thinking, "How was your evening? And your morning?"

The Merry Widows bubbled over with excitement. This was the good stuff they had been waiting for Alexa to divulge for over a decade. Finally, they had caught her in the act, so to speak. With the mayor! The George Clooney of politicians. This was a layer of romance they hadn't suspected.

"So. . . tell us everything," Ming insisted, as more coffee arrived.

"First, I must let you know, he is up to speed on the plan for tonight. He will execute his end of the plan," Alexa confirmed, antagonizing her friends on purpose. They could wait for the juicy stuff.

Mitsy took the lead. "Well, that's grand to hear, but that's not why we all got up at the crack of dawn."

Alexa dragged the moment out by taking a long sip of her weak hotel coffee before saying, "I can confirm that Timmo Lynch is a very charming man with a stunning apartment who can make a very good old-fashioned. And that is all I am going to divulge." There was a round of boos and disappointed faces.

"Is he still operational?" Roxanne asked, making a gesture with her hands that was considered impolite in most countries. Gasps all around followed by laughter.

Alexa realized she owed them more. They had, after all, come to New York to support her plan, so she delivered. "Yes, still fully operational. And, I can tell you this, it was my idea to spend the night and his idea to drop me off this morning. In addition, he informed me that he would have quite a bit of free time in January and might like to spend some of it with me on the Aegean."

This is what the table had wanted, and they offered up a small ovation.

"Brava," said Toots.

"A fine head of hair!" said Roxanne.

"Nice catch," said Ming. "And he doesn't need your money."

"I'm sorry that Sarah had to get that van back to the lacrosse team in Connecticut," Frannie said. "Or else she would whoop it up and scream, 'LFG!'"

"What does that even mean?" Roxanne asked.

"I don't know. But something good."

The women all toasted with their coffees. "LFG!"

***

AFTER BREAKFAST ALEXA only had a few minutes to get ready for the day before Penny arrived in the lobby expecting an art tour, not an ambush. Alexa had her get-ready-quick drill down: dry shampoo, body-only shower, moisturizer, and foundation. Then she slipped into her New York travel outfit of black on black on black with a decent bag and good, European-chic sneakers. She blew out her hair, put on makeup, slipped the Operation Butterfly baseball hat and a pashmina into her bag. She was ready, at least physically.

She took a second to breathe deeply.

Her stomach was in knots at the thought of seeing Penny. Her daughter. Her heart and soul.

She needed this to work. She needed to get back to the closeness they shared. She needed to hear Penny say that she was forgiven for whatever had caused the rift. She wanted her daughter to be happy again.

She let out one last, long breath. *Please let this work, please let this work.*

Chapter 30

THE SCHEME

The Mother of the Groom

"Mom? What are you doing here?"

"Supporting you!" It was the answer that Abigail had rehearsed, knowing this moment would come when she and Alexa had finalized the plans. Her son was going to ask, so she had better be ready, she told herself. "We respect you. We adore you. And we want you to be happy."

"What is going on?" Chase said, looking around at the assembled crew, which included his parents, his boss and his boss's security detail, a cellist, two aging ballroom dancers, those DAR friends of his mom's in wellies, and his college buddy, who was holding his little sister's hand. None of this made any sense to a logical, one-step-ahead guy like Chase. "Is this an intervention?"

"A love intervention!" Sarah answered, and everyone laughed. Everyone but Chase.

"Could someone please explain this to me?" Chase said, looking directly at his father.

George started to step forward and tell his son the plan, even though he had the barest connection to Operation Butterfly. But the mayor opened his glorious mouth first. "What we have here is a group of concerned citizens. And we're concerned that in the aftermath of breaking off your engagement, you've broken your own heart. And Penny's heart. And this team of people is going to help you put those hearts back together again."

Abigail took over from the mayor, explaining the timeline of the evening with just the right level of detail. She explained that Penny was in the museum, that everyone present was rooting for them, and that the sushi was from the place they went on their first date. She finished with emotion in her voice. "We all believe you and Penny should give this relationship one more chance. Don't let planning a wedding get in the way of planning your life. The wedding, your wedding, won't be the most important day of your life by a long shot. There will be so many other days that will define your union that won't involve caterers and bouquets. But a wedding will be the start of something new, and we are all here for you."

Chase looked at his mother with amazement and then hugged her deeply. The same for Sarah, followed by quick handshakes with his father, his friend, and his boss. "I'm all in. Let's do this."

"No cheering," Sarah stage-whispered. "Penny's upstairs!"

The mayor took the warning to heart and said quietly, "Now, does someone have a drink for the young lad?"

Lloyd, who had put together a bar cart for the evening, rolled it toward his friend and said, "What can I make you?"

***

Just as the mayor, Abigail, and Sarah triple-teamed the explanation, the text came that the Merry Widows were done with their tour of the second floor and headed down to the first floor and garden.

"It's go time!" Sarah announced with great energy but low volume, directing the mayor, her parents, and the Daughters of the

American Revolution design team to exit the building through the back door. "It will be more romantic if Chase is alone in the garden with the lanterns and the music and the dancers. He doesn't need to look like he's at a cocktail party, standing around here with his boss and parents. Off you go! We'll see you at the restaurant afterward," Sarah said, alluding to the meetup spot arranged by Alexa.

But Abigail turned to Chase, getting in a hug and a few words of encouragement. "The right partner in life is a tremendous gift. Especially where you're headed. Don't let Penny slip through your hands."

"What made you change your mind? I thought Penny wasn't our kind?" Chase asked in the least judgmental tone he could muster.

Abigail was humbled, but she didn't have time to explain it all to her son at this moment. She would soon. She thought of everything she had learned about Penny and her family since the day they announced the engagement. Their strong family connection to relatives in Greece. About the tragic death of Alexa's mother and how that shaped her as an adult woman. How hard Penny worked from the time she was a teenager until now, never feeling entitled to anything. Plus, she learned of Penny's warmth and genuine care for others from the Widows. Abigail had made snap judgments based on old stereotypes, lack of knowledge, and her own biases. "I was wrong. She is as special as you are."

"Yes, she is." George echoed the sentiment with a nod. "The key to any successful relationship is to keep growing and changing. And admitting mistakes when it's the right thing to do. And forgiving whenever you can. Right, dear?"

"Right." Then the two of them, Abigail and George, walked out of the museum hand in hand, followed by the mayor and his bodyguards, leaving Chase to change his destiny.

The Blakeman siblings stood side by side watching their parents leave the building, actually touching each other in public.

"What has gotten into them?" Chase asked, and then turned to his sister and his best man, gesturing to the couple. "And we need to talk about the two of you because this is weird, too."

"Love is in the air, bruh," Lloyd said, squeezing Sarah's broad shoulders. "What can I say? She swept me off my feet."

"It was more of a stick tackle," Sarah claimed, mimicking the move, then she put on her coach voice. "All right, Chase, hustle up and go stand over there," she commanded, pointing to a particularly lovely section of the garden lit by lanterns. "I'm counting on you to turn this setback into an opportunity. You got this?"

Now that was a pep talk a third team all-state former high school lacrosse player understood. He high-fived his sister and his friend. "I got this."

Chapter 31

THE SCHEME

The Mother of the Bride

"I thought we were going to do the galleries on the first floor and then drinks in the garden?" Penny asked, confused by the sudden change of plans. All day long, she'd been her usual pleasant self. Alexa was relieved that she'd received a genuine hug, while Penny whispered in her ear, "I'm so happy to see you." Then, their golden girl greeted the Widows with hugs and smiles, dishing on her work project and sharing in group jokes. She added facts and stories to their walking tour of the shops, galleries, and historic sights of Queens, leaving Chase's name out of the details. The Widows made sure to heap praise on the neighborhoods they drove and walked through, exclaiming over the little two-family houses in Astoria as "charming" and "a great investment opportunity." They oohed and aahed over the redeveloped streets with high-rise condos, the movie studios and trendy bars. Here and there, Penny pointed out the shops catering to the large Greek population with signs indicating "Greek spoken inside." And they declared the entire borough to be "unexpected" and "the best part of the city."

Alexa gave the group a look, worried they were laying on their enthusiasm for Queens a little too thick, but even she had to admit that Queens looked like a very nice place to live. After Penny led them to a taverna for a traditional Greek lunch of meatballs in egg and lemon sauce, lamb fricassee, country salad, stuffed peppers, and roasted tomatoes, Alexa could no longer deny her approval. "It's like being in Athens. How wonderful. I think you would do fine here, if you and Chase come to an agreement."

"That's a big if," Penny said softy, then her voiced turned playful. "But I told you that you would feel right at home in Astoria if you gave it a chance. Plus, the Greek cheeses here are better than the ones on Patmos. Did you taste the kefalotyri on the salata horiatiki?"

"Those are fighting words," Alexa retorted in her native language.

Penny translated for the crowd and they all laughed.

It was like the old Penny, the pre-engagement Penny, was back. Maybe because she started the day in the hotel lobby with a declaration that it be free of conversation about the "breakup or the pause or whatever Chase wants to call it." (Her snarky tone sent a chill through the California women.) But now, there was an edge in her voice, like she was suspicious of the rerouting. "Why are we stopping the tour now? We've only seen half the museum."

"Well, you know Roxanne. Metabolism like a hummingbird. When's she hangry, she's hangry. We should have anticipated this," Toots vamped. "She needs food now, right, Roxi?"

Roxanne, who was the definition of a good soldier, was happy to be thrown under the bus for the success of the mission. Everyone secretly knew she always had a packet of peanut butter crackers in her bag to combat her "low blood sugar," a medical condition she'd never actually verified. "Thank you, Toots. You all take such good care of me."

Alexa snapped into tour guide mode with an ulterior motive.

"Yes, we moved up the timeline. Everything is waiting for us in the sculpture garden. Why don't we all stop in the ladies' room to freshen up first? Penny, you look pale. Do you have lipstick? Put some on."

All eyes turned to Penny, in a black maxi dress and jean jacket with a blue silk scarf looped around her neck, hair up in a bun. A classic New York look, but a swipe of color on her lips was a good idea. She rolled her eyes at her mother, who was expecting that response. While Penny had been warm and cheerful when they first saw each other after weeks of chilly communications, the suggestion that she could use some lipstick was all Penny needed to mock her. "Do you think I'm going to meet Mr. Right at the reception? Like a cater waiter or something?"

Toots to the rescue. "Your mother's right. I want a group picture. Everybody needs lipstick!"

"Fine," Penny agreed. "We should all get matching T-shirts for the next trip that say, 'Everybody Needs Lipstick.'"

Mitsy made a mental note to do just that.

***

THE GARDEN AT the Noguchi Museum was beautiful at night without any amendments. The sensuous lines of the sculptures, the contrasting textures of large and small rocks and lush greenery, and the winding paths that invited wandering à deux. But the scene that Abigail, Sarah, and the Connecticut cohort had created was magical. In a short time, they'd added flickering lanterns, classical music, ethereal dancers waltzing in white, and an anxious but handsome Chase, standing cocktail in hand with his vulnerability in full view. It took their collective breath away.

Maybe for the Widows, it stirred a memory of such a moment from long ago. Of being young and beautiful and in love. Of anticipation or regret. They took it all in without speaking.

For Penny, it took only a second to understand the implications of what she saw before her. Tears sprung to her eyes. She turned to her mother. "Did you do this?"

"We all did. And Abigail and Sarah, too. We love you both," Alexa replied, and as soon as she said it, she knew it was true. *She loved them both.* Penny, of course. But also Chase. Instead of seeing him as this stranger poised to come between her and her daughter, she saw him as a good brother, steady friend, and loyal son. Maybe, if she was honest with herself, she was a little jealous that Penny had found a good life partner when she never had.

But it was the time she had spent with Abigail and Sarah, with Timmo, even with Lloyd that had convinced her that Chase was worthy of Penny. Her Penelope. He was funny, smart, a hard worker. He genuinely cared about other people. He was caught up in his career, but it was a worthwhile endeavor. He was a good man. She thought back to Homer, to the ancient poem. There was no need to unwind the scarf tonight. Yes, Chase was the one Penny was waiting for. She hoped her daughter would see the same thing. "Go to him."

"I should, shouldn't I?"

"Yes."

"Thank you, Mama," Penny whispered. "And you were right: The lipstick was a good idea."

She watched as Penny called out to Chase and he turned to see her, not in an ethereal Kalliope Moon white dress, but in a well-worn jean jacket and sneakers. This was it. The first-look moment. But not the pre-produced one for the wedding photographer's camera. No, this was genuine. Alexa's skin tingled. Chase was seeing Penny, truly seeing her, as his bride, the woman he would marry and share his life with. There were tears and wonder. So much wonder.

Alexa couldn't see Penny's face from her vantage point, but she recognized the confidence in her walk. She strode to the man she loved and wrapped her arms around him.

They looked like a sculpture, Alexa thought as she wiped her eyes. Two bodies fitted together as one. She turned away, leaving the reunited couple alone. Well, alone with the cellist, the dancers, Sarah and Lloyd, and the museum staff.

Operation Butterfly appeared to be a success.

Part Three

WINTER

Dearly Beloveds and Betrotheds . . .

With all those holiday weddings in the offing, the volume of mail queries about wedding questions has ratcheted up to an all-time high. I'm hearing from all members of the wedding party on various topics that bubble up the closer the wedding date is.

To Short-Waisted Bridesmaid Louise: Literally the whole deal about being a bridesmaid is WEARING THE DRESS. Or the suit. Or the caftan. Or whatever your friend, the Bride, has decided her attendants will wear. If the dress is as unflattering on you as you describe, you might ask your dear friend, the Bride, if you can wear a cut more comfortable for your body in the same color. Same color, different dress. Understood? And do so in a voice that says, "I am concerned about your wedding photos, not my personal preference." And no to the Doc Martens unless they are white.

To the Conscientious Maid of Honor: You are my hero. I hear your concern about the upcoming toast at the wedding and appreciate being your sounding board for ideas and concepts. I wish every person who plans on giving a toast actually planned the toast they are giving. As opposed to the "drunk and winging it" approach that so many take, to the distress of the Bride and her mother. Is Ten Positions to Try on Your Wedding Night a fun toast idea? It's not, dear MOH. Even Three Positions is three too many. Double entendres aside, this is a terrible idea. In general, toasts that involve sex, politics, old flames, side pieces, college debauchery, mooning the audience, and references to the Bride's breasts are NSFW. (Not Safe for Weddings. And yes, I have gotten letters about all these kinds of toasts.) My tips for a can't-lose toast:

- Keep it short

- Keep it warm

- A few words on why you love the bride or the groom (that don't include subjects mentioned above)

- A few words on why you love the couple (that don't include subjects mentioned above)

- Best wishes for a long and happy marriage.

To Concerned Aunt Nellie: Are you really concerned about your nephew, the Groom? Or are you concerned about you? Because wanting to do a sit-down with the Bride about the table seating prior to the wedding doesn't really sound like you're that worried about the Groom not liking the table for his family. It sounds like you might not like your table. Now is not the time to impose your will on the wedding couple. I'm sorry that you had to sit at "the Old People's Table" at the last family wedding. But did it ever occur to you that you might be the old people? Get right with that before you go. As a mature guest, be gracious, be grateful, and be getting out onto that dance floor as soon as the music starts.

To the many beautiful brides that wrote in about this one: You are not the only one who has a mother or a future mother-in-law who wants to invite a few additional guests now that some of the invited guests have declined. This is classic MOB/MOG behavior. Shut it down with a simple no. As in, "All the invitations have been sent out. We won't be sending out any more to anyone." Practice this ten times in the mirror in a firm, full voice.

To the Left-Out MOG: Technically, you are not in the bridal party like the Mother of the Bride. That's the protocol. MOB, yes.

MOG, no. The bride has no obligation to include you in any little thing, never mind every little thing. Let her be the Bride and you get to be the wise gracious influence in her life. The good news is that if you behave with love and grace through the wedding planning and on the big day, the chances are much greater you'll be a part of their lives going forward. But throwing a hissy fit (your words, not mine) to attend the final wedding dress fitting? It's a tiny slice of the rest of your relationship. Let it go.

To the High and Mighty MOB (my words, not yours): You know who you are. You claim, in very demeaning language, the MOG has terrible taste and picked a dress that clashes with yours for the wedding. You insist the Bride has been trashing the dress behind the MOG's back but won't tell the MOG to her face. Should you step in? Absolutely not. This isn't your wedding. You know that, right? Here's the truth: After the first ten seconds of the ceremony when the MOG walks down the aisle before the music starts, no one will pay attention to what she is wearing. (Photoshop can fix the photos.) The Bride is the star of the day. The rest of you, merely supporting players. Even you, High and Mighty MOB.

Big Kiss & Wedding Bliss,
Your Aunt B

Chapter 32

THE ARRIVALS

The Mother of the Bride

Alexa leaned against the luggage cart in the baggage claim area at LAX, a giveaway that she was beyond fatigued from being on her feet for the last few days. There had been site inspections of the wedding venue and her final dress fitting. She had shopped for gift baskets for multiple guests staying in multiple locations, like Simon and his family and Timmo Lynch. She walked through Roxanne's beach house, where her family would be staying, to inspect the linen and the bathrooms because her family was in the hospitality business and very demanding about such items. (She swapped out the hand soap, candles, and other amenities for extraordinary ones from Hudson Grace at the Country Mart.) And last night, she stood in the kitchen, baking loaves of her signature bread, her only culinary skill. Now, as she waited for her family to make it through customs, she used the cart as a barre so she could stretch out her hamstrings. She'd been obsessed with her walk down the aisle and keeping her muscles flexible for the task. She didn't want to creak down the aisle like someone's yaya.

Although she hoped to be a yaya fairly soon.

It was then that the Diamandis family emerged from the tunnel leading from passport control like an army of well-traveled merce-naries ready to add their energy to any event. The clan included her older brothers, Nikos, Yiannis, and Theo; their wives Thalia, Demi, and Calla; and cousins Chloe and Iris, who were close in age to Penny. (They opted to shop in California rather than ski in Italy.) Rolling their bags like pros, dressed in black puffers and Euro sneak-ers, they appeared to have all slept well and been fully caffeinated on the plane. The Diamandises were a force.

Alexa's heart burst. She had underestimated the joy she would feel at seeing her family on her turf for Penny's wedding. Normally, it was she and Penny who traveled to see them, making the thirteen-hour flight and arriving on familiar soil with anticipation of experiences to come. But not this time, and it made Alexa grateful and humbled to have her people on hand to witness the next step in Penny's life. For the first time in all the planning, she had the feeling that this wedding weekend might actually be fun.

As soon as they spotted Alexa, the noise level rose in the arrivals area, with calls of "Yia sas!" and spontaneous cheering, as if they were in a contest to outdo the large Korean and Brazilian families in the waiting area. The Diamandises came to conquer.

After hugs and kisses, Alexa went into tour guide mode, pop-ping up a collapsible white flag with the distinct Odyssey Vacations logo, leading her family out in the chaos that was the LAX curbside pickup. "Let's go! Páme, páme!"

"You're not driving, are you?" her brother Nikos asked, immedi-ately settling into old family patterns about her inferior road skills. Everybody laughed, even Alexa.

"Of course not," she said, leading the group to a black Mercedes motor coach stocked with water, coffee, and snacks. "We do things first-class here in the Golden State. You have a driver all weekend. Meet Ricky!"

And with that, the family piled into the bus to start the two-hour drive north to Montecito.

***

AFTER THE LONG drive followed by a leisurely lunch at Jeannine's, where Alexa's family marveled over the generous California salads and all the people in great sunglasses, she delivered her family at Roxanne's house and instructed them to make themselves at home. Roxanne was staying at the Miramar with Toots, but she had stocked the fridge for her guests, which was a lovely gesture. They immediately organized a late dinner at their place, contacting Penny and insisting she and Chase come. Ricky was tasked with taking the women to the grocery store to supplement their supplies while the men napped. They were resting up to do the cooking, her brothers claimed. Alexa could tell the chaos was going to grow from there, so she ducked out quietly. She loved her family but they were a lot.

Plus, she had one more guest to get settled.

***

ALEXA WAS WAITING for Timmo Lynch at the rental house she had secured for him, which was walking distance to her own place but in an entirely different stratosphere in terms of price and prestige. Set back off the street, it was an immaculate midcentury modern with ripe citrus on the trees, a heated lap pool, and a view of the Pacific Ocean from the dining room. It was the latest celebrity rental house, a trend that had infiltrated the neighborhood. The owner was a designer from Sag Harbor who had recently relocated and was trying to put his stamp on the town. He didn't live in this house, but it was all part of his online presence. He was the type who not only had his own line at Target but shopped there, too. At least according to his social media. He'd offered the neighbors first dibs on the rental over the holidays at a reduced fee as a show of good faith and appreciation. Alexa snapped it up on Timmo's behalf.

At first, the mayor had balked about not being at a hotel, but she informed him that many of the wedding guests and the Widows would be staying at the Miramar and she would hate to run into them in the elevator. A private home, she reminded him, would be more *private*. He signed on immediately. They wanted to make the most of their three nights together.

Timmo had a driver and security for the weekend, and she watched as his black car pulled into the driveway. The candles were lit and the champagne was chilled. Earlier in the day, she had felt a little guilty leaving her family for . . . for what? Was Timothy Lynch her boyfriend? Her lover? Something more? Time would tell. But for now, he was both a distraction and a destination. There were the long calls at the end of his day. The flirty texts. The anticipation of their next meeting. But there was also planning their first get-away somewhere after his reign as mayor was over. The suggestion of spending August together at his place on Long Island. She scanned real estate listings imagining her own little place in New York. They were enjoying both the grand and the intimate moments together.

She opened the door. "I'm so glad you're here."

And she really meant it.

He allowed security to check the house before sending them off for the night.

"Where is your team staying?" Alexa asked.

"I have no idea. For three more days, I'm the mayor of New York. And I'm going to let my executive assistant make all the arrangements. Next week, I'll be an old out-of-work Irishman, taking cabs and scraping by."

"I doubt that."

"As do I," he said, then took her in his arms and kissed her. Deep, exciting, but familiar in the best way. "You smell good, like the sea."

"I swam today. A quick plunge. But I didn't rinse my hair. Knowing how much you like the salt air." She kissed him again, tasted the whiskey he must have had on the plane. "Maybe you'll come with me in the morning down to the beach."

"If you'll stay with me tonight."

She thought of the overnight bag she had already stashed in the primary bedroom. Of course she would stay with him tonight. "Yes. That's my plan."

***

LATER, WHEN THE champagne was gone and the dishes done, the couple relaxed on the couch, a fire roaring in the fireplace and some sort of light jazz coming through the speaker system. Timmo's eyes closed, but he wasn't quite asleep. He was on New York time, and even a night owl like himself felt the effects of the three hours' difference. She thought about giving him a shake and then dragging him to the bedroom. But when his breath got heavy, she knew he was past his peak performance hours. She laughed as she thought about aging and romance. Timing was everything.

"Timmo." She shook him gently. "Let's go to bed. You'll need your sleep for tomorrow morning."

He stirred. "That I will." And then he asked for the second time that night, "You'll stay with me, won't you?"

"Yes. That's my plan."

Chapter 33

THE MOTHERS' TEA

The Mother of the Bride

Amid an elaborate tea service in a paneled room at the Nottingham Forest clubhouse filled with flowers, women, and women dressed in flowers, Alexa finished her walk around the tables to say hello to all the guests. Abigail circled in the opposite direction, stopping to introduce herself to a Montecito-heavy crowd, pointing out her daughter, Sarah, her aunt and three cousins who had made the trip from Simsbury, and her dear friend Bernadette. She received a warm welcome from all, including the Merry Widows. Penny weaved in and out, giving hugs and kisses to the mothers of her high school friends, the shop owners and business associates of Alexa's, and the other local luminaries who had no place else to be the week between Christmas and New Year's. The social choreography of all wedding events was complex and exhausting, exacerbated by high heels and shapewear. But the three women performed their roles with enthusiasm and grace.

The Merry Widows had insisted they be allowed to host a mothers' tea for Alexa and Abigail. Months ago, when the subject came up, Alexa protested that they were already doing so much for the wedding they didn't need to host another event. But they refused to back down. "We all host so many charity events for people we barely know or hardly like," Mitsy had said that day. "Let us do something for people we truly enjoy."

Mitsy explained further, "It's not a shower. There are no gifts, no games. People come, they chat, they nibble, they meet Abigail, and then they leave. We'd like Penny to make an appearance if she has time, of course, but this tea is for you and Abigail. A chance to relax before the hustle-bustle. It also means one less day of activities you have to schedule for out-of-town guests. The women can come to the tea and the men can play golf or bridge here at the club." She made it all sound so sensible that Alexa couldn't say no.

Ming, who loved any opportunity for cucumber sandwiches and mini cheesecakes, jumped in. "We'll invite the Montecito crowd who aren't coming to the wedding. If they're not going to Hawaii or Palm Springs for the holidays, they'll be so glad to get an invitation to go out during what is normally a dead week that they'll forget you excluded them from the main event. Now that your family is coming from Greece, your sisters-in-law and your nieces are invited, and Abigail's friend Bernadette, her family, and those two who did all the flowers at the museum. What were their names again?"

"Lucinda and Martha," Mitsy said, as if proper New England names were her specialty. "I loved talking to them at the Greek restaurant. We've stayed in touch. They're staying with me. They're on the flower team for the wedding. They've been drying hydrangeas since September."

The months between that conversation and the actual events had been a blur for Alexa. As soon as Penny and Chase reconfirmed their wedding, the planning had been nonstop. But the first order of business was to get Penny to agree to limit the stress that had caused her to melt down in the first place by tightening the guest list, whittling down the bells and whistles, and putting aside the anxiety of what she should do versus what she wanted to do. Alexa was convinced that with a smaller, simpler wedding, Penny would thrive as a bride, just as she had seen her do in the office. Alexa suggested they each sit at their own big conference table with a calendar and a whiteboard to work out the entire plan, like their days together at Odyssey Vacations. Penny agreed, and the two connected over videoconference to hammer out the details.

But what Penny didn't know was that Alexa had already solved the size and demographic problems. It had hit Alexa like a bolt of lightning: Go with what you know. "Penny, I understand you feel like you must reciprocate all those invitations from your twenties. You were in so many weddings with all those showers and hen parties and bridesmaids' dresses. Now you never even see most of those couples. You said yourself that you don't want your wedding to be a bunch of college friends partying. So, I have an idea on how to keep the wedding guest list small and intimate but include people from college and work in another capacity should they wish to join you. Here's my pitch: Invite them on your honeymoon."

"That sounds romantic," Penny deadpanned.

"It's called a buddymoon and, according to Aunt B's website, it's all the rage. She's not for it, but I am." Alexa went on to explain her idea of putting together a reasonably priced package to Greece for twenty or so friends of the couple so that they could share in the honeymoon but be left out of all wedding-related activities. "No showers, no gifts, no expensive destination wedding at the holidays. Instead, invite them to spend five days on Patmos with you and Chase. All vacation, no drama, very reasonable cost. We can block out the whole hotel for five days so it's like your own private villa but you're not in charge of anything, and everybody gets their own room. The family will host a party with food, music, dancing—but easy, easy. Imagine one long table in the stone courtyard filled with your friends and family on the island, a view of the sea, white lights. A celebration but not a wedding! Pure fun. Simple but lively. I've talked to your uncles and they would love to do this for you. As a gift."

"Is this in exchange for me inviting them to our wedding?" Penny wagered with warmth in her voice.

"That's not how families work, Penny. You know that. But, yes, you should have some Diamandis family at your wedding. You'd regret not sharing your day with them. Not all the cousins, of course, but the core group," Alexa responded smoothly, having thought out this entire presentation for this specific exchange. "After the Patmos party, you and Chase can slip off to someplace private for your real honeymoon. For your friends who want to stay longer, Odyssey can put together five days on another island, something sexy like Santorini, if they want to opt in. We are in the travel business, after all. With our connections and your uncles' hotels and restaurants, it's cheaper for your friends to go to Greece than to come to Montecito. They get a holiday and you get to include them in your new life as a couple."

What Alexa didn't say was that it was cheaper for her, too. Even with the generous help of the Widows, the wedding was still going to cost a small fortune. Redirecting the college friends and others to Greece and keeping the numbers in Montecito smaller and more manageable on every front was a win for Alexa, too.

Penny looked at her mother with a mixture of admiration and relief. "Mom, this is a brilliant idea. You're a genius. And yes. Yes! This is the solution! Who wouldn't rather go to Greece on vacation instead of sitting through another wedding? I'll be a hero bride! But first, I have to talk to Chase."

"Yes, absolutely. Chase should be on board. High season would be very expensive. Are you okay with June or September for your honeymoon?"

"June is perfect. Before the campaign gets overwhelming. Late June if we can so it's a bit warmer."

"And don't worry, you'll have the top team at Odyssey working on this. And the best trip leaders."

"You mean you?"

"Oh, no. I'm too old for your crowd. I couldn't keep up with the day drinking and the disco nights. Plus, I'm considering cutting back on work," Alexa said, thinking of last night with Timmo and hoping she wasn't blushing. "I tried to lure Madison away from the wedding business. But she's committed to commitment, I guess. But she has another sorority sister who she thinks would be a great trip leader. I'll get her up to speed, send her on a few low-stress trips before June."

"I think this could be a giant travel trend, Mom. Maybe this is our new business avenue. Think about it. The Odyssey Wedding!"

"Or the Wedding Odyssey." Alexa felt a surge of parental pride. She had solved a major issue for her adult child without making it obvious she was solving a major issue. And the way Penny said "our new business avenue." Did that mean they might be a team again? Alexa hoped so. She would wait until after the buddymoon to ask her about work. But from that moment on, the wedding planning was smooth sailing.

Now, at the mothers' tea, surrounded by the women in her life who had gotten her up, gotten her going, and gotten her through all those years as an only parent, a business owner, and an outsider in an insider's town, Alexa felt at peace.

So far, everything had gone to plan. Her family was ensconced in Roxanne's beach cottage, already treating it like their own real estate by hosting an impromptu dinner last night. Abigail's family and guests were taking up every available room at La Mariposa. Simon, Hazel, and the twins had arrived from England before Christmas and swore they might never leave, nestled in a rental house near the beach but with its own heated pool. Simon and the boys spent hours on the beach, kicking the soccer ball or flying kites. Hazel, with the help of a list from Mitsy, mapped out all the shops and restaurants that the local royals were said to frequent in hopes of a sighting to impress her friend in Ledbury. No luck yet, but in the meantime, she had acquired an entirely new wardrobe of beachy separates and flowing dresses. At the tea, Hazel was wearing some sort of floral maxi dress that made her look ten years younger and like she was on vacation in Mallorca. Alexa even spotted her and Simon in a steamy embrace as they parted ways earlier—she for the tea, he for the tee. There was some magic in the Montecito breeze.

The rest of the guests were arriving tomorrow and would be scattered throughout Montecito, Santa Barbara, and Summerland in hotels and rentals. Setup would begin at the wedding venue in the morning. The rehearsal dinner would be for family only. The after-party, for "the young people," would be at a brew pub with an outdoor firepit and sponsored by Lloyd in lieu of a bachelor party because a congressional candidate couldn't risk one wild night in today's political climate. Ricky had secured a fleet of cars and vans to move the wedding guests around from event to event without clogging up the streets of Montecito, which frowned upon parked cars in private neighborhoods. And all the details of the wedding day timeline had been approved and committed to an Excel spreadsheet by Madison Meadows, from morning coffee to hair and makeup to the walk down the aisle to the first dance. The brunch on the morning after would be hosted by the Diamandis clan at the beach house and feature the breakfast burritos that Penny requested. It would all be perfect.

For now, Alexa's only job was to sip tea and relax. Penny had arrived to say hello before heading out to get her nails done with some high school friends. She floated around the room in another white dress from a seemingly endless supply of white dresses. "Retail therapy at sample sales," she had explained to her mother as she unpacked her suitcases back at their condo, the two of them living together again for the last few weeks.

Alexa was so proud she could have watched her daughter all day, but the drop-in was short and sweet. It seemed mainly to say hello to Toots and thank her again for her generosity, a fitting gesture. Now, it was back to being the MOB and engaging with the MOG and each other's people. The guests at her table were already involved in lively conversations. The Greek cousins settled in seamlessly, comfortably conversing in English. Iris was fascinated by Hazel Fox's apple orchards, and Chloe was chatting with two of Alexa's most trusted employees about a new hot spot in Athens. Mitsy caught up with her former daughter-in-law Helen, who had driven up from Pasadena with her newish husband Patrick, an archaeologist. Frannie and Roxanne recounted the details of Operation Butterfly to Charlene, the mother of one of Penny's high school friends. Toots and Ming had their heads together about some new scheme that might involve Sarah and Lloyd. There was laughter and love bubbling up throughout the room.

She caught Abigail's eye and they shared a smile and a wave. They both knew that this was the kickoff event of a nonstop three days. Damn the weather report. A little rain was a good omen, wasn't it?

Chapter 34

THE REHEARSAL DINNER

The Mother of the Groom

"An atmospheric river. What are the chances?" Abigail Blakeman asked as she dressed for the rehearsal dinner in the guest suite at La Mariposa. The sky was clear for their party, but the weather for the wedding was threatening, with updates coming in from Madison every hour. Abigail wondered why even have a wedding coordinator if she was just going to roil everyone up about a little rain? Wasn't her job to calm everyone down? To the bride's credit, she responded to every text with an umbrella emoji and a heart. Chase simply shrugged his shoulders and said, "We're inside and wearing clothes. No need to panic."

Just in case, in a nod to due diligence, George had spent the morning at La Mariposa supervising the tent setup with Antonio's cousin. He reported that while it wasn't the most glamorous tent, it would "do the job."

Meanwhile Abigail had spent the morning at the Padero Surf Club with Sarah and Lloyd finalizing details, stringing additional lights, and supervising the table setup even though it was the exact same setup that the club used for every event. The rental blue-and-sand tablecloths and napkins registered "beachy vibes," just like the bride wanted. The flowers arrived, and Flora the florist took the tables over the top with muted tropical tones that paired with the blues. The bride and groom insisted that there be no wasteful or extraneous monogrammed party items, so, sadly, Abigail didn't order the monogrammed bucket hats for each guest as a party favor. (But that decision did save hundreds of dollars, which she put toward top-shelf tequila.)

"At night, with the twinkle lights on, it will look like a movie set. Amazing," Madison promised, as she looked around the casual, chic clubhouse.

The theme of the night was "Moonlight Surf" and the dress code was California Cowabunga, a ridiculous pairing of words concocted by Madison as a placeholder for the event that somehow stuck and ended up on the invitation. Chase and Penny loved the romantic overtones of "Moonlight Surf" and thought California Cowabunga sounded casual, ironic, and on point to describe the vibe of the Padero Surf Club location to out-of-towners. Surely, guests would know they didn't mean to literally come in surf wear, Penny had said, dismissing Abigail's concerns about the descriptor. "Everyone will know to dress up by dressing down."

But to the mother of the groom and host of the party, it was a meaningless turn of phrase meant to guarantee that a few guests would wear Hawaiian shirts, board shorts, and flip-flops despite the real, mailed invitations meant to indicate an elevated surf event. The theme did allow Abigail an excuse to wear a blouse splashed with color, velvet pants, and a bedazzling puffer vest because while the surf club was chic, it was also unheated. She had spent hours in resale shops buying up the bits and pieces for the wedding weekend. She'd taken Lola from the senior center with her, which helped enormously. Lola was an unrelenting vintage shopper who knew to check the backs of shelves and other unexpected spots for the good items other shoppers had hidden until they could come back later. The strategy paid off: a stunning Roberto Cavalli blouse hidden under a drab gray blazer. Lola had even managed to find some vintage Hermès ties for George at astonishingly low prices in the bargain bin. Abigail had emptied her entire secret bank account to outfit the family for multiple events, and she felt it was worth every penny.

Was it worth every penny to sell her mother's Queen Anne maple highboy to cover the cost of the lobster tacos for tonight's guests? Probably not. But, in all honesty, Abigail was getting rather fatigued by all the proper, early American antiques that decorated her Fair Harbor home. Where was the fun in mahogany? She was looking forward to the day they could sell the house, ditch Aunt Eleanor's period pieces, and move to a condo with comfortable couches and cozy fabrics.

Ping. Another text from Madison alerting that all the latest models had the rain starting after the event. "More weather updates!" Abigail mocked.

"It's fairly predictable."

"What is? The weather?"

"The atmospheric river," said George, who monitored the weather as a hobby. Even the weather in places he had never been to and was never going to visit made it onto his daily rounds. George was your man if you wanted to know the temperature in Denali National Park at any given moment. Or the precipitation expected in Pompeii. He'd been monitoring the storms out in the Pacific for months because of El Niño. "These sort of extreme weather events are happening with more frequency, and this is the season for heavy rain here. But most of the guests live nearby or are already here, the ceremony and dinner are inside, and we have a tent! The dancing can carry on. Don't worry, sweetheart," he finished. And then taking in his wife in her silk blouse and velvet pants, he kissed her on the lips with the passion he usually saved for Saturday night.

"What was that for?" Abigail said, pulling away and smoothing her clothing and hair.

"You've done an amazing job on the wedding, all parts of it," he said, inching her back toward him with a gentle tug. "You've risen to the occasion to embrace a new daughter. The party tonight is going to be wonderful. You haven't bankrupted us. That extra legroom in coach was a game changer. This house is paradise. And you look hot in these pants," he said, running his hand down her back and over her backside. "Senior center Pilates, my ass. You are not a senior with this bod."

"Language, please, George!" Abigail blamed a pre-dinner drink for the friskiness, but she blushed all the same. "Later," she promised. "Is your speech ready?"

"You know it. Picked out some choice California quotes."

"That turns me on," she purred. "You're not going to quote Reagan, are you?"

"I'm not. But if that crowd I met at Ming's club was any indication, he still has a lot of fans here." George had played bridge at the Nottingham Forest clubhouse and picked up a few potential clients who needed online lessons or paid partners in tournaments. It had been a fruitful afternoon while the Merry Widows and others gathered for the mothers' tea.

"You know you're up against Baron Plumley," Abigail reminded him, as Simon was also giving a toast. The traditional father-of-the-bride slot, though by now, after so many glasses of wine and long talks with Alexa and the Widows, Abigail was resigned to the fact that Simon Fox was not Penny's biological father and the Blakeman grandchild would not inherit a title. Their grandchildren's lineage would include a random tall, dark-haired volleyball player/grad student who needed cash. She had made peace with that, most days. But George going toe-to-toe with Simon in the toast department was an exciting prospect. Never mind the mayor of New York appearing as the officiant. "And everyone's favorite late-night-talk-show mayor, Timmo Lynch."

"I feel like I can compete with the apple farmer," George said, referring to Simon by the nickname they'd given him after a few

G&Ts. "But I saw the mayor's schtick at the rehearsal. He swore he was going to play it straight. But you know he's going to bring all the quotes from those goddamn Irish writers."

Abigail opened her mouth to speak, but the phone pinged again. She checked the message instead of commenting on Timmo Lynch's role in the proceedings. "Oh, it's time! Ricky will be out front in ten minutes with the car. Can you go meet him and I'll get Sarah and Chase?"

"Anything you say, MOG."

***

"LET'S GET A photo! Mignette!" Abigail called out to the house manager as she waited for her family to assemble in the front hall of Toots's house. That is, the whole family plus Lloyd, who was staying with them at La Mariposa for the festivities. It should have been awkward, seeing as he was Chase's friend before he was Sarah's boyfriend, but Lloyd was such a lovely man, so enamored of Sarah and her cankles, that he smoothed over any awkwardness. Abigail hoped Lloyd was a permanent addition but stashed that thought away for another time.

Tonight was about Chase, and when he descended the front staircase, ready for his rehearsal dinner the night before his wedding, it brought tears to Abigail's eyes.

She loved being Chase's mother. From the minute he was born thirty years ago to this moment right now. Watching him grow from the sweet blond little boy who'd loved watching the trash trucks on collection days and riding his bike while creating his own sound effects into this smart, sophisticated young man about to marry a lovely young woman and begin his adult life in full. What a good job she and George had done with Chase.

And, as if she needed any further proof, he had interpreted California Cowabunga as a chance to wear a custom blue blazer, pressed jeans, and a striped blue button-down shirt. His thick dark hair was freshly cut, and he smelled like salt and sand. Not a flip-flop in sight.

"You look so handsome," she said, hugging him with an extra squeeze.

"Penny will only allow me to wear blue clothes for the rest of the wedding events, as per the theme. Damn good thing I look so good in blue," Chase answered. And because he'd been particularly grateful since Abigail had staged the Chase and Penny Reunion, he added, "You look beautiful, Mom. This look is daring for you!"

"I have to move out of my comfort zone to keep up with these Diamandis women."

"Don't we all?"

George arrived in the front hall and tucked the notes for his toast into the pocket of his blue blazer. Not custom like his son's, but a serviceable off-the-rack Brooks Brothers. Then Sarah and Lloyd bounded into the front hall, bringing that golden retriever energy with them. Leave it to Sarah to take California Cowabunga to its natural extreme. She was in a vintage 1980s Body Glove wetsuit dress, and Lloyd was wearing a wild pink and green floral-print Mr Turk suit. They looked like a couple on the verge of a costume, but not quite over the line. In fact, Abigail thought, they looked fabulous. Young, fun, and fabulous.

"Cow-a-bunga!" Sarah screamed, then started humming "Wipe Out."

"Won't you be cold at the bonfire? It's freezing here!"

Sarah pointed to a backpack in the corner. "Sweats, beanies, and puffers for both of us."

Lloyd gave Sarah a thumbs-up. "She's really into gear. What do you think of this, Mrs. B?"

Before Abigail had a chance to answer, her son the politician took the question.

"I love it, man," Chase said to Lloyd, extending a hand and a slap on the back. "Let me guess. Sarah made you wear this?"

"No! I picked it out myself! I'm going to get a lot of wear out of this suit," Lloyd deadpanned. "My good luck suit for pitching investors for that third-round funding."

"Tomorrow we're wearing the clothes you want us to wear. Tonight, the real us," Sarah said.

"Mignette!" Abigail called again.

"I'm here, Missus. Here to take the photo," Mignette said, calmly standing in the corner taking care of business like she had been doing for the past week, as La Mariposa transformed from home to wedding venue. All the while, Mignette provided excellent care and food and beverage service for the Blakemans in her stealth-like manner.

"Of course you are!" Abigail gushed, thinking for the zillionth time how lucky people were to have good help.

"Look here, family!" Mignette instructed in her French-Canadian accent. "Say 'Cowabunga!'"

There was joy and laughter on the faces of the Blakeman family as Mignette snapped the photos. Yes, tonight they were themselves. Tomorrow, part of the scenery.

***

"THERE IS A lot of love in this room," Bernadette said as she typed a few notes into her phone and then waved the server over for another margarita. Her interpretation of the dress code was a black dress with pearls, a look she assumed for every rehearsal dinner. She took in the glowing room with the glowing couple and the glowing young people and sighed. "Everyone seems to feel like this is a good match."

"You sound surprised," Abigail said, shaking her head when the server asked if she wanted another "maggie," as they called the concoctions at the Padero Surf Club. Because it was too much of an effort to say a four-syllable word when there were waves to catch. The mother of the groom knew all that sugar and salt on the rims would result in a bloated face for the wedding photos, so she was sticking to champagne.

"A bit. At the engagement party, there seemed to be two separate camps, the Pro-Chase Team and the Pro-Penny Team. But now, all I see is family and friends from all over the world crowded into this charming room and celebrating those two gorgeous people," Bernadette said as she pointed to Penny, in a white, blue, and gold flowing silk dress, and Chase, holding tight to her hand as they made the rounds.

"I love how traditional this guest list is as well," Bernadette continued, turning her professional eye to the party. "Not every person you have to make conversation with tomorrow in the receiving line. But the small, select group of people who will support the couple."

"That's what Penny and Chase wanted," Abigail claimed, though really, the size of the place dictated the guest list. And the cost. She was so grateful that the Merry Widows volunteered to take themselves off the guest list, saving them money and opening a table for Alexa's family. "Don't invite us. We've had enough PSC lobster tacos to last a lifetime," Toots offered. And Abigail thanked her. But no reason to explain all that to Bernadette. "It feels . . . traditional. Right for us."

"And Alexa's family may be the most attractive family on the planet. Good genes going into the pool, Abby." The Diamandis men were stylish in an array of handsome linen jackets in shades of blue, their dark hair and tanned skin set off by white shirts and good teeth. The women, blonder than Abigail assumed they might be, paired long dresses with sleek leather jackets to protect them from the cool winter weather. The two cousins looked like Penny's twin sisters and wore sophisticated, midriff-baring ensembles that screamed "youth with money." As a group, they were striking.

Abigail nodded in agreement. There was nothing more to be said on that front except, "A lot of good hair."

"Many families don't come together to support the couple. They are entrenched in their own needs and wants. Eighty percent of my mailbox is family conflicts. I'm more therapist than etiquette expert. The tiniest grievances become life-or-death issues around a wedding. One bride threatened to throw her future mother-in-law out of the wedding ceremony if she did an attention-stealing choreographed dance with her son. There's unity for you," Bernadette said, accepting a shrimp kabob from a server who might also be a male model. "And don't get me started on all the MOB versus MOG incidents. I hate playing into the women competing with other women stereotype, but if my mail is to be believed, it's a real issue. But you and Alexa, you've found middle ground. You've risen to the challenge, Abigail. It's good to see."

Her old friend held new admiration for her. That warmed Abigail from the inside.

She thought back to her initial reaction to the engagement and knew Bernadette was right. She had been headed in that direction, toward Full Entrenchment. But now look at her! Open to new ideas—within reason. "Thank you, Bernadette. That means a lot to me."

Madison appeared so suddenly by her side, it startled Abigail. "Go time for your husband's toast. We're passing champagne now. Sound good?"

"Perfect."

Madison nodded and she and her clipboard slipped away. Bernadette commented, "She's good. She filled me in on the whole history of this place and the house tomorrow. Invaluable to my story. Also, the Odyssey Wedding concept for the young people who didn't want to stand in one more buffet line. Send them all on vacation together to drink and dance! Brilliant. That's all they want to do anyway. I told Madison we'd stay in touch. I'm always looking for spotters for interesting weddings. And believe me, I'd like to come back here in the summer!"

Abigail felt a swell of pride. Madison had been the glue holding the whole event together. "She is terrific. I'm sure she told you that she's transitioning to wedding planning from corporate events. Any help you can give her to build her client list would be appreciated." Two old friends networking at a rehearsal dinner. "And did I tell you Sarah is moving here in June? She's taken a new job at a prep school nearby, teaching and coaching. I've lost her to Lloyd and California."

"Will there be a Fair Harbor wedding at Water Street?"

"No engagement yet. But they are going to get a dog together, so we shall see. Though, you know Sarah. She'd be happy to get married on a field hockey pitch and have a kegger afterward," Abigail said, but she was already scheming about what she could sell off to afford upgrading the electrical in the house to accommodate a caterer.

Madison signaled and Abigail responded.

"It's showtime! Excuse me. George wants me to stand with him. How does my face look?" Abigail said, standing up straight, smoothing her clothes and sucking in her stomach—her three-pronged approach to looking younger and taller.

"Glowing. Go forth and MOG."

***

ABIGAIL WISHED SHE could focus on George's speech, but she was mesmerized by the view. Standing at the front of the room, staring out at the guests, who looked happy to be included, she felt satisfied in a way she hadn't in a long time. She watched Chase as he concentrated on his father while holding Penny's hand. Abigail knew that some people operated better on their own, like Alexa, independent and admirable. But some people needed to be a unit, part of a team. She and George. Chase and Penny. Sarah and Lloyd. That was a legacy she was passing on, and it pleased her. *Teamwork makes the dream work.*

The laughter of the crowd made her aware of her surroundings again. George was finishing strong, with his wish that Penny and Chase could both remain in this moment and, at the same time, grow with each other in the years to come. "Joan Didion wrote that 'Marriage is memory. Marriage is time. Marriage is not only time; it is, paradoxically, the denial of time.' Penny and Chase, look at each other and then look around the room at the people who love you. Imprint this. This is memory. This is time. This is marriage. We wish you a healthy heaping of all three. To Penny and Chase!"

With a lump in her throat, Abigail lifted her glass and she was back at her own country club wedding thirty-one years ago. In her white dress with the capelet and George by her side in his gingham tie. Memory. Time. Marriage. Her George had done it again. Let Timothy Lynch come at them with Irish poets. And Lord Simon Fox with that accent. Her George would not be bested. "To Penny and Chase."

Chapter 35

THE DAY OF

The Mother of the Bride

The guest quarters above the pavilion at La Mariposa were quiet. The buzz of the MOB, the MOG, and the bridesmaid having their hair and makeup done was over. The popping of champagne and blaring of music was done. It was only Penny and her mother in the ready room waiting for the signal from Madison that it was time. Alexa and Penny, as it always had been.

Alexa was afraid that if she studied her daughter too closely, a flood of tears would ruin her carefully crafted makeup. She couldn't have tears running down her neck to stain her silk dress. (Kalliope Moon had sold her a mermaid-silhouette dress, more figure-hugging than the original flowing caftan Alexa had bought. The designer named the swirling blue creation the Thetis dress, after the sea nymph in Greek mythology.) The moment was so much bigger, more meaningful than Alexa had imagined. Had the venue and the pomp and circumstance made it so? Or would she have been as emotional at a City Hall ceremony with a Chinese restaurant reception? Based on the weight of her emotions, Alexa surmised that she would have cried either way.

"Penny—" she started.

"Don't. Please. We can't cry. It will ruin all the photos," Penny answered, her voice thick.

"I want to say one thing. Please."

Penny, her face framed by her deep brown hair against the white tulle veil embellished with light-blue butterflies, nodded. "Is this where you tell me about you and Mayor Lynch?"

"No, it's not. I'll tell you about that another time. It's where I tell you what this day means to me."

"Fine," the bride said, turning toward the window and the darkening skies. "But I can't look at you. And no crying."

Alexa took her hand. "You are my greatest joy. And this day is your gift to me." She stopped before she got sloppy. She didn't tell her daughter what it meant to see her find her life partner, who loved and respected her. What it meant to see her in that stunning dress, a grown woman but still blooming with youth and possibility. What it meant to see her healthy, happy, and so, so capable. That would have wrecked them both. Instead, she squeezed her hand and said in her native tongue, "S'agapó."

Penny turned to look at her mother, "Ki egó se agapó." *I love you, too.*

Lord Simon Fox, dapper in a blue suit, white shirt, and a handsome blue Gucci tie with purple butterflies, knocked before popping his head in the door. The sight of the two Diamandis women, mother and daughter, in their wedding finery took his breath away a tiny bit. "Stunning. Very good. Both of you. This is such an honor for me." And then he added, "It's time. Alexa, Madison informed me that all the guests are seated. If you'll kindly go downstairs and meet Madison for your entrance. Then Penny and I will follow. Ready?"

***

A GROVE OF evergreens, the deeply discounted Christmas trees that Mitsy and her crew scooped up on the twenty-sixth of December, provided a privacy screen for the bridal party to assemble out of view of the guests. Madison, headset on, clipboard in hand, motioned to Alexa to take her place at the head of the line, next to Abigail and George.

It had been Penny's ideas that Alexa walk down the aisle with the Blakemans instead of on her own or with a groomsman. As mother and daughter met on Zoom to plan the timeline of events with the same care and decisiveness as a tour of Delphi and Olympia, Penny had said, "Chase and I were talking about everything our parents have done for us, including getting us back together. We said we didn't want gimmicks, but we want to ask you to do something special for us. We thought maybe all three of you could walk down the aisle together to symbolize unity, two families joining. Is that too much? Would you rather walk alone?"

Alexa was taken aback. She had assumed she would walk herself down the aisle. She fancied her own moment, a quiet nod to how she had raised her daughter, but then she remembered the advice Aunt B had given her months ago at the engagement party: *It's not your wedding.* So instead of protesting, Alexa agreed like it was a brilliant idea, the best notion ever. "As long as I get to pick the entrance song."

"As long as it's not the Cure," Penny had answered, rolling her eyes at her mother's former goth sensibilities.

Now here they were, the two mothers ready to walk down the aisle together. Alexa, tall and proud, took her place next to George. Abigail, on the other side of her husband, looked stunning in a vintage Lela Rose midnight-blue floral gown that she'd picked up on the clearance rack at Saks after selling a set of nineteenth-century Windsor chairs that had been stacked in the basement since the seventies.

"You both look amazing," Madison said, then spoke into her

headset. "It's go time. Cue the music." The first chords of a string quartet playing the Cure's "Pictures of You" could be heard. Madison gestured to the trio to proceed, informing whoever was on the other end of the headset, "Here come the MOB and the MOG."

George asked the women on his right and on his left, "Ready?"

And the MOB and the MOG snuck a look at each other and said at the same time, "LFG."

Wedding of the Year:

Penelope Diamandis and Chase Ellsworth Blakeman

LA MARIPOSA
Montecito, California
December 29th

It was a rainstorm of epic proportions that sealed the Montecito wedding of Alexa Diamandis and Chase Ellsworth Blakeman with a (soggy) kiss. Maybe you've seen the viral video? The one with a happy couple leading an enthusiastic crowd of family, friends, a baron, a mayor, and a cabal of well-heeled women in the Cha Cha Slide when a suspicious tent gave way under the weight of the water and doused the crowd with rain, glorious rain? Yes, that wedding. Yours truly, a lifelong friend of the Mother of the Groom, was in attendance, sheltered by a portico when the deluge happened. Did that fact go viral? No, but I can vouch that before the tent collapse and in its aftermath, the Diamandis-Blakeman wedding was filled with love, butterflies, beautiful people, dancing feet, wonderful Greek food, romantic Irish poetry, sly British wit, and enough love and goodwill to take on the rain. And win.

The Diamandis-Blakeman ceremony and reception were held at the home of Toots Bixby, a well-known interior designer and dear friend to the bride and her mother, who renovated the stately Spanish Colonial Revival home in

the latter part of the twentieth century. The renovations
to the Mediterranean masterpiece included a spacious
entertainment pavilion that Flowers by Flora transformed into
a Grecian greenhouse of sorts, with the foraged florals from
roses to lavender from local gardens in Montecito and Fair
Harbor, Connecticut, the home of the Groom. The backdrop
was a dramatic forest of evergreen trees lit with white lights
and filled with Grecian-blue paper butterflies handcrafted by
schoolchildren on the island of Patmos, the ancestral home
of the Bride. The table decoration was simple and elegant
with white linens, ample use of silver pieces and china
from the collections of the Merry Widows of Montecito, as
the friends of the Mother of the Bride call themselves, and
rustic arrangements of white and blue hydrangeas, clipped
and dried especially for the occasion from the Mother of the
Groom's garden in Fair Harbor. The aisle flowers and arch
that decorated the ceremony space featured greenery, roses,
and crisp bows of various shades of blue. The seating and
ceremony area for the sixty guests was snug and convivial,
ensuring that there were no gaps in the decor or the
conversations.

The ceremony began with a break with tradition. George
Blakeman, the Groom's father, walked the Mother of the
Bride, Alexa Diamandis, and the Mother of the Groom, Abigail
Ellsworth Blakeman, both wearing shades of blue, down the
aisle together. It was an emotional moment for all the women in
attendance to see these two mothers united by their children.
Maid of Honor Sarah Blakeman made her way down the aisle
in a vintage Betsey Johnson dress covered in the winged
creatures of the theme. The Groom and Best Man, Lloyd
Chandra, stood at the altar in blue suits and silver ties, a
sophisticated modern look.

When the Bride appeared in her ethereal Kalliope Moon dress, an elegant bohemian affair with hints of blue amid the ivory layers and a matching tulle veil, there were audible gasps from the guests. The effect of the Bride in her dress against the backdrop of evergreens was breathtaking. The guest next to me, Lucinda Bufford Morrison, a member of the Connecticut wing of the floral foragers and of the Daughters of the American Revolution, whispered in my ear, "What a triumph!"

The Bride was escorted down the aisle by her godfather, Baron Plumley, Lord Simon Fox, to the waiting arms of Chase Blakeman. Timothy Lynch, then mayor of New York City and Mr. Blakeman's (now former) boss, married the couple with a flourish and a bit of the Seamus Heaney love poem "Scaffolding," as the first drops of the downpour began.

Nobody seemed to enjoy their wedding more than the newlyweds, Ms. Diamandis, who will be keeping her maiden name as a nod to her mother and her heritage, and Mr. Blakeman. The wedding had very few contrived theatrics. There were no videos that touted "The Story of Us" or choreographed social media moments. But there was a tearjerker of a toast from Baron Plumley, a beautiful Greek song and traditional dance from the Diamandis uncles, who traveled from Athens and Patmos for the occasion, and the most wonderful lemon wedding cake from Room for Cake set among a meadow of florals. The couple chose the Kacey Musgraves song "Butterflies" as their first dance. The families of the couple joined them on the dance floor as the song faded into "Empire State of Mind" with Mayor Lynch escorting Ms. Diamandis.

Even when the rain came down and then the tent came down, the Bride and Groom stayed up. Guests packed the reception rooms at La Mariposa, dozens of towels appeared, hot beverages were served, a supply of pashminas materialized to warm chilled guests. The dancing continued far beyond the acceptable quiet hour in that neighborhood. As Toots Bixby, owner of La Mariposa, said, "I'm happy to pay the fine for such a glorious event."

So when you search for the video online and gasp at the volume of water drenching the wedding party, know that all was okay. In fact, better than okay. It was a triumph.

Acknowledgments

There was a three-month period during the pandemic when it looked like the worst was over and life could get back to normal. (Spoiler! It wasn't and it didn't!) But during that Summer of Love, it seemed like everyone on my social media feeds got married, hosted a wedding, or went to a celebration. The joy! It was contagious. I couldn't get enough of the wedding industrial complex! Big weddings! Micro weddings! Weddings on land, on sea, and on mountaintop. Weddings of exquisite taste and/or extravagant budgets and weddings cobbled together with duct tape and fairy dust. I soaked up every photo of beautiful brides, handsome grooms, elegant MOBs and MOGs, first dances, glorious bouquets and floral arches, bridesmaids in matching dresses (or not) and groomsmen in linen blazers. And so many dogs as ring bearers. Thank you all for still believing in wedded bliss. You were the inspiration for *Abigail and Alexa Save the Wedding*. From your Instagram pages to my book proposal. A toast to you!

My editor, Rachel Kahan, said "Yes!" to the idea of a wedding story told from the point of view of two mothers instead of the happy couple, recognizing the value of a story about two grown women thrown together through no fault of their own. I'm grateful for her confidence in the concept and for her guidance, enthusiasm, and steady hand during the editing process. I'm honored to be part of the William Morrow family and to work with professionals who love books, heart and soul. A huge thanks to my entire team:

Alexandra Bessette, Amanda Hong, Marie Rossi, Hannah Dirgins, Amelia Wood, Jennifer Hart, Michele Cameron, and Hope Ellis.

My agent, Yfat Reiss Gendell, said to me one day, "You know, Lian, most writers complain that they can never get their agent on the phone. Do you ever complain that you can't get your agent *off* the phone?" Reader, I do not. I'm grateful for her wise counsel, her power-brainstorming skills, and her ability to drill down on good ideas during our long calls. Thanks to Ashley Napier at YRG Partners for her assistance throughout the entire process, from ideation to publication. You're both wonderful to work with. Don't stop calling!

The winner of the Most Impressive Emails Award goes to Tanya Farrell, Emily Afifi, and the rest of the team at Wunderkind PR. Every few weeks I get a lengthy list of all the events, the press, the publicity hits that Wunderkind has made happen. It's hard to describe how much my list-loving heart adores those emails and working with the Jersey Girls of Wunderkind.

A huge thanks to the women of Birnam Wood in Montecito for their enthusiasm, sharp observations, sense of fun, and fabulous style. I've loved spending time with you and dipping into your world. Thanks to Fannie Flagg, Penny Bianchi, Pam Breedlove, Beth Wood, and my personal conduit, Diana Nixon. Thanks to the lovely events team at BWGC, including Tiffany Grummer, for hosting me on multiple occasions.

This book is my sixth novel and my eighth book. In the twenty-four years since my first book was published, I have spoken to thousands of women through hundreds of philanthropic organizations, service clubs, book groups, library events, and charity functions. It's been such a privilege to have long-term relationships with engaged women across the country who welcome me back time and time again. I value the friendships that have developed over the years. Special thanks to the Library Foundation of Los Angeles and the Friends of the Pasadena Public Library for continued support.

Booksellers are the best. Shout-out to my Southern Cal sisterhood: Vroman's in Pasadena, Zibby's Bookshop in Santa Monica, Lido Village Books in Newport Beach, and Pages in Manhattan Beach for their enthusiasm. To the booklovers on social media who have championed my works, big kiss. I'm grateful for the book love.

My support system is deep and wide. I'm very lucky to have Satellite Sisters coast-to-coast who have encouraged me, supported me, pitched me for local signings or hosted me for book clubs, schlepped my luggage or boxes of books, done my hair and makeup, driven me to events or the airport, and bought me so many glasses of wine. From Pasadena to Portland, Oregon, from Santa Fe to Dallas, from Minneapolis to South Dakota. And the entire tristate area, from New Jersey to Long Island to Connecticut. I couldn't do it without you. Cheers!

To my family, you're the best. To my siblings, my siblings-in-law, my nieces, nephews, and niblings, never forget: no free books. To my sons, Brookes Treidler and Colin Treidler, no pressure, but I know a LOT about weddings now so feel free to have one. And to my husband, Berick Treidler, thank you for saying "I do."

The book is dedicated to my dear friend John Chris Connor, who died unexpectedly as I was completing the final draft. I met Chris on our first night of college, and we remained friends for forty years, thanks to a shared love of Ralph Lauren knitwear and floral design. He was intellectually curious and always had a thoughtful but sharp opinion on most aspects of life from politics to party invitations. He worked in finance, then did a turn in public service working at the White House, followed by a third act in architectural preservation. He was a world traveler and lifetime student of Japan. He was a walking Art History 101 textbook. He was a great dancer, a wonderful storyteller, and a bespoke dresser. He loved Mary J. Blige, rose gardens, great restaurants, and his people—all of them. What I've realized since his death is that the JCC slot in my circle of friends will never be filled again. The slot for the person who can text me the specific color of carnation pink to paint my front door. Or send me a Kashif song on Monday morning to start my week off right. Or explain the four stages of the economic cycle to me for novel research while he cooked dinner. I think he would have approved of the wedding flowers in this book. The hydrangeas are for you, Chris. xo

About the Author

Lian Dolan is a writer and talker. She is the author of six novels, including *The Marriage Sabbatical* and *The Sweeney Sisters*. She has written humor columns for *O, The Oprah Magazine*; *Working Mother*; and *Pasadena Magazine*. She also created and hosted *Satellite Sisters*, an award-winning podcast with her four real sisters. A graduate of Pomona College, she lives in Pasadena, California, with her husband and family.